Praise for *Changers Book One: Drew*

'*Changers* should appeal to a broad demographic. Teenagers, after all, are the world's leading experts on trying on, and then promptly discarding, new identities' *New York Times Book Review*

'"Selfie" backlash has begun: The Unselfies project wants to help people quit clogging social media with pictures of themselves and start capturing the intriguing world around them' *O, The Oprah Magazine* on the We Are Changers Unselfies project

'This is more than just a 'message' book about how we all need to be more understanding of each other. The imaginative premise is wrapped around a moving story about gender, identity, friendship, bravery, rebellion Vs. conformity, and thinking outside the box' *School Library Journal*

'A thought-provoking exploration of identity, gender, and sexuality . . . An excellent read for any teens questioning their sense of self' *Publishers Weekly* (starred review)

'A fresh and charmingly narrated look at teens and gender' *Kirkus Reviews*

'Everyone should read this, regardless of age. The book discusses important topics about growing into your skin (literally and physically), and gender identity . . . Go get a copy of this right now' *Huffington Post*

'Changing bodies, developing personalities, forays into adult activities – where was this book circa the early 2000s when I needed it? But something tells me my adult self will learn a thing or two from it as well' *Barnes & Noble Book Blog*

BOOK ONE

CHANGERS

DREW

**T COOPER &
ALLISON GLOCK-COOPER**

ATOM

First published in the United States in 2014 by Black Sheep,
an imprint of Akashic Books
First published in Great Britain in 2016 by Atom

1 3 5 7 9 10 8 6 4 2

A CIP catalogue record for this book
is available from the British Library.

ISBN 978-0-349-00242-2 (paperback)
ISBN 978-0-349-00243-9 (eBook)

Printed and bound in Great Britain by
Clays Ltd, St Ives plc

Papers used by Atom are from well-managed forests
and other responsible sources.

MIX
Paper from
responsible sources
FSC
www.fsc.org FSC® C104740

Atom
An imprint of
Little, Brown Book Group
Carmelite House
50 Victoria Embankment
London EC4Y 0DZ

An Hachette UK Company
www.hachette.co.uk

www.atombooks.net

*For anybody who has looked in the mirror
and not recognized the person s/he sees*

Before he became the one he was meant to be, before he lived through those four years called high school, those four years where everything he ever knew evaporated into air, where the ground dropped away, and he fell in love, and he saw people die terrible pointless deaths, and he saved lives without even knowing how, and he did everything wrong until he got a few important things right, before he understood that he wasn't any more chosen than anyone else (even though they told him otherwise), and harnessed his power, the power he never wanted, never believed he could comprehend, before any of that and a hundred other awful, wondrous, ruinous, magical things happened, he was just a kid in Tennessee named Ethan.

PROLOGUE

ETHAN

"**G**ood*night*," I say, and then "*Geesh*," under my breath. It's about the twentieth time Mom and Dad have come into my bedroom and wished me goodnight. Like they don't want me go to sleep or something. It's not like I'm enlisting, or getting married; it's just high school. Every kid has a first day of high school. *I know, I know*, except for the ones who have to spend their days carrying water on their heads for twenty miles roundtrip to their families for survival, so they aren't afforded the luxury of education. I just mean most regular American kids like me.

"We want you to know—" Dad starts, but then Mom interrupts.

"We love you, Ethan," she blurts. There are tears in her eyes. *Again.* "You've been so great about this move, and your father and I ... I guess we just want you to know how much we appreciate who you are."

I hug and pat her (I admit, a little condescendingly) on the back. Hit the light switch over her shoulder. Then my dad gets in on the hugging, and now we're man-hugging with me standing in nothing but my skull-and-crossbones boxers, and it's getting a little too Lifetime Original Movies up in here, and suddenly I can't remember whether I washed my favorite jeans or not, the skinny ones with the rip in the left knee from when I busted on my skateboard, attempting a simple kickflip off some stairs the day before we moved to Genesis, Arkantuckasee. Okay. It's Genesis, *Tennessee*, but what's the diff, really? There's no art house theater here. No skate park. No cereal bar. It may as well be the moon. The moon with about a thousand fried chicken restaurants on it. Not that I have anything against chickens. Or frying them. But would it kill anyone to, I don't know, open a decent taco joint?

They close the door, *finally*, and I jump into bed, pushing over our pit bull Snoopy, who stands and circles, then curls up at my feet, letting out a giant doggy-sigh, like I've really put him out by making him move over three whole inches. It's only my second night in this room; I don't even know the patterns the light plays against the walls yet. (I'd had it memorized in my old room in New York, where headlights moving left to right on my closet doors meant they were actually going right to left on the street.) The stitches in my knee are itching like mad. As in, I know I'm not supposed to scratch them, but not doing so is quite possibly going to send me to the loony bin. Come to think of it, I wonder where I'm going to get the stitches taken out, now that I can't go to Dr. Reese anymore. "I delivered you into this world," he says every time I'm in his office, "so don't forget I can take you right out of it if you give your folks trouble." (And then he sticks me with a needle.)

There are tons of boxes that still need unpacking— my drum kit all broken down and stored in the building's basement. Weird how my entire old life is literally contained within four or five stacks of beat-up cardboard. My soccer participation trophies, my first broken board, even Lamby-cakes (the stuffed animal who apparently accompanied me home from the hospital the day I was born). Something makes me want to leave the boxes packed and just start over. *You can, you know,* I'm thinking to myself, lying on my back in the dark, cradling my head in my palms. Damn, my pits stink. I guess sex ed was no joke: *Unsettling changes that are nonetheless completely natural.* Nothing "natural" about the swamp funk swathing my entire body. Not enough deodorant in the world. I'll shower in the morning.

Maybe I could just wake up tomorrow and be the dude I always wanted to be: confident, funny, tall (grew two inches over summer!). Got game with the ladies. Nobody here has to know that I've never gotten to second base, or that I sucked my thumb until fourth (okay, fifth) grade—or anything about me, really. Mom hasn't even started putting up embarrassing family photos in the apartment yet, which is peculiar now that I'm thinking about it, because for as long as I can remember, our houses have always been filled with pictures of me staring back at myself through every year of my life. Sooo many bad haircuts.

I keep lying here, watching the occasional light dart in random directions across the walls, no rhyme or reason to it. Each flash startles me. Crazy to be living in some bland apartment complex outside a city I've never visited before. Crazy not to be able to skate down the block to Andy's house and get an Orangina out of his fridge in the garage. Crazy I can't sleep—I usually crash as soon as my head hits the pillow. *Thanks, Mom and Dad,* for giving me insomnia with your interminable "Goodbye and Goodnight" marathon.

I flip and flop, flip again. Flop one more time for good measure. It's hot. And humid, even with the A/C on. This isn't my normal pillow. This pillow sucks. I decide to make a list in my head of all the things I want to accomplish during freshman year:

1) Get a girlfriend. Like a real one. Not a *girl* who is a *friend* who calls to tell me all about the dude she's crushing on who doesn't even know she's crushing on him and, by the way, should she get bangs?

2) Get really good at algebra. Kidding! I don't give a donkey about algebra—except knowing enough of it that my parents don't ride me about grades this year.

3) Complete a laser flip.

4) Make it onto a team. Don't care which, so long as it's athletic and not the debate team or robot-building club, or marching band, or something terminally *Glee* like that.

5) Lift weights/get muscles. *Low-key* muscles. Not too roided out or anything. I'm not an animal.

6) Get a girlfriend. Wait, I already listed that one.

That's about it. And . . . ? I'm still not tired. What the hell is my problem? The stitches keep bugging me, and I'm trying desperately not to claw them out with my fingernails.

I slap the wound with the flat of my hand. Doesn't work—in fact, makes it itch even more. My stomach hurts. Not really *hurts*, more queasy. And I'm clammy. I better not be getting sick. Not for my first day. I toss off the sheets and go into the bathroom, pop on the light, and look at myself in the mirror. My cheeks are red. But my hair finally looks fly. Thank jaysus I got to a dope barbershop before we left New York.

I splash some water on my face. Stare at my reflection, check for any whiskers on my chin. Is that a little reddish one, glinting in the light on the left next to the cluster of three freckles? *Nope.* Oh well, there's always tomorrow.

I guess my stomach feels a little better now. I go back into my room, dig Lamby-cakes out of a box. He needs a wash. He's still kind of cute. But I will *not* bring him to bed with me. I'm three years too old for that. I put him on the desk where I can see him from bed.

Dang, I hate this pillow. Where's my old pillow? I grab my iPod, cram the buds in my ears, and flop back into bed. I press shuffle. Another few lights shoot into the room, dart from wall to wall. I close my eyes, try to do that relaxing breathing thing I saw on *Oprah* when Mom was watching. Four-seven-eight. Or is it seven-four-eight? I breathe in for seven seconds, hold it for four, then exhale for eight. No, that can't be right. Breathe in for four, hold it for seven, then exhale for eight seconds. Yeah, that's it, that feels nice . . .

෨

I can hear my mom and dad skulking around on the other side of my bedroom door. *What's going on with them?* Is this their midlife crisis? Is Mom going to beg for another baby and Dad going to trade in his wagon for a *(fingers crossed!)* Z4 roadster convertible? I squint at the digital clock: *6:57.* I have eighteen minutes of bliss left, and they're ruining it.

I can hear Mom whisper, "Do you think he's up yet?" but Dad doesn't answer. I yank the sheet over my head just as the door opens. Silence. I know they're watching me. I can almost hear them breathing. It's getting humid under the sheet from my own dragon breath. When did my parents become stalkers? The door shuts. I listen a few more seconds to make sure I'm alone, then pull the sheet back down. I notice Snoopy's not at the foot of my bed, where he is pretty much every morning I've woken up since we rescued him when I was seven. *6:58.*

Next thing I know my alarm is stabbing into my brain, and for a split second, like it does every morning that a shrieking noise wakes me, the world feels like a horrible place, and living in it seems entirely impossible. I pull the crappy pillow off my face and paw at my end table until I land a finger on the clock, silencing it. *7:15.* Yay, time to enroll in a giant, unfamiliar school and be the anonymous new loser in town. Getting lost on the way to classes, enjoying solo lunches in a corner of the cafeteria, fighting with impossible-to-open lockers, changing for gym class in front of dudes who look like NFL running backs. You know—general awesomeness.

I sit up, reach down for the black vintage Slayer shirt I'd left out on the floor the night before. Pull it over my head while stumbling toward the bathroom. My eyes are barely slitted as my head pops through the neckhole, and I catch a flicker of somebody in the full-length mirror behind the door—*WHAT THE*? Someone else is in the room with me. I manage to pry both eyes open. *Hel-lo there*. I pull my shirt all the way down and step a little closer to the mirror. She's wearing the identical Slayer shirt, faded, with holes in exactly the same places. That blows; it was supposed to be one of a kind.

Wait, is this what my parents were fussing about? Some long-lost cousin or something? Some hillbilly relative come to live with us and enrich our lives with her down-home truisms and smoking hot, Daisy Dukes–wearing friends? Her name is probably "Brittney" or "Sunflower" or something innocent and dirty at the same time. This could be sweet.

I raise a hand, attempt a wave. She does the same. I rub my eyes like they do in cartoons, and look again. Cousin Brittney is kind of a babe, if I can say that in reference to a cousin without being too incesty about it. Long, straight, white-blond hair—the kind that doesn't come in a bottle—and wide, wild green eyes, a nice body. A little shorter than me. She's also . . . wearing my skull-and-crossbones boxers. That's weird.

Enough Cirque du Soleil mime routine. I swing around to open with something like, "Hey, I'm . . ." But nobody's there. I turn back to the mirror: Brittney's still in it, looking at me. I step closer. She steps closer. I feel a whoosh in my stomach, like I could cough up a lung.

Okay, I get it. This is a dream, the weirdest freaking dream I've ever had. And it's still going on. Duh, of course, because I was obsessing over getting a girlfriend before I fell asleep, now I've conjured myself an imaginary dream girl. Pathetic, sure. But hey, I'll go with it. I reach out to touch her, and she reaches out to touch me. We get closer. My eyes float down to her chest. My fingertips touch her fingertips in the mirror, and then for some reason my hands do a U-turn and land on my own chest. I look down, start lifting up my collar to peek inside.

Holy . . .

"MOOOOM!!" I scream in a high voice that startles me.

My mom is in my room in seconds, takes one look at me, and commences jumping up and down like a three-year-old at a birthday party. She squeals over her shoulder to Dad, "It's a girl!"

She starts hugging me and crying. In the mirror, I can see her hugging this girl, but I'm nowhere in the picture. I'm watching a movie with actors playing the parts. My knees buckle. My dad comes in, tears in his eyes too. It's like I've come home from war. Everyone is so thrilled to see me— even the dog has poked his head into my room to see what all the commotion is about. I pull back.

"I'm not dreaming, am I?"

My mom shakes her head. I've never seen her weep so openly. "We didn't know for sure you were going to change . . . " she blubbers.

"So we didn't tell you," my dad finishes.

"Tell me *what*?"

They look at one another, and my mom sits down on the bed, gesturing for me to join her. I prefer to stand, cross my arms (soft flesh grazes my forearms, *WTF?!*), and lean against the wall. My dad wheels over the desk chair.

"Well, Eth—" my mom starts, but abruptly stops herself. "We hoped this would happen, but—"

"I'm Ethan!" I interrupt her, again in the squeaky voice I can't control. "Why won't you call me Ethan?" I sound like a Teletubby.

"But you never know if you'll be chosen for sure," Mom just keeps going.

"*Chosen?* Chosen for what? What are you talking about?" I ask, looking back and forth between them.

"Sit down," Dad says, and I don't want to, but I feel like I might face-plant if I don't. "You're a Changer."

"A *what?*" I say, finally sitting. I notice Snoopy won't come into the room.

"A Changer, sweetie," Mom repeats.

"No, I'm an Ethan."

They look at me pathetically.

"Changers are an ancient race of humans," Dad says. "You are here for a purpose. To make the world better."

"You're crazy," I say. "Are you punking me? Is this an elaborate practical joke? Because it's not funny. It's not funny at all."

"I'm a Changer too," Dad continues, speaking slowly and deliberately in the voice he usually reserves for our ninety-eight-year-old great-uncle. "Your mom's a Static, and one day you'll partner with a Static like her, and hopefully your child will be a Changer too."

My head feels like it's about to implode.

"You're going to help make the world a better place!" Mom echoes rhapsodically, clearly having drunk the Kool-Aid.

19

I look into her glistening eyes, her sensible bob curling at the ends, just above her *I Hiked the Grand Canyon!* T-shirt. Which she never actually did. She said she bought it for the color. But it's a lie. The shirt. Just like this must be.

"I don't give a crap about the rest of the world. I just want to go to high school."

"You will!" she blurts enthusiastically, like this is the best thing that's ever happened in her entire life. "And on the first day of every school year, you'll wake up a different person, and then live as that person for that whole year."

"Wait, you mean this, this . . . *thing* is going to happen to me *three more times*?"

"Yes, and after graduation, you'll choose who you want to be forever," Dad adds, as though what he is saying doesn't sound completely and certifiably crazy.

"Oh good, so after this trip into the bizarro world of unknown horrors, I can go back to being me," I say, relieved at the tiny light at the end of a four-year tunnel.

"No. You cannot choose to be the person you were before the changes started," Dad says, shrugging a little, as if to say, *I don't make the rules*. He sighs, pats down his hair, which he hasn't brushed. It stays stuck in the air. A miniature teepee.

"This is bullshit!" I can tell I'm starting to piss Dad off. Mom tries to hug me again, but I dodge her.

"I know it doesn't feel like it now, but this is an incredible gift you've been given," she says. "You get to take a journey few are able to. Who hasn't fantasized about being someone else?"

"Sure. Like Jay-Z. Or Tom Brady. Not a girl. A *blond* girl . . ." I can't finish.

"Think of all the insight you'll gain!" Mom says.

"Have you met any fourteen-year-olds, Mom? All those kids at the mall? Not shopping for insight!"

She just stands there, arms folded over herself, staring at me approvingly. Dad puts his hands on her shoulders from behind.

Then it hits me: "You mean you guys have known this could happen to me all along and chose not to tell me?"

My parents look at each other for a beat, before Mom says, "You're meant to have as normal a life as possible."

"Normal? Really?" I look at Cousin Brittney, I mean myself, in the mirror again.

"And," she continues, "there's always the possibility a Changer-Static union won't be permitted Changer offspring."

"I don't know, seems like something you might want to share, you know, like, *Your dad's a FULL-ON MUTATING FREAK. And you might be one too!*"

I run to the bathroom and slam the door behind me. Look at myself in the mirror. Everything I do, this damn girl does. Raising an eyebrow, blinking alternating eyes, making kissy-fish face, sticking out my tongue. I'm the girl in the Slayer shirt. No way around it. I feel dizzy. I pull up my long hair and let it drop over my ears. I yank my toothbrush out of its holder and squeeze some toothpaste on it. I jam the brush into my mouth, looking at this girl, at *myself?* I listen at the door, but my folks aren't saying anything. I finish up, spit, rinse. Swish some Listerine. Spit again.

"I didn't mean to call you a freak," I say to my dad as soon as I crack the door.

"We know how weird this is," Dad says, "and it's going to be hard at first, but trust me, you'll get the hang of it."

"I just wish somebody had told me."

"They don't like us to say anything until we're certain," Dad says.

"*They*? Who are *they*?" I ask.

"The Changers Council," he replies, as Mom picks up a thick envelope.

"The what?"

"The Council moderates and governs the Changer race. They guide and protect us. Without them it would be chaos," Dad explains.

"This just arrived by courier." Mom hands over the package, and I open it. Inside: *The Changers Bible*, a thick book with densely packed, opaque white pages and a symbol on the front, like Leonardo da Vinci's *Vitruvian Man*, but with four bodies instead of two. Also a birth certificate, which I pull out immediately.

"Drew Bohner?"

"It'll be your name for the year," Mom says.

"Really. Drew *Boner*? Great."

"Well, I'm sure you'll *rise* to the occasion," Dad tries. I'm not laughing.

In the package are middle school and elementary transcripts, medical records, a Social Security card, birth certificate, passport—all in Drew Bohner's name. Old photographs of this made-up girl, of me, at different stages of life over the last fourteen years. Mom and Dad are droning on about how the Council has pre-enrolled me in school, how I'll eventually, when it's safe, get to meet other

Changer kids like me, how I should spend the first few days studying *The Changers Bible*, and things will start making sense. That they're always there for support and to answer questions, blah blah blah.

I'm just flipping through the photos of this little girl: tap dancing in a red top hat and leotard, winning a bronze medal in the freestyle swimming relay, standing in the first row, second from the left in Mrs. Johnson's fourth grade class picture. *Who the hell is Mrs. Johnson?*

"So I have no say in any of this? Like, what if I don't want to be a girl?" I ask.

"I think you'll find that what you are transcends gender," Mom says.

Barf.

"And Drew," Dad adds. I don't know who he's talking to. "Ethan!" he says louder, and I snap to. "That's the last time I'll call you that, by the way. Listen to me: you cannot tell anybody who or what you are."

But I don't even know what I am, I think. Dad's tone is serious as nut cancer. So I don't say anything.

"This is why we moved so suddenly, left everything behind," he goes on. "Later we'll receive alibis for your future V's—those are the four different versions of yourself—but for now, we're new enough here that Ethan never existed. You just moved to town with your folks from outside New York City for your dad's new job in Nashville. Got it?"

"I guess." But I am leveled by a rush of sadness like when Pappy died as we all held him in the hospice; except it's me, Ethan, who's gone, and I never even got to squeeze a hand or say goodbye.

* * *

Minutes later in Mom's closet, my mind is racing, totally unfocused, but she keeps pulling out clothes, expecting me to make some sort of decision. I can't envision myself in anything she suggests. A silky green blouse ("It'll complement your eyes"). A blue cotton tank top ("High in the mid-nineties today"). Something called a "romper." I am paralyzed. As she closes the closet door, I notice the full-length mirror on the back of it. She stands there looking at me in it. Again with the tears. The woman is going to convert to dust if she keeps losing liquid at this rate.

"Maybe those," I say, pointing to some stained khaki shorts she does yard work in.

"Honey, it's your *first* day."

"And?" I stare at her.

She exhales, hands me the shorts, which feel so wrong I can barely stomach touching the fabric. I unbutton them (they even *button* the wrong way) and step in. They are pleated and bulgy, while at the same time entirely too tight. And they ride too high up on my waist. Nothing about any of this fits. And then . . . "I'm so sorry, but," Mom begins shakily, "it wouldn't be right to send you out of the house without—"

"What?" I cut my eyes at her as she starts fishing through her top drawer. My heart is pounding. After a few seconds she pulls it out . . . a *bra*. A white silky strappy thing that looks like two yarmulkes sewn together.

"No," I say. "Nuh-uh, not doing it." I shake my head.

"It's part of the deal, sweetie. Let me show you," she says, trying to lift up my Slayer shirt. "It's easy once you get it adjusted right."

I slap my shirt down and her hands drop, the bra falling to the carpet between us. And then, the weirdest thing happens out of nowhere and with no warning: I begin to cry.

"Oh, baby," Mom says, gathering me into her arms again. A heavy drop falls on her shoulder from the rim of my right eye. "I have a jog bra; maybe that'll be easier your first day."

She gives me a tight squeeze, then goes back into the top drawer and pulls out a black spandex mini–tank top thing, with pink stripes under each armpit. "Just put your head through here and your arms—"

"I know where it goes!" I say, louder than I'd intended, snatching the bra from her. "I'm not an imbecile."

She winces. Chews her lip. "I knew it was going to be difficult if you were given a girl for your first V," she laments, seeming genuinely sad. I look away, feeling like a jerk. The phrase *your first V* hanging in the air between us.

I turn my back to Mom and pull off the T-shirt myself, then wrestle my way into the too-tight jog bra, which feels like a medieval torture device, not to mention my *things* are going every which direction in it, but there is no way I'm reaching down there to do anything about the situation. The spandex so tight I swear it's even changing my breathing pattern. I quickly put my shirt back on, then turn to study myself in the mirror. A too-big men's vintage thrash metal shirt and Mom's middle-aged housewife frump shorts. This is my outfit for the first day of high school.

Today is going to suck dog balls.

Oh wait. It already does.

"Maybe we'll drop by the mall together after school?"

Mom offers, gathering my hair into a ponytail on the side of my head. "That will help, yes?"

"Not really."

"Maybe your Vans with that?" she suggests, working a rubber band around the ponytail. Yanks at my scalp. She steps back and studies me. "A side pony suits you." And then, "You really are beautiful."

I shake it off, yank out the rubber band, and my hair falls across my face. Then she reaches into her pocket and comes out with a shiny silver lipstick tube. *There is no way I'm letting her paint any of that on my face*, I'm thinking.

It's then I notice in the mirror that both my knees are perfectly intact—no cut, no caterpillar of stitches from the gnarly fall off my skateboard. No more torturous itching. I bend over to inspect, and wowzers, the wound is completely healed! There's not even a scar—

OWWW!

My left butt cheek is suddenly on fire, and Mom is quickly recapping that lipstick tube. There's a singeing electrical odor in the puff of smoke hovering between us. As I'd bent over to check out my knee, Mom yanked down the back of my shorts and boxers and branded me (*branded me like livestock!*) with one end of the "lipstick" tube. Which obviously wasn't lipstick at all.

"The Council included this," she says, looking sheepish. "Had to be done before you left the house."

I twist around and look down. The same little emblem that was on the cover of *The Changers Bible* is now seared into my flesh:

"Are you freaking kidding me?" *This is some BS.*

"It's for your own good," she insists. "Like a vaccine."

I stretch to get a better look. The brand is small, dime-sized but detailed. Vaguely creepy. Completely embarrassing.

"You must promise never to reveal this mark to anybody except the Static you'll one day choose as a partner."

"Don't worry," I say.

My dad comes in then, starts unbuckling his belt.

"Dad, no, please," I try, but his pants are open, and the elastic waistband of his Jockeys is inching down his butt, and he is displaying a very pale ass cheek where the same emblem is seared into his skin.

"Nobody's ever seen mine but your mother," he says, pulling his pants back up and smirking in that PG-13 way he does sometimes. (And I thought I couldn't feel any more nauseous.)

"Breakfast's waiting, and you have to be at the registrar's office in twenty minutes. I can drive you," Mom offers.

"I think I'll just take my board."

"You sure?" she asks doubtfully.

I nod, and then, *Thank Lordy above*, they leave, and I am alone in the closet.

I peruse Mom's clothes, most of which have already

been unpacked and neatly organized—so many shapes and colors, all with a vague perfumed whiff. My usual "wardrobe" consists of essentially square T-shirts and (depending on weather) shorts or jeans—in blues, blacks, grays, and whites. Maybe a red sweatshirt now and again when I'm feeling reckless. And I own one piece of jewelry, a wristwatch, my big black G-Shock that I've had since my tenth birthday, which, I notice for the first time, is practically falling off my wrist, since it was set to size, uh, Ethan. I reach down and cinch it tighter by a couple holes—the smallest it'll go. It's still a little loose.

I notice Mom's necklaces, which are draped over a mirror, rings piled in a small antique saucer on the dresser. It's all so . . . *girlie*. I check my whole look in the mirror again: *Ridiculous*. But I guess I have to get this carnival on the road.

All of Mom's shoes are a little too small—not to mention ugly—and all of my kicks are now too big. I fish out a couple pairs of Mom's thicker socks, double them up over my feet, then go with my old checkered Vans that Mom placed outside the closet door for me at some point while I've been in here hiding and quietly trying to make a deal with a god I've never been acquainted with to please let me wake up from this nightmare so I can start ninth grade and get on with the life I thought I was living.

At the breakfast table, I quickly study the first few pages of Drew Bohner's history, so there will be no surprises when I fill out paperwork at school. I feel my parents' eyes drilling into the top of my head.

"*What?*"

"Nothing," they say in tandem, then go back to gawking at me, their child, the Coney Island freak show exhibit.

"I'm not hungry," I announce, pushing my plate away. And I'm not. My stomach is roiling, and the last thing I want to put in it is two fried eggs over-medium on toast with turkey bacon.

"You should eat something," Mom pleads with me.

"I think I'm good." I feed an egg and piece of toast to the dog, who takes them, hesitantly. *Great, even Snoops doesn't recognize me.* I wonder what the Dog Whisperer would say about all this.

Then Mom produces a Hostess cupcake with a single candle on top. "Happy Birthday, baby!" she shouts, holding the plate and cupcake in front of her like a waitress. I stare her down. Then shift to Dad, who is shrugging: *Wasn't my idea.*

I lick my thumb and snuff out the candle. "Maybe later," I say, grabbing my backpack and skateboard. I kiss Mom on the cheek and blow by Dad, who reaches up and pats me on the forearm in a way he's never touched me before. Like I'm made of glass.

"Remember: don't tell anybody!" he hollers when I'm almost out the door. "It could mean death for all of Changerkind! Love you!"

I walk as quickly as I can down the hall, trying to outrun what just happened. My shoes slip a little, rubbing the backs of my ankles and bunching up the socks. As I wait for the elevator, I try vainly to fix them, to seem normal, the way I was before my alarm went off and I woke up changed. The elevator dings, and this corporate-looking dude and I ride to the ground floor. The door opens. Neither of us moves. The doors start to close again, and he reaches to hold them back. I realize he was waiting for me to exit.

"Sorry," I say, even though I'm not really sure why I'm apologizing.

Out in the lobby I glance down at my chest again. Still shocking. I hold my board in front, a shield. The doorman smiles. Andy and I always used to boast that if we were girls, we'd never leave the house because we'd be touching our boobs all the time, but now I'm not so sure about that particular hypothetical. Careful what you wish for. Wait, *Andy* . . . Can I never be friends with him again?

I walk outside, and the air is already oppressive. I decide I'll just keep e-mailing and talking on the phone with Andy, pretending I'm still me, until I can figure a way out of this mess. I mean, I am me, still (*right?*), but I'll just be Ethan on the inside and leave out the whole whoever's-on-the-outside, so then nothing will have changed between us except geography (not to mention *top*ography). Wait, my voice. Frack, I can't figure this out. I guess I can't talk to him on the phone. Okay, just e-mail and texts.

Right outside the gates of our building complex, I drop my board on the sidewalk and plant my left foot on it, but before I can get my right foot on the deck, the board goes shooting out from under me, and all of a sudden I'm bouncing on my butt on concrete.

What the hell? When did I get so lame? *Oh yeah.*

"Here," a girl appears, offering a hand. I take it, she helps me up.

"Thanks."

"I'm Tracy," she says, brushing off the back of my shorts for me. I twist around to get away from her. "And no, you can't be in touch with an old friend by e-mail and pretend the Change didn't happen."

Holy cow, how is this chick reading my mind?

"I can't read minds," she says nonchalantly, digging my board out of a bush, "but when I was Change 1–Day 1, right about at this point is where I started scheming to stay in touch with my best friend Maddy from middle school."

I start looking around suspiciously. It feels like we're being watched.

"Wait, are you . . ." I whisper.

Tracy nods her head and smiles, smugly putting a finger to her lips in the universal *shhh* sign. Ten seconds in and she is already the most annoying person I've ever met. She's dressed in a white frilly blouse with a navy sweater-vest over it, a plaid skirt, and knee-high socks—with a matching plaid headband and loafers, and a shiny little leather backpack. She looks like Mormon Barbie.

Dropping my board on the ground, she indicates that I should try again. "I guess you didn't read your file that closely. You're left-handed now."

"I'm *not* goofy-footed!" I insist.

"I don't know what that means," she says, "but if it has something to do with not taking this seriously, yeah, all signs point to that."

I cannot put a foot on the board, I cannot move. My butt is burning in two places—where my new freaking *brand* is, and also where it collided with the ground. I start becoming aware of the weight of my body, saddled around my hips, underneath my rear—on my, *gag*—chest—*gag*. Even my arms flop differently.

"You really should have spent a little more time with the materials," Tracy chides, pushing her headband back with her index finger. I shoot her my best *eff-you* glare. She is unmoved.

"It is in your best interest to read all the paperwork provided by the Council."

Great, I'm already in trouble with the Council.

"Let me guess. The first rule of Changers is that you never talk about Changers?" I say, kind of loving and hating myself at the same time.

Tracy, ignoring. "Since you didn't bother, I'll fill you in. I've been assigned to be your Touchstone for the next four years. That's like your fairy godmother. At least, that's how I see it."

"Where's your wand?"

Tracy sighs, her tolerance waning. "Did you at least read the Day 1 page in your *CB*?"

"My *CB*?"

"*The Changers Bible.* Gawd." She shakes her head, starts walking.

I pick up my board and follow. "Wait, this isn't, like, a religious cult or something, is it?" I call from behind.

Tracy laughs, kind of at me, in the way I used to laugh at Andy's little brother when he tried to pop and lock. Back when my biggest problems were bothersome little punks and worrying about looking fly in the skate videos we filmed. You know, yesterday.

Tracy is saying something that starts with, "Joke all you want," and ends with *yadda yadda "intolerance."* I begin to suspect she loves nothing more than having all the answers. She is *that* girl. The sitting-in-front-of-the-class, hand-in-the-air girl. My fairy godmother is a Grade-A brownnoser. And she is apparently all mine for four years. Unless I can put in for an exchange—I make a mental note to look *that* up in *The Changers Bible* when I get home.

"World religions could *benefit* from a little more Changer philosophy, IMHO," she continues, pulling farther ahead. "But that's perhaps a discussion for a later time."

"Awesome. Can't wait."

Tracy stiffens at the sarcasm. This probably isn't her best day either. Not that I care. Because I totally don't.

"Soon you'll realize that you've been put here to serve a much higher purpose," she says, taking a few more steps before adding, "I know this is scary. I was scared too. But if you just trust me and give it a little time, everything will make sense in a way it never has before." Her eyes dart around in every direction. "We need to find a private place." She starts walking even faster.

"Listen," I say, trailing, "it's just, it feels like I've landed in the middle of Siberia, and everybody's shouting at me in angry Russian." As I talk, my eyes well up again. I try to concentrate on the ground and keeping my idiotic floppy shoes on.

"I know," Tracy sighs, making what seems like a conscious decision to share something personal in return, like it probably says to do in the *Touchstone Handbook* companion to *The Changers Bible*. "I remember thinking my parents were acting so strange. My mom, especially, was a robot. She's the Changer, my dad's a Static."

"My dad's the Changer," I offer somberly, then quickly add, "apparently," because I don't know *what's* real anymore.

For the first time since I met her, Tracy lets some silence blossom in the air between us, and I start feeling like I should be a little nicer. Having determined which way we're headed, she leads me past the Speed Queen Laundromat, a KenJo gas station, and a convenience mart. We cross the parking lot where I'd skated two days before while we were waiting for the moving van to show up. I can feel moisture building up beneath my jog bra, which is starting to itch.

"You'll want to know about this place," Tracy says, pointing out ReRunz, a used clothing store at the far corner of the plaza. "You can buy and sell there at the beginning and end of each year, and they always have current fashions for like, less than half of what you'd pay new."

The two window displays on either side of the door are decorated in a back-to-school theme, and I spot a really nice, worked-in pair of brown Carhartts on the boys' side of the display. But, I remember with dread, that is not the side of the display I'm supposed to be looking at anymore. There is nothing on the girls' side that interests me, not a single stitch of clothing, not a belt, a shirt, nothing—except maybe the purple pair of Vans the broken mannequin is sporting. I didn't even know they made girls' Vans.

Tracy gets closer, whispers, "A couple of Changers in this region work there after school, it's kind of an unofficial outfitter, if you will. Anyway, at your first mixer next month, you'll see who's there and then you'll recognize each other from the meeting, and I bet they'll hook you up with a discount."

We continue around behind the building, a seemingly popular shortcut to school because there is a well-worn dirt trail snaking through the weeds and strewn with broken glass, crushed and faded Red Bull cans, splintered pens and pencils, a few cigarette butts.

"Over here," she says, walking with purpose. "Do you have any questions you want to ask me before we get there?"

Any questions doesn't cover it. "Uh, are you going to be in school with me?" I ask weakly.

"No. I graduated from Central two years ago— valedictorian!" she chirps.

No kidding.

"I could have gone to Yale, but I elected to stay on as a Touchstone. I work for the Council now," she babbles on.

"Sounds fun."

"I find it supremely rewarding. So you know, I changed into Tracy in the tenth grade, and let me tell you, the minute I opened my eyes on Change 2–Day 1, I knew she was going to be The One."

"You mean the you that you're supposed to pick after graduation?"

"Yeah, my Mono, which is the V you're going to live as forever, after you've experienced all four," she instructs. "I've heard other Changers say they felt something like that too, almost like a tingle along your spine or something. But don't worry if you don't feel it now, or ever—you'll figure out your Mono when it's time."

I try to take in what she's saying, but the out-of-control

35

flutter in my chest is somewhat distracting. "So, to recap: you're telling me I'm actually going to be this Drew person for just a year, and I can't tell anybody, and can't make any real friends because I can only know them for a year anyway—well, as far as they know. And then I'm just going to disappear and come back next year as some other random person, and essentially I have no choice in the matter? I'm just stuck here at the corner of Life and Sucks?"

The queasy, gonna-yak feeling in my stomach surges back.

"I guess you could see it that way," Tracy answers, calmly. "But it'd be great if you in fact did make friends and embrace life to the fullest. Time is relative. You are only just entering the possibility of being."

"And that means . . . ?"

"Don't stress so hard. High school is tough for everyone. Just be yourself."

"How the hell am I supposed to be myself if I don't even know who myself is?"

"Release the story you are telling yourself," she insists, sounding like the cult member she keeps insisting she's not. "You know who you are."

"No, I don't," I argue, stopping in my tracks just as the façade of the high school appears behind an abandoned Quonset hut with a crooked sign on it: *Lube, Flush, A/C, Oil Change*.

"You need to get enrolled, and you don't want to be late," she says, adjusting her tone and the subject. We hear a couple kids coming up the path behind us. "And there's one last item we need to take care of before I let you go." She glances toward the Quonset hut, then takes off toward it. When I don't follow, she turns around and rapid-flaps her hand at me.

"For a fairy godmother, you're bordering on lame," I say, my voice cracking on the last word.

The kids pass behind me, and after an appropriate pause which I'm hoping makes a point, I plod toward Tracy, who's just entering the hut. Once inside, it's obvious from the vintage rusted car parts sitting around, the old garage hasn't been used since the Bee Gees were getting laid.

Tracy removes her backpack and takes out a frilly looking handkerchief, carefully spreading it atop a dirty work bench. She proceeds to remove a few silver medical-looking instruments from her backpack, arranging them on the fabric. "Shut the door behind you."

"What are you doing?"

"Just shut it," she repeats, and now she's snapping a rubber glove onto her left hand.

Before I nudge the broken door shut, I peek out and glimpse a few more kids mindlessly heading up the path that leads to school. Their biggest worries are finding the right classrooms and generally not making fools of themselves. I squeeze my eyes tight and wish I could go back to being one of them.

When I open my eyes, Tracy is straightening the instruments and checking her inventory, referring to a page of a small pamphlet.

"Okay, I don't know what weirdness you're doing," I say, "but I have to get to class, so I guess I'll just be seeing you around?" I put my hand on the door.

"The Council has one more requirement before you are allowed to proceed with this V." She is sounding like an android now, and quite frankly, not that I couldn't take her, because I totally could, but . . . she's kind of scaring me.

Tracy picks up a small, high-tech pillbox-looking doohickey, presses the thumb of her right ungloved hand on the top of it, and it seems to scan her print, then beeps. The top flips open.

"I don't want to be this . . . whatever it is!" I shout. My voice echoes in the cavernous shop.

She snaps on a second rubber glove, carefully extracts from the box a tiny piece of metal the size and shape of a grain of rice. She holds it aloft, pinched between thumb and forefinger, studies it closely. "Change happens to everyone, Drew. You might as well embrace it."

"But I didn't ask for this. It's not fair!"

"Drew . . ." Tracy's shoulders rise and fall as she inhales deeply and exhales slowly. "You've been chosen. Ours is not to wonder why, but to embrace the opportunity." She picks up a large stainless-steel-syringe type of contraption and loads the rice grain into the top of it, inspects the tip, and looks squarely at me.

I'm not Drew is all that's going through my head. *I'm not Drew, I'm not Drew, I'm not Drew.* I consider bolting, making a break for home, but I have a feeling my folks—not to mention "The Council"—would have a few things to say about my not accepting this important *mission* I've been blessed with. Why couldn't this have been something simple, like being bitten by a radioactive spider that suddenly transforms me into a human-arachnid hybrid that can catch criminals and make chicks fall in love with me?

"Drew, as I'm trying to tell you, there's one more key component of Change 1–Day 1."

"Yes?"

"The Chronicles," she says, screwing a capped needle onto the end of the syringe. My eyes must be popping, because Tracy adds, "You'll barely feel it."

"Uh-uh," I say, backing away. "No ma'am."

"All Changers are required to keep a journal through the course of every Change. At the end of your cycle, after graduation but before your Forever Ceremony, you'll be given the Chronicles containing the entries you wrote during the four years of your lives—so you'll be better informed before declaring your Mono."

I back toward the wall, keeping my eyes on the needle.

"Chronicling is a crucial aspect of the process," she rambles on. "It's an essential human tendency to forget who we were on the way to becoming who we're going to be."

"Do you even hear yourself?" I'm sweating more now, wondering if I ran how soon my sneakers would fly off, and whether I could make it home anyway.

"Trust me, you're going to want to remember every single thing you went through as your four V's. Picking your Mono is the most important decision of your life. Well—" she stops, blushes.

"What?"

"I was just going to say, picking your Mono is the most important decision you'll make—*until* it comes time to pick your Static mate," she explains, and it's clear she wants me to ask her about it. Which I will not do. "I've got my eye on someone kind of special—"

"I'm not good at keeping a diary," I interrupt. "In seventh grade we had to write about our feelings for Human Development, and I forgot every week."

"Well, the best part about Chronicling is that you don't have to do anything but think," she says, carefully unsheathing the needle. Which. Is. Enormous. Thick as a porcupine quill. I suddenly realize the rice grain is supposed to get pushed through that needle.

"You're not sticking me with that thing," I say.

"The technology is amazing," she continues, ignoring my protests. "All you do is think what you want to say, and it gets recorded into your file and securely stored in the mainframe. Hold up your hair."

I shake my head.

"Come on, Drew, stop being such a baby. Turn around."

I slowly begin gathering my hair, but the strands are so weblike and wild, it feels like I'll never be able to contain it all. I'm Medusa. If only, so I could turn this girl to stone and bail. Tracy nudges me with an elbow, and I slowly give her my back.

"The more relaxed you are, the less you'll feel this," she mumbles, ripping open something between her teeth and the fingers not wielding the giant syringe. I feel cool moisture at the base of my neck, where Tracy is rubbing really hard, scrubbing me raw with alcohol like I'm some dirty gutter punk. It smells like Dr. Reese's office. "Just breathe. In and out, big deep breaths."

I inhale and exhale for a few cycles while she futzes

behind me, flips through the pamphlet some more. I'm getting light-headed.

"It can take as little as five minutes a day," she says, placing a hand on my head. "Or it can take as long as you want. But every day, at some point, you need to put some time into thinking about who you are and what's happening to you—just focus your attention on it and you'll know when you're recording. Lean your head forward a little."

"Will it come out, like, complete sentences, or just thoughts, or fragments or—"

"Just think of it as recounting what happens to a really close friend, someone you don't hide anything from. Or if it helps at first, imagine you're capturing the story of this new person's life, like a character. But the person is you. Okay, here goes. Really deep breath . . ."

After a few more seconds I feel the beginnings of what seems like a scalpel carving an incision into the base of my neck—this goes way beyond a "prick"—and soon after, the oddest sensation comes over me, almost like gears churning at the base of my brain. I can feel Tracy start to push the plunger in—it takes two thumbs for her to get it in there, and as she does, she whispers, "In the many, we are one," and I'm holding my head up against her, and the pain is like nothing I've felt before. It's not even pain, it's something way past pain, and my head is whirring and feels like it will explode, but then I feel a *click*, the needle is out, and off in the distance, somewhere from a galaxy far, far away, I hear Tracy's muffled voice trailing off.

There, that wasn't so bad, was it . . . ?

DREW

CHANGE 1-DAY 1

Is this thing on?

Is it even working?

How do I know when it's recording . . . ?

————?

Hello? Um, well, hi. So, I guess this is Ethan, or whatever, Drew, reporting in from, uh, to be honest, my private corner of hell. I don't really know what I'm supposed to be saying here, but Mom and Dad are making me sit here on my bed and *quote* "think about my day" *unquote* (do I have to "think" punctuation?), so I don't really know what to—

Seriously, is this working? How do I get in touch with Tracy? She didn't even give me her cell. I need to ask how to start using this thing. Maybe it's in the bible guide I'm supposed to read. She told me I have to study that thing pretty much cover to cover, which I don't really know how I'm supposed to do considering I have to do this journal every day, which I don't even know if it's recording, but anyway there's that, plus homework, which three out of six teachers actually assigned today, on the first freaking day of school, and then I'm supposed to be glued to my *CB* the rest of the time. I guess I'm not really allowed to sleep.

Anyway, so, well, today sucked. And the back of my neck where Tracy stabbed me is still throbbing. There you have it.

Not much else to say. So, I guess I'm done "Chronicling."

Oh, wait, here's something that happened. This creepy kid basically tried to molest me while I was walking by him to register for school. So that was great. And Tracy told me, "You haven't been given anything that you cannot handle, and things are only going to make more and more sense as time goes on. Not less." Which sounded like cheesy lines from a superhero movie, the kind delivered by some wrinkled old lady right before the superhero does something tragically stupid. You know, to *learn his lesson*. Hubris! Which I remember from eighth grade English class. Thinking you are all that just before you trip into a ditch or unleash some awfulness into the universe, and anyway, Tracy is clearly wrong, since I couldn't handle a single thing from pretty much the second I opened my eyes this morning and thought I was looking at some hot girl who turned out to be my own reflection in the mirror.

I'm guessing not a lot of people can say that about their first day of high school.

I wonder what's for dinner.

Mom and Dad just told me to go back in and do some more, that they timed me and I'd spent only three minutes Chronicling, so there was no way I could've actually gotten anything recorded. I told them I didn't even know if it was working, and that I'll just ask Tracy about it and catch up tomorrow, but that I'd done all I possibly could for the first night. They didn't believe me, and said the early days of Chronicling are some of the most critical. Dad was in fact a little uppity about it, because he said they didn't have this technology back when he was cycling through his V's, and he had to actually sit down every night and write down what happened in a paper journal for his Chronicles requirement. With an actual pen! And ink! Ye Olden Days. So I'm supposed to be happy all I have to do is sit there and *think* everything I want to be recorded.

I told him I have no idea what to say, and he said I should try to Chronicle what makes the biggest impression on me. Okay, fine.

So that guy at registration. I go into the office after Tracy said her schmaltzy thing to me and sent me on my way, and there's a long line of scruffy and bored delinquents waiting under a handwritten sign on the wall that reads, *New Students: Unregistered.* There's also another sign that says, *New Students: Preregistered,* so I start walking up to that desk, because there wasn't a line. Next thing I know, this kid in a German army surplus jacket and a ski cap (keep in mind it's like ninety-five degrees with one hundred percent humidity), steps in front of me, blocking my way.

"S'up?" he slurs right into my face. He has sour garlic bagel breath, stringy black hair snaking out from under his cap.

"Hey," I say back, and stop. Because there is nowhere else to go.

"Hey," he repeats, but sing-songy, like making fun of my voice or something.

"Don't be a wank, Chuckie," the chick behind him says. She's the girl version of him in the face, maybe a year older, and much cleaner. He ignores her and goes so far as to plant his leg on the wall in front of me, penning me in and getting dangerously close to rubbing his junk up against me.

"Let her go," the girl says.

"Only if she asks nicely," he says to me, not budging. Of course, I want more than anything to clock him in the jaw. But something tells me I probably shouldn't.

The girl smiles at me apologetically. "Please excuse my brother, he forgot to take his medication this morning."

Chuckie relents, maybe because he's a little embarrassed. "Catch you around," he whispers as I pass. I can practically feel his lips on my ear, which gives me an all-over body shudder.

Then, after I maneuver around Chuckie the toad, there's the next horror of negotiating my new name. (Thanks for that, Changers Council.)

"Howdy, sugar!" this old lady behind the desk squawks at me. Her hair stiff from root to end, defying gravity. "What's your name?"

"Uh, Drew Bohner," I say, trying to keep quiet.

"Boner?"

"Bah-ner," I repeat, inventing a blue-blood pronunciation on the fly.

"Spell it for me, honey?" the lady asks, pecking into a PC that looks like somebody might've invented *Pong* on it.

"B-o-h-n-e-r," I spell out slowly, hoping that Chuckie can't hear me.

"There you are, right ... *there*," she says, slipping on some reading glasses and leaning closer to me. "I'm sorry, doll, it's just this menopause is seriously screwing with my hearing or something."

And my cheeks go hot and I don't know what to say

to that. Ethan never had to hear about menopause. Or the dating life of somebody he just met. He also never had random crusty dudes getting up in his business in the hallway. Or girls being kind to him—unless they needed something urgent, like directions to the toilet or CPR. Two hours into this Change, and I'm wondering whether that's what being a chick basically is: a constant stream of Too Much Information.

"Okay, you're all set, just need you to fill out an emergency contact card, and . . ." The lady squints into the screen, and I'm just sitting there waiting for some sort of problem with my paperwork. "Looks like we have your medical forms. Yep. And your schedule is set? Yep. And I just need to snap your picture for your ID, and then you'll officially be matriculated with us here. Welcome to Central High, Miss Drew!"

She looks up and pushes a pink 3" x 5" file card across the counter, with a chewed-up pen. "Isn't that shirt just *darling*," she says, as the sputtering printer spits out my paperwork at her hip.

I look down and laugh, but then realize she was possibly serious. Or seriously trying to make me feel good about myself, like they do on *Sesame Street*. I glance around the office; all the other girls getting their photos taken are wearing fancy blouses, tank tops, even dresses.

I start writing *E-T-H*. Shoot. "May I borrow another card, ma'am?"

"What, you don't even know your own name?" she accuses, and for a split second I panic, but then I see her smiling as she slides over another pink card and crushes the first one, tossing it into the trash. "You're just nervous since it's your first day. I see y'all moved from . . . *New York!* Wowie, girl, this is going to be quite a change for you, isn't it?"

"You don't know the half of it," I mutter.

I start filling out the card, *D-R-E-W* . . . I notice my writing looks more slanted and round; I couldn't switch back to Ethan's handwriting if I wanted to.

When I'm done, she punches a few more things into the grubby keyboard, then gives me my schedule and other random paperwork about drunk driving or something, and then directs me to stand behind a peeling strip of duct tape on the floor. Starts messing with a little eyeball-like camera atop a cardboard box and looks into the monitor. "Okay, hon, let's get a nice, pretty smile."

I sort of manage to curl up my lips. She starts gesturing to her own cotton-candy hair. I'm waiting for the picture to snap, waiting, waiting, but she doesn't take it, just keeps patting at her hair while looking at the screen.

"You want to fix your hair, hon?" after a few more seconds.

"Me? What?"

"It's a little . . . You want to do something with that hair?" Her accent makes *hair* sound like *higher*.

"Oh, I'm okay," I say, and she gives me a confounded look before finally taking the picture.

"You want to check it?" She gestures toward the monitor.

"I'm good," I say, and she looks deflated, which makes me feel bad for some reason, maybe because I've made her feel useless by not accepting her help, so I pretend I've changed my mind and say, "Actually, may I see it?" Which seems to make her happy.

She swivels the screen toward me, and there's the photo of a 2" x 2" Drew, all pixilated with a jacked-up *hairdon't* and the eyes of Dead Freshman Walking. Just the top third of the letters *S L A Y E R* run off the bottom edge of the square, and Drew's head is cocked to the left ever so slightly, the way I've seen myself do in photos—like my first Little League picture day when I was on the Orioles, or posing by the old maple with Andy when he was Darth Vader and I was Luke Skywalker for Halloween. There's a sliver of Ethan there on the screen, even if it wouldn't be visible to anybody but him. *Me*. Him?

"You like it?" the lady asks. I have no idea how to answer that honestly. But I nod my head enough for her to process the ID, and while she sets up the camera for another girl who's just reapplied lipstick for the third time and made her eyes look even more ridiculously raccoonish than they had been before, the laminator lights up and Drew's face slowly emerges from the slot onto the counter.

"Ready?" the lady asks the other girl, who snaps to and gives a perfectly flirty and fake smile as the flash goes off.

"Cute!" the lady says, and the girl echoes, "Cute!" and looks overjoyed after peeping herself on the screen like I just did, and then the lady cuts around the laminate of my ID and hands it to me, still warm.

"That boy likes you," she whispers, indicating Chuckie. I must look horrified, because she quickly adds, "I know it's hard to tell with these boys sometimes, but he just don't know what to say to a pretty girl like you."

Join the club, Chuckie.

Although I'm fairly sure you're not supposed to do what

Chuckie did when I had to walk back by him to get out of that office. I tried not making eye contact, instead just sort of nodded at his sister while he was leaning up against the wall with his arms crossed and a knee jutting out into the walking space. "I'll be smelling you later," he growled at me, making a big show of sniffing the air around my hair.

Which was revolting. And really, what's the end game there? What girl would that actually work on? Who wants to be smelled? Luckily, his sister pushed him aside and whipped out a flyer and handed it to me.

"No thanks," I said, attempting to flee the office, but she jammed it into the mesh side pocket of my backpack anyway. I pulled it out as soon as I was in the hallway: cheerleading tryouts.

Now, I won't lie. Can you even lie when you Chronicle? Anyway, I have always, always wanted to attend cheerleading tryouts. For obvious reasons. But as a *fan*. An admirer. One for whom school spirit is best expressed by observing athletic girls doing splits and leg lifts in pleated skirts. The idea that I could become one of those girls was simultaneously horrifying and intoxicating. I mean, if I'm stuck being a girl, I may as well be one who cheers. Right?

If this were a real journal like Dad used to have to keep in the bad ol' days of yore, I would tape the actual flyer into the pages. But I guess I just have to think it into the page. It went:

Show your true colors!
Grab your spirit stick and
Come shake what your maker gave ya!

49

Be positive! Have fun!!
All abilities welcome!
(Some gymnastics background a plus!)

So many exclamation points! I have no idea what a *spirit stick* is, though I certainly have my ideas. And as far as my maker goes, not quite sure what he, she, or it was thinking by giving me *this,* whatever it is. Mission, I guess. Gooo Changers! Rah freakin' rah.

P.S. [C1–D1] My parents think they understand, which is what they just told me about a thousand different times in a thousand different ways over dinner. (Quesadillas, by the way—my fave—so someone at least feels a little guilty.) Not to sound like every other teenager on the planet, but: my parents *don't* understand. Any of this. The only one who has a chance of understanding is Dad, but he went through his changes so long ago, he acts like it's no big deal, and plus he thinks of his cycle as the best years of his life. I'd like to get a peek at a page out of *his* Chronicles from Change 1–Day 1, to see if it was all as "fantastic" as he remembers.

Mom thinks that because she's a therapist and lived life as a female, she knows everything I'm going through right now too. Like taking me to Delilah's at the mall tomorrow after school is going to change a single thing. Like I'm not already forever going to be THAT GIRL, the sad one wearing her mom's soil-stained gardening shorts, whom the rest of the girls set upon like a pack of feral dogs the second I cross into scent range.

Yeah, I forgot before (a.k.a. blocked it out). So after

roving up and down the beige medicinal-smelling hallways, getting looked up and down repeatedly like a piece of damaged merchandise on the discount table that my peers couldn't decide whether or not to buy, I located my first class. Homeroom English.

First thing I do is scan the layout, hoping to plant myself in my customary back row seat, preferably near the door so I can exit ASAP. No such luck. The only open desk is in the second row, center. As I thread my way through the cluttered aisle—*Excuse me, pardon me, sorry*—a girl with Ming the Merciless eyebrows snipes, "Nice outfit, Peppermint Patty," which makes several other girls seated around her snicker conspiratorially.

My ears heat up. The old me would have shot a joke right back, but then again, the old me wouldn't have been wearing a jog bra.

The teacher, Mr. Crowell, an unassuming late-thirties dude dressed in skinny ankle trousers, dress shoes, and a striped tie with a stained polyester short-sleeved button-down I assume is ironic, starts talking about the syllabus and where to buy books. I struggle to pay attention. It seems like everyone is staring at me. The new girl. The new *girl*.

I don't know how to sit. Am I supposed to cross my legs? I discretely survey the room. Most girls are leg crossers. A few at the ankles. Another couple sitting *on* their ankles, like they are around a campfire roasting marshmallows. I opt for the ankle cross. It feels awkward. Maybe I can just press my knees together. For the zillionth time, I was making a mental note to look up something in my *Changers Bible,* when Mr. Crowell started calling roll, and I hear him saying that name.

"Drew Bo-ner? Boner? Boner?"

Oh Christ. The room is already tittering. "*Genius*," the Ming eyebrow chick trills (her name is Chloe), thrilled to have won the easy-mark lottery.

"*Bah*-ner. Present!" I correct, clearing my throat.

"New to the area, Drew B.?"

I nod.

"Stand, please, and introduce yourself to your future friends." I sense the quotation marks around the word "friends," but do as I am told.

"I'm Eth—ah, um, Drew *Bah*-ner."

"And Drew *Bah*-ner, what is it that makes your life worth living?"

"Well. *Madden NFL*, I guess. Skating, *Call of Duty*. BMX." I look around the room, detect major dissonance. I was obviously doing it wrong. Crap. What did Drew's file say she liked? I'm trying to remember. "And tap dancing. Music. Uh. Tacos?"

"Thank you," Mr. Crowell says with no hint of judgment. "Quite a well-rounded young lady."

As I sit down, one of the Ming dynasty snickers, "Dyke much?" And again, the laughter.

I wanted to punch somebody in the throat for the second time prior to nine thirty in the morning. Instead, I studiously avoid everyone else, craning my neck way to the left where, much to my chagrin, a very pretty redhead with curly hair and curly eyelashes and lips as glossy as sardines is smiling right at me.

"Hey, I'm Audrey," she whispers, extending her hand.

"Hey." I reach to shake, but realize I don't know how to as

a girl. I scan my memory for images of women touching each other. Handshaking does not materialize. I end up grabbing just Audrey's fingertips and pressing them together like I'm in some Victorian period movie that makes my mom cry.

"BMX is the bomb," Audrey says, smiling with her eyes. "Don't let the alphas bring you down. It's kind of their job."

"Yeah. I guess."

"That and peaking too early," she adds.

I laugh. I hadn't been sure I remembered how.

After class, the contents of which are a blur, Audrey and I stroll the hallway, with me beside her realizing that no girl had ever voluntarily spent this much time with me before. I begin strategizing about how I can capitalize on Audrey's interest when I remember: I'm not a dude. Audrey is looking for a friend. Not a prom date.

"I gotta have a slash, er, pee," I say to her, nodding toward the bathrooms.

"Okay, see you around," she says, grabbing my arm. "Wrong door, silly!" She points at the *BOYS* sign hovering above my head.

"First day," I offer, shrugging.

"Yeah," her hand still on my forearm. It's soft, warm. "The first day is always the hardest . . ." Then our eyes meet, and when she doesn't drop my gaze I'm thinking hopefully, *Maybe she's also—*

"Of school, I mean. The first day of school is always hard," she finishes.

Duh. School. What else could she have meant? The first day of finding out you are a genetic alien freak charged with changing a world you don't even care that much about? Of course not. Because that would be ca-razy.

"Life's a beyotch, and then you die," I say, sounding more idiotic and desperate by the second. Audrey smiles charitably, her eyes narrowed slightly in confusion.

"M'kay. See you later, Drew Bohner." She says it with the "ah," then winks, vanishing into the thick hallway crowd as I duck into the girl's bathroom.

Holy hipster, is this joint C-L-E-A-N! Sure, the bins overflow with hastily wadded paper towels, but that's because these girls actually wash their hands. They are bent cheek-by-jowl over the sinks, jostling for position and eyeing themselves in the mirror, dabbing on lipstick or pinching their cheeks, spritzing gel into their hair and scrunching it over and over. The place smells like spring and laundry detergent and mint gum. And it's loud. Like a tin can of kittens. Two older girls are turning around, examining their butts in the reflection.

"I see a line!" says one, tugging down her sequined T-shirt in a fruitless effort to cover her rear end.

"You should have worn a thong," her friend comments.

"On the rag, Michelle? *Really?*"

"You totally still can. Just double up on the cotton mice."

"My vag is not the Grand Canyon, skank."

"That's not what I heard."

They both start giggling, then rush out, the one still tugging at the hem of her shirt.

I have never wanted to call Andy more in my life. But I can't call Andy. I can't text Andy. I am dead to Andy, and he doesn't even know it yet.

I am dead to myself.

So I'm just standing there paralyzed watching this soap opera, and before I start seeming too creepy, I remember I should probably find a stall. I go inside the one on the end and lock myself in. I sit down on the seat—no reason to stand anymore.

And with that realization, the horror of my situation washes over me again. I'm a girl. Only, I'm not just a girl. I'm some kind of hybrid; I'm everything and I'm nothing. And I don't know what I'm supposed to do. Why me?

Why not you? I hear Tracy saying in my head.

I can think of a zillion reasons *why not me,* starting with I'm just an average kid. I was never special at anything. Solid B average. I wasn't captain of any team. There are no home movies of me playing Mozart on the piano at age five. No teacher ever pulled my folks aside and said, "This one is *special.*"

Obviously the Council made a mistake. I'm a mistake. This whole tragic thing is a mistake, and I want out. I want, I want . . . oh crap, the tears again. I'm trying and trying, but I can't stuff my feelings in. I let out a wailing staccato moan like an animal snared in a trap. And then the tears pour out of me, and I just sit there with no choice but to let it all go.

"What's going on in there?" some girl asks another. "Is she all right?"

"Are you okay?" the second girl hollers in to me.

"Fine," I gurgle out, unconvincingly.

I wad up some toilet paper and dab at my eyes. It tears apart in my fingers like shameful confetti. Public school toilet paper. Like trying to wipe yourself with a cloud. I give up. Use my shirt as a tissue. Not like an oily snot stain is going to ruin my tremendous outfit.

A bell rings and the room empties. Alone at last.

I don't know how long I sat there. Long enough to eventually stop weeping. And to read all the graffiti on the back of the door, which was terrifying. Note to self: do not get on Rhonda Shiv-you-in-your-Honda's bad side. Bigger note to self: never open that little mailbox container hanging on the sidewall of the john. Horror. Freaking. Show.

I left the soothing isolation of the stall and headed, very late, to Biology, which, *Ha*! I'm thinking Intro to Bio isn't going to have much to offer me this year, given that I am a walking, talking defiance of its foundational principles. Double-helix my Changer-branded behind.

Why even go to classes? What's the friggin' point?

The minute I got home, I flipped open my *CB*, page one, and read:

THE EIGHT COMMANDMENTS

AS PUT FORTH BY
THE CHANGERS BIBLE
TO BE UPHELD AND HONORED HENCEFORTH
FOR THE BENEFIT OF ALL CHANGERS
AND ALL SOULS TO FOLLOW,
AUDIRE ALTERAM PARTEM

1. *Thou shalt not reveal yourself a Changer to those who are not Changers.*
2. *Thou shalt not lie down with other Changers.*

3. Thou shalt not misuse the power thus granted.

4. Thou shalt keep an open heart to all souls, even those who may wish evil upon us.

5. Thou shalt honor thy father and mother.

6. Thou shalt put the welfare of the Changer race before that of thyself.

7. Thou shalt not worship false idols.

8. Thou shalt create the future by completing the past.

And thus do we know:
IN THE MANY, WE ARE ONE.

What a load of crap.

All I wanted to do today, all I want to do right *now*, is go back in time. I want to wake up as Ethan. I want to text Andy and tell him this insane dream I was obviously having. I want to walk around knowing who I am and what I like and what I don't like and what I'm good at and what I want. I don't want to have so many questions. I don't want to be furiously scanning this *CB* for answers that aren't even there. I don't want to feel so stupid. To have to change the planet. I didn't choose this! I would NEVER choose this. I'm not Tracy or Dad, or any of the other good little Changers who probably snap right in line.

This whole thing? It isn't right and it isn't fair and I don't care what that *Changers Bible* or Tracy or my parents keep insisting, but it will never, ever, ever have been worth it.

So, to conclude, I hate my life. And I hate you. Suck on that, Chronicle Overlords. You may be some all-knowing,

Alien-Gandalf-Spockian leaf-on-the-wind secret society with God or *whatever* on your side, but you screwed the pooch this time, Council! You got the wrong guy. You can't force me to be someone I'm not. You'll see.

I feel like "jeggings" might be the worst word in the English language. (Aside from the v-a-g word. And its sister in ick, "menstruation." "Cycle" ain't so great either, come to think of it.) Never mind. I just know that given how today went, the introduction of jeans-plus-leggings into my life is no question a definitive sign that everything in my world is going downhill.

First off, jeans are not supposed to be miniscule, they are supposed to be roomy and comfortable and rugged. Not so tight around your knees and ankles that you cannot squat, or even sit comfortably. It makes no sense to wear a piece of clothing that clings so desperately to your skin it may as well be paint. Who invented this hybrid of tourniquet and denim? It probably has origins in Nazi Germany.

And yet. Here I am, sitting on my bed (uncomfortably, like, it's really pushing into my stomach and making it feel like I have to fart) in a new pair of jeggings, one of three pairs Mom bought for me today, insisting that I'll "be glad I did." I can't believe this is the kind of crap I am going to be wearing every day for the rest of the school year (and probably another).

Sure, I could just take a stand and wear what's comfortable, the kind of clothes I used to mindlessly throw on each morning. But then I'd be facing nine months straight of the kind of abuse I experienced all day today (not to mention yesterday), courtesy of the reigning queen bee Chloe and her clan of doting and fearful beyotch Bees. I now know one of them is named Brit and has a twin, whose name I haven't caught yet (Twit, maybe?), and their dating pool consists exclusively of varsity boy athletes. Chloe's thing is to say she's "over it!" An expression of insolent disdain she applies to everything from Boo Radley to emo boy bands to wedge-heeled flip-flops, usually only after someone else has made what I'm learning is the biggest mistake you can make as a girl in high school—expressing genuine enthusiasm for something.

Example I saw this morning in the hall: Normal-seeming girl wearing hoodie with hearts all over it: "I just got this—sweet, right?"

Chloe, sidling by: "Hearts? For reals? *Over* it." (The normal-seeming girl played it cool, but then I saw her wad up the hoodie and stuff it into her locker before PE.)

Of the Bees, Chloe is by far the meanest, a fact which Audrey highlighted in a note she passed to me in English class that pictured a pencil drawing of a snub-nosed Chloe-monster (surprisingly accurate), and a mouth bubble thing which read, "*I'm over-compensating.*" It was the funniest note I've ever received in class—not to mention with the biggest word—and it definitely made me feel better after Chloe announced loudly as I came into the room (in my mom's shorts again, plus a red golf shirt), "Shrek have a yard sale?"

The whole catty clan laughed in my face. When Mr. Crowell turned around and asked, "Something funny, ladies?" they shut up, and Brit cooed, "I like your tie, Mr.

Crowell. Is that new?" in a bit of an inappropriate tone if you ask me, at which the corner of his mouth twitched, and he turned around to finish scribbling, *T-H-E O-D-Y-S-S-E-Y,* real big at the top of the chalkboard.

At lunch I asked Audrey, "Why do they care so much about what I wear?"

She tilted her head charmingly, as if it was the first time she'd been asked to consider the question.

"I mean, nobody at my old school ever said a word about my clothes, and here—"

"What school did *you* go to?" she laughed. "Kumbaya Prep?"

"No, it was just, like—" I stopped myself. I had a feeling I wasn't supposed to say any more, according to rule number 354.16-A in *The Changers Bible.* "It was just a regular school."

Audrey looked into my eyes and said in what seemed to be all seriousness, "I like your style, Drew."

I laughed it off.

"No, seriously," she said. "Sometimes I wish I had the courage to just wear whatever and not give a toss what people think. Maybe it would free up my mind to think about other more important things, you know?"

Which meant that, *great,* I was now a source of political inspiration, with some (okay, a lot of) pity tossed in, which made me feel even grosser about my Shrek outfit, and why the minute I got home I ditched my backpack, scarfed a piece of string cheese and some chocolate milk, and told Mom I'd changed my mind. "Take me to the mall!" She was happier than Andy at Comic-Con.

Hence, jeggings. And so, so, so much other stuff I never

knew I needed. Like scarves. And ankle socks. And more than one belt. And knee socks. And bump-its. And flats. Which are really shoes with no support, slippers basically, that some genius has figured out a way to charge fifty dollars for. There are more styles of flats than types of beer in Max's Liquor Palace. Not that I've been in Max's Liquor Palace. But I have waited in the car while Dad went in, and that joint is gigantic. You could house elephants in there. And yet, it couldn't begin to hold the number of freakin' flats I saw in one day at the GD mall.

"Maybe one pair?" Mom tried. But I wasn't having the flats discussion. The only item of clothing that seemed gender neutral was good ol' Chuck Taylors. Exactly the same for boys and girls. No nonsense. No bunnies or kittens or sassy, frizzy-haired cartoon girls printed all over them. I got three pairs.

I also got jeggings. In the span of merely twenty-four hours, I've already learned you have to pick your battles.

CHANGE 1–DAY 3

I couldn't have felt any stupider today had I actually tried. (It's becoming somewhat of an unofficial theme for me.)

Here I am, embarking upon the great experiment, heading to school in my new black-and-white striped shirt with a purple tank top underneath, black jeggings with a faint cheetah print, and off-white Converse high-tops. Trying to keep my head up, instead of glued to the ground, taking stock of the trail of discarded items as I had been doing the first two days. Even Tracy didn't recognize me when I spotted her waiting by the Quonset hut to catch me before class.

"Hey!" I yell over.

She turns in my direction, but it takes her a second to register. "Oh my goodness! You look ah-mazing. I'm glad you're getting with the program."

"Whatever," I shrug, looking down, startled by my twiggy legs. It's still like I'm seeing somebody else.

"Well, you look like a completely different person," she says. Totally sincere. I decide to skip the jokes. Tracy, not a friend of comedy.

She holds out an envelope sealed with the Changers emblem. "This is in three or four weeks. You need to go with your folks. It's at a secret location."

"Ah, the famed Changers Mixer I keep reading about."

"Hey Drew," a floppy-haired kid I recognize from Bio class calls from behind me, saluting with the hand not holding his skateboard.

Tracy gives me a look.

"Shut up," I say, snatching the envelope from her.

"Been delving into your *CB*?" she asks, her eyes maniacally darting to and fro the way they always seem to when we're near school. I furrow my brow.

"Expecting someone?" I ask.

"That's just it, Drew. They want us not to expect them."

"They?"

"*CB*. Abiders chapter."

"Abiders. Got it. Anything else?" and when she doesn't answer, I head up the path, a few paces behind the kid with the board. Which reminds me, I miss my own board, and I realize Tracy was the last person who saw me with it, but when I turn around to ask her where it went, she's vanished.

Up at school, I'm waiting for Audrey on the steps, when all of the Bees plus a couple hangers-on stroll by (minus Chloe). I brace myself and look the other way, pretending to spot somebody. Brit and Twit make a point of ignoring me, but one of the nameless Bees surveys me head to toe as she passes. *What?* I mouth at her. Which catches her off guard—"What?" she snipes back, because she can't think of anything to say about me today.

Mission a-freakin'-complished.

I'm feeling really self-satisfied, thinking maybe I'll ask Mom about something to make my hair look a little less like a rat's nest tomorrow, when Audrey comes up. In—I'm not kidding—pretty much the same frumpy outfit I wore the first day (crappy khaki shorts and an oversized black T-shirt, busted tennis shoes). She notices me in the striped shirt and skintight pants, seems like she's about to say something about it, but then: "We're going to be late for first period."

I don't know what to do, so I just follow Audrey into school. "Those suitors really know how to throw a righteous party up in Ithaca, huh?" I call after her, thinking she's probably the only other student who actually read the first two books of *The Odyssey* as assigned. But she's already pulled far ahead and doesn't respond.

In English, Audrey sits one seat over from me, and Mr. Crowell starts getting all worked up about how the goddess Athena takes the form of Odysseus's old friend Mentes and then suddenly shows up at Odysseus's house in Ithaca. As the dude Mentes, Athena convinces Odysseus's son Telemachus to try to kick out all of his mom's suitors who are basically squatting at her house, eating up all of her salted mutton and alcohol and just generally being d-bags because they think the man of the house died in the Trojan War—and that they're going to be the lucky one to nail his wife.

"Meanwhile, where's Odysseus again?" Mr. Crowell asks over a shoulder as he scribbles on the board. I raise my hand.

"Disney World!" some dope wearing a maroon plaid shirt shouts from the back row. Mild chuckling.

"Anyone?" Mr. Crowell turns around. "Yes, Drew?"

"He's stuck on an island with Calypso, who's in love with him and won't let him leave," I say, my voice kind of going up at the end, almost like I'm asking a question—even though I know I'm right.

"*Baum chicka baum baum,*" the same kid in the plaid shirt adds in a porny voice, thrusting his hips forward in his chair, and the classroom completely erupts. Except Audrey, who I notice is slouched over her desk, her demeanor now perfectly matching her outfit.

"Yes," Mr. Crowell says. "And not that I appreciate the outburst, Jerry, but Homer is likely alluding to something a little *untoward* in his description of Calypso and Odysseus's relationship."

I scrawl a note to Audrey, *What's wrong?* and then sketch a little picture of Odysseus handcuffed to the side of an island. I fold it up real small and angular like a paper football and toss it behind another student's back, and it lands right in Audrey's lap. She picks it up, tucks the little origami into her copy of *The Odyssey* without even opening it.

Mr. Crowell is going on about how Zeus and Athena and all the other gods are out there essentially controlling everything in the Greeks' lives, and how they're basically forcing Telemachus to grow up and instantly become a man in his father's absence. For a minute, I can kind of relate, and take heart in the fact that in ancient times it was no biggie for folks to suddenly morph into other folks, but then the bell rings and class is over, and I try to make eye contact with Audrey one last time before we go our separate ways for second period, but she completely ignores me again.

Packing up my books and slinging my backpack over a shoulder, I realize this morning was the first time since waking up as Drew that I'd felt even a teeny, tiny bit better about myself on the outside. But now here I am feeling pretty crappy on the inside, like I said or did something wrong and scared away the only person who'd shown kindness to me because she wanted to—and not because she had to (like Tracy or my parents).

I think about Andy back in New York. How this weirdness never happened with him. We just did what we wanted. Not what we thought other people wanted. We never worried about whose feelings might be hurt by something we said or did, let alone wore to school. I mean, how do you even factor all that in? Doesn't that turn every single decision into one of those crazy-making math problems where the train is going 100 mph, and the passenger is walking backward at .3 mph, and how long before you reach the station and realize the jeggings you chose for the trip are going to ruin your new friend's day?

Being a fourteen-year-old sucks. Full stop. But being a fourteen-year-old girl? Exhausting. You know what might be useful in that *Changers Bible?* A crystal ball and a decoder ring. Because I don't see any other way I'm going to figure this stuff out.

Audrey and I pretty much avoided one another for the rest of the day, but after school I spied her waiting for her ride, so I decided to give it one last shot.

"Are you going out for cheerleading next week?" I ask.

"I don't know," she says, as though she's never considered it, even though we've talked about tryouts, like, seven times.

"I'm thinking about it," I offer, "even though I know it's stupid."

"You should," she says, digging gunk from under her fingernail.

"My mom got all this for me," I say, pawing at my shirt and jeans.

"You look nice."

Then a red Mustang, a three- or four-year-old model, pulls up with the top down, blasting some corny country music, and stops in front of Audrey with a screech. The guy inside doesn't even look at her, just checks himself in the side-view mirror while he waits. He's got aviator sunglasses on, a torn Central High football jersey, beefy forearms jutting toward ten and two on the leather steering wheel in front of him. His skin is seriously tanned, the color of pancake syrup.

"Gotta go," Audrey says, clutching a notebook keeper. In my head I'm like, *What the hell*, which obviously shows on my face because she adds, "He's my *brother*," before stepping toward the car door, which I have to stop myself from opening for her.

"See you tomorrow," I say.

"Yeah, see you," she echoes.

"Who's that?" syrup arms asks accusingly, sucking his teeth.

"The new girl, Drew," she answers, and he looks over his shoulder at me.

He pulls his sunglasses down to the bridge of his nose with one finger. "Hey, Der-eww," he says, somehow managing to stretch the name into two syllables.

"Hey," I reply, but by the time I do, they're already peeling out, V8 engine growling, his spiky blond hair vibrating in the wind.

CHANGE 1–DAY 6

Yo Andy,

You will never believe what happened to me on Monday. You know how girls are like essentially aliens, and we never understand anything they do? Yeah, well, I am one now.

I'm not lying. I'm this (kind of hot) girl named Drew, and on the first day of school I woke up and realized I was her. (I mean I'm still me, I guess, but I'm actually her, or that's what I look like on the outside.) Anyway, right after I woke up and saw her in the mirror, I thought I was dreaming and was even thinking to myself as it was happening, "Damn, I have to call Andy right this minute and tell him what boobs actually feel like," but then my parents came into my room acting all crazy and informed me I am a member of this weird secret race called Changers, my dad's one too, and if you can't tell from the name, basically we change into four different people during high school, and by doing that we're supposed to be making the world a better place or some ridiculousness like that. I'm not supposed to tell anybody about any of this, and "The Changers Bible" (it's like a handbook) strongly suggests that I not be in contact with you at all because I can never be the person you knew. I can never be Ethan again.

So you have to absolutely positively promise, swear on your life, not to tell anybody. Seriously, because there's also this Changers Council out there who will like have me arrested or disemboweled or something if I tell anybody who's not a Changer what I am. Okay? So only write me on this new e-mail account, and I'll write more as soon as I can. Not to be paranoid, but it feels like I'm being watched sometimes, so I have to figure out what I can and can't do.

One more thing, and I can barely write this to you, so I'll just go ahead and say it: I can't skate anymore. Yeah, um, Drew's goofy-footed, and when I tried to skate to school on Monday I totally beefed and landed on my butt. All my skills are so yesterday. One cool thing is you know that gash I got before we moved, and I had to get all those stitches? Totally disappeared, it's like not on this girl's, okay MY, body anymore. No trace of anything like that. I mean anything.

DO NOT tell anybody. Swear, dude.

Your homie,
Ethan

Yeah, right. I totally didn't write that to Andy. Not that I didn't want to. I typed it, and was about to press send, but at the last second I chickened out and deleted it. Here's what I really wrote instead:

Yo A-Rod! What's up? How's school? Have you gotten to second base with any babes yet? I totally have. What's

*been up, man? What's Sleepy Hollow High like? I wish
I could go there with you. This is my new e-mail address,
write me, K?*

*Peace out,
E*

CHANGE 1–DAY 10

Just when I thought I was sort of hitting my stride, things were totally cool with Audrey, I was figuring out how to walk around school and not have to look away when random people made eye contact with me, and I felt like I was dressing how I actually wanted to dress, talking how I wanted to talk, Tracy was buzzing off for the most part . . . today happened.

Cheerleading tryouts.

I'm in the locker room, trying to find a quiet space where there aren't dozens of squealing girls sailing around the room talking about things you don't even hear on late-night TV. Not that I'm not digging this sudden all-access pass into the formerly forbidden sanctuary of the girls' locker room, but Tracy has me all paranoid that when I change my clothes in public, I have to make sure nobody sees the Changers emblem on my badonk—which is still red and raised and nowhere near healed, definitely an attention-grabber. I mean, *I'd* do a double take if someone else was sporting one while drying off next to me.

So I came up with the idea to tell the PE coach Ms. Harmon that I'm new in town and having a "rough" day and am wondering whether I can use one of the tall lockers in the smaller changing room. This seems to work magic on her and she looks at me like she really understands something, but ultimately she declares, "Those are reserved for the *varsity* cheerleaders, hon." Who, as even a casual viewer of any teen movie filmed after 1974 knows, occupy the highest rung in the school social order. (Like so much else about high school, the unfortunate stereotypes bear out: nerds get their heads shoved into lockers, punks get singled out for trouble they didn't start, jocks act like the stars of their own music videos, and cheerleaders dance in the background.)

None of which explains why I am here at junior varsity tryouts. My neck is clammy, a headache starting to squeeze its way in, but I find my way to a slightly less populated corner of the locker room by the showers, carrying the short stack of red, black, and white practice gear that Ms. Harmon had signed out to me. Not a stitch of clothing is free of *CHS* or our mascot the falcon. I put the clothes on the bench, jam my backpack into the tiny square locker, and already I'm deeply regretting the decision to "get involved" like *The Changers Bible* instructs. I mean, how will they know if I actually do "a minimum of one activity per semester"? Oh yeah. Tracy.

The most confounding part of the practice gear has got to be these bloomer things. They're almost like regular underwear, but thicker, with *CHS* emblazoned on the butt, which I guess is supposed to be visible when you're jumping up and down. Like that's a good thing. Central High, *how you doin'?* I mean, I admit I definitely didn't mind catching a glimpse of these when Dad would take me to the occasional Giants game, but I guess I never thought about what it might actually feel like to wear them. Well, they feel like a polyester diaper. Huzzah! Mark that down:

my Changers life lesson of the day—girls' clothes *always* suck.

I leave on my underwear and then I'm wriggling into the bloomers when I hear Audrey joke, "They should hand these out at church." Then some brunette sophomore snarks, "Granny's secret," and I squeak out a laugh and pretend not to notice all the other girls, including Chuckie's sister, who gave me the tryout flyer at registration, buzzing around, their various bare shoulders and thighs brushing up against me like it's no big deal. Like it doesn't make me tense up and chirp, "Sorry, my bad," every time. Like it doesn't feel incredible.

I suit up quickly as possible, acting natural, you know how you do when you're the one-time dude trying out for girls' cheerleading. Oh, forgot to mention there's also a scratchy red skirt that has to go on top of it all (I stepped into it backward at first, until I saw Audrey's, then spun it around 180 degrees, zipper in the back).

The practice outfits are transformative. Girls begin bouncing around like pogo sticks, flipping their hair. It's like that experiment I saw on PBS where they gave some college kids police uniforms and other ones jailbird jumpers, and in no time the police kids started acting all superior and in charge, and the fake criminals started drooping under the weight of their self-loathing. Everybody is twittering about pom-poms—*do we get pom-poms, when do we get our pom-poms, what color are our pom-poms*—and then Chloe comes in wearing the full cheerleading squad outfit and announces that there will be loaner poms for the rookies on the field, and all the girls cheer, *Woo-hoo!* like they've just been told they were voted Homecoming Queen.

Audrey and I look at one another like, *What are we doing?*

"Come on, Ellen and Portia," Chloe sneers, "you don't want to be late for getting cut from the squad."

"I thought cheerleaders were supposed to be cheery," I say.

"Wait, is homophobia even a thing anymore?" Audrey asks loudly, while Chloe, standing perfectly upright, glares at me.

I start to chuckle. Then try to cover it up, which only makes it worse. Audrey takes one look at my contorted, laugh-suppressing face, and cracks up too.

"I'm so *over* you two," hisses Chloe, huffing toward the field. As she spins around, I notice she's braided bows in the school colors into the back of her hair.

Outside, we're all warmed up and stretched out and I'm standing next to Audrey. We've composed ourselves, the angst of the audition settling in full force. My stomach is sloshing somewhere beneath my navel, and I'm hoping I'm just nervous, that the cafeteria tacos aren't Montezuma's Revenging me or something. On the field, the red football side is pounding into padded sleds upon the periodical whistle while the white jerseys are running patterns. The varsity cheerleading squad is spread out on the far side, hollering in unison, flipping here and there and generally looking like the women's Olympic gymnastics team with bigger breasts.

We wannabes are lined up in five rows of five. Chloe has been tapped to teach half of us a simple routine, while the others go off with some older coach-type girls who are going to assess their tumbling skills. Chloe is smug as hell as she prances over to a boom box on the ground and presses play: *All the single ladies . . . All the single ladies,* Miss Bey is call-and-responding. Chloe sings along a couple bars then starts barking directions at us, but I can't hear a thing. I look at Audrey, whose arms are in the air, her stomach showing, where I notice she's got a tiny silver belly button ring. She's trying to keep up with Chloe, but glances over at me, notices me noticing her.

"What?" she scowls, then nods back toward Chloe, who is counting *5-6-7-8*. "Pay attention!"

I *am*, I think. Just not in the way she means. I try to study Chloe's ridiculous high-stepping pattern, and to my surprise, after watching a couple cycles and sort of mimicking it in my head, I can move along with her (and the beat). This from a dude who never, not even once at a friend's bar mitzvah, danced. Not in front of the TV, not alone in my room, not in my dreams. Never. I wonder if dancing is a Changer perk. Sure, your life is going to be in utter shambles, but as a consolation prize you'll be able to grapevine with the best of them. *Dancing With the Freaks!*

Mercy, it's hot out here. I am sweating like a linebacker. My underwear, both pairs of them, grow sodden and itchy. The skirt keeps slipping around, the zipper ending up on my hip. I keep trying to yank it back in place while still flipping my hand back and forth *putting a ring on it*. My hair is sticking to my cheeks. Oh god, I hope I don't have pit stains. Do girls get pit stains? I turn and *yep*, big ol' rings of funk. I'm assuming pit stains are not cheerleading material, but I press on, shaking what my maker gave me.

"I want to see more teeth!" the head coach shouts. She has piles of makeup on, her hair pulled back so brutally she looks like she's been caught on the wrong end of a vacuum. Her voice is *so* enthusiastic, I realize it was likely she who wrote the tryout flyer that obviously cast the hex on me to bring me here today. I mean, *Today!!!*

"More facials, play to the top row!" she screams over the music, her expression a mask of what is supposed to be joy, I guess, but more resembles that dude's face in the Indiana Jones movie right before it melts off and drips down his shirt. "Teeth! Teeth! Teeth! No squinting! You look confused! Happy teeth! Happy teeth! And 5, 6, 7, 8 . . ."

We are taking a break, Coach screeching at another group of happy teeth in waiting, when a football ping-pongs between the rows and comes to a stop in front of me and Audrey.

"Subtle, Jason," Audrey mumbles, which makes me look up. It's her brother in full pads, shirt soiled, helmet dinged up, trotting over to us.

"Hello there, Drew," he says after spitting out his gross rubber mouthpiece. It has dead brown grass stuck all over it.

"What do you want?" Audrey asks him.

"Just retrieving the ball."

"So fetch already."

"What, she don't talk?" He nods at me.

I'm just about to respond when, "Boner twins!" Chloe is snapping at us from the front row. "Coach. Lois. Is. Speaking," she snarls, never happier.

Jason tucks the ball into an elbow and jogs off, Audrey

shaking her head at him, as Coach Lois starts bellowing again.

"If you're serious about making this squad, we have expectations, no exceptions!" She clocks each and every one of us. "No drinking, no smoking, no inappropriate behavior, ever! The Internet is public, ladies! School spirit on and off the field! You are never not representing!"

I watch Jason get reabsorbed into the sea of white jerseys. He flips the ball to another player, and a coach slaps him on the butt as he sets up on the line of scrimmage. A rush of envy rolls over me.

"And practice, practice, practice, no excuses!" Coach Lois hammers on. "All my girls will do a left and right split! All my girls will do a back handspring. Scrunchies should be red and white only! I don't want to see facial piercings, I don't want to see tattoos, and if you have any designs on making the auxiliary varsity squad, you better be up on the first page of this list of skills!" She raises a flapping stack of purple paper. "Take one of these before you leave today. And now I want to see some herkies! Chloe?"

Chloe practically skips into place in front of the group, claps, snaps her arms straight into a Y form above her head, swings them around, and then all at once sticks her left fist on her hip, her right one out perfectly straight in the air, and then at the same time jumps up really high with one leg bent out to the side and the other straight in front like a fancy unicorn. It is one of the craziest, most contorted things I've ever seen, but the next thing I know, I hear, "Let's break it down into two steps. Boner, come up and let me see your jump."

It's just so funny every time she calls me that. I wonder whether it'll ever get old.

Audrey nudges me forward with a shoulder.

"I've never done one of these before," I say, loud enough so everyone can hear.

"Okay, so don't worry about your hands right now, but do the jump," Chloe instructs, all nice for once because the coach is watching, and she cuts her eyes at Brit, who's in the first row, fake gagging herself with a finger.

I figure what the hell. I really want to show Chloe I'm not afraid of her, so I step up and just go for it and attempt the crazy unicorn-prancing thing, and to my surprise, I get really high and don't fall down when I land.

"Good job, girl!" Coach Lois barks, and she seems genuinely surprised (as am I), but I notice one of Brit's hands is covering her mouth and she's pointing at my skirt with the other.

"Let's see it again," Coach says. "And try to add the hands."

Before I register what's going on, I'm up in the air again, and I think I've switched my arms, leaving the wrong one on the hip and the wrong one punching the air, because all of a sudden everybody is laughing at me with these half-horrified/half-hysterical looks on their faces, and Audrey rushes forward and puts an arm around me, leading me in the direction of the field house like I'm an escaped mental patient.

"What's the deal?" I ask, freaked out. "Did my bloomers rip or something?"

"Worse," she whispers after a few paces. "You're bleeding through."

I almost twist an ankle in the turf.

"I'm what?" I look frantically up and down my sides, at my legs, wrists, down my shirt.

"Funny," Audrey says. "Good to see you're keeping your sense of humor." And then: "I think I have some tampons if you're out."

My mind explodes. *Tampons?* I flash on those goofy commercials with women playing tennis in white shorts and lounging poolside in white bikinis. Then I remember my mother's bathroom, that cardboard box that sometimes materializes by the toilet. The one with sizes on the side. *Jumbo.* Or *Super.* Yeah, *Super.* Oh god.

Once in the locker room, which is mercifully empty, I step out of my skirt and in the mirror notice a considerable amount of blood on my underwear. Like, practically as much blood as came out of the gash on my knee when I fell skating. As in, an alarming amount of blood that my instincts are telling me require a visit to the emergency room. But Audrey is completely calm.

"It used to happen to me all the time," she says.

"I—" I cannot speak.

"Wait, is this your first?" she asks after registering my silent scream.

"Um. Um. I guess," I stammer.

"Wow, you're *so* lucky!" she says, fishing around her purse for some change. "I'll get you a pad."

Audrey heads over toward the sinks, pops two quarters into a machine, and turns its silver knob. A plastic pouch drops out.

"I've had mine since I was twelve. I'd be so psyched if I were just getting it now. Welcome to Club Red!"

I still can't eke out more than monosyllables. She hands me the purple plastic thing. The packaging crinkles in my hand. For some reason I think, *Hot pocket.* Then feel nauseous.

"You know how to put—"

"Of course," I interrupt. But I have no clue.

"Did your mom talk to you about it, or, do you want me to show you?"

"NO!" I shout, too loud.

"Okay," she says, in a way that doesn't make me feel stupid.

I head into a bathroom stall, and Audrey stands outside at a respectful distance. "So those little flap things wrap around . . . you know?"

I don't answer, and she leaves me alone to struggle with the hot pocket. But soon she is back.

"Uh, Drew? I have an extra pair of underwear in my bag if you want them. It's no big deal, seriously."

"Everybody saw," I respond, digesting for the first time that this mortification is not mine alone, that the news has probably already been texted to every freaking kid at Central High. Maybe the alumni list too. Possibly even a photo of me in midair. I can't breathe.

"This has happened or will happen to every single one of them." Audrey's hand reaches under the door, her spare panties pinched between her fingers like a handkerchief. I snatch them from her, ball them into my fist.

"I need to be alone," I say, but remember to add, "Thanks."

And then I am, for the second time in a single week, collapsed on a toilet and sobbing from behind a graffitied-up stall in an echoey tiled girls' bathroom—a place I never in a decade and a half of life (not to mention a million years) thought I'd ever (no seriously, *ever*) find myself.

When I got back from school, Dad wasn't home (thank You-Know-Who up above—or wherever You are), and I didn't stop to talk to Mom in the kitchen; I just went right into my room and closed the door behind me. The only person I could imagine talking to was Audrey, but I wasn't about to wait around for her after tryouts.

Soon my mom taps on my bedroom door. "Everything okay, honey?"

"I'm fine."

"You don't sound fine."

"Well, I am. So."

I could hear her padding back down the hall. I pull out my *Changers Bible* and flip to the index. *Our bodies, Girls: p. 157.* I turn a few pages, to a ghoulish illustration of a lady's body cut in half down the middle, in a side view, and lines pointing to various body parts—*bladder, cervix, uterus, anus.*

Anus? Really?

This is precisely the kind of image Andy and I used to cut out of the pamphlets we got in middle school reproductive health class, then affix to each other's notebooks, lockers, skateboards. Once I taped a pair of what I now see are called *fallopian tubes* to Andy's back, and he walked around school for half a day before anybody told him.

I quickly scan back:

Usually heaviest during the first few days . . . More sexual thoughts and urges . . . Sometimes we think love relationships will help us feel stable, but not everybody is ... Some choose to experiment with masturbation to release sexual feelings, while others wait for the feelings to pass ...

I frantically flip another page.

Every single individual is different ... Remember that there are no right or wrong questions or answers ... Making art, music, playing sports, cheerleading, acting, and, most importantly, daily Chronicling will help redirect any anxiety ...

I can't focus on a single complete sentence; it is all blurring together in my head. Another gross graphic, this one about using tampons. Running along the bottom of the pages in bold lettering, I notice:

The best place to start is always your Touchstone. That's why he or she is there! And you can be assured they've been where you are now, possibly two or three times.

Tracy? I'm positive Tracy has never had a stray eyelash, never mind bled all over herself, let alone in front of half the school mid-herky. The thought of telling her about this makes me want to go to sleep. For four years.

P.S. I feel fat. What the hell is *that* about?

CHANGE 1–DAY 12

I take back every time I've said (or even thought) that girls are annoying. Any time a lady has been snippy with me over the last almost fifteen years, including Mom, I hereby totally, retroactively understand. First off, having your period once in a lifetime would be hard enough, but EVERY MONTH. WTF?! I can't believe I survived a day without stabbing someone in the retina. (Another life lesson, Changers Council? Is that all you got? Cause this is almost *too* easy.)

I couldn't have done it without Mom. I finally broke down this morning and told her what was happening. It wasn't like I had a choice, but she was totally cool and told me that when she got her period, Granny advised her to keep an aspirin between her legs so she wouldn't get pregnant. Which is disturbing. But also funny, in a retro-denial 1950s conservative kind of way.

You know what's not funny in any kind of way? Putting a tampon in. I think, for me, that little advancement in the womanly sciences will have to wait a few more months. Or V's. Maybe I should ask Tracy about *that*. Just to see her squirm.

I went back to cheerleading tryouts this afternoon, and all I had to say to Coach Lois (in a soft, shaky voice) was, "I'm sorry about the other day, but I got my period—for the first time," and all was forgiven. Clean slate. She practically blurted that I already had a place on the JV squad, but I'm still worried that when the list goes up on Monday, my name isn't going to be on it.

I don't know why I care, but I do.

CHANGE 1—DAY 14

So this thing happened today. I mean, it wasn't a *thing*. That's making too much of it. A moment maybe? I'm probably exaggerating it in my head, now that I think back. It was nothing. Just a guy and a feeling. Which makes no sense, I know. Hormones. That's all. Topsy-turvy Changer hormones. Make typical puberty look like the hiccups.

Anyway, I'm shopping with Tracy at ReRunz. We decided to meet there instead of our usual hideaway, the craptastic Quonset hut. Mostly because the Quonset hut smells like dead livestock and gasoline and I get no small amount of PTSD every time I go in there from my involuntary human kebab moment. I had just said "s-h-o-p" when Tracy clapped her hands together in quick succession and cheeped, "Perfect! I need some new cardigans."

We meet in the *New Arrivals* section, which I joke about, and true to form, Tracy doesn't get.

"What's the latest?" she asks, flipping through the hangers with such ferocity they snap.

"Oh, not much. I started my period in front of the entire freshman class."

"Yeah. I heard."

I consider asking how, but decide I'd rather not know.

"At least you're on track, developmentally," she says,

pulling out a plaid vest with sequin epaulets. She holds it to her chest. "Too much?"

"Not if you're enlisting in Prince's army."

"What else?"

I'm about to say, *What do you mean, what else? Every day, all day is what else,* when over the racks I see this dude walk in, arms full of garbage bags, denim jackets and sweaters spilling out of the top—girl clothes. He is grimacing, the bags slipping and sliding, stuff falling. He barely makes it to the resale counter where he drops the whole lot like it's nuclear waste, throws his arms back, and sings, "Ta da!"

Then he smiles.

Thinking on it now, I can't recall ever noticing another dude's smile. Not counting the Joker, or freaks like that. But some random guy in a shop?

And yet. This smile imprinted on my brain. I was mesmerized. When I blinked, I could reproduce it exactly, as if a flash had exploded before my eyes and seared the image onto my visual cortex. Which is exactly what I was doing when—

"Drew? Drew? *Drew!*"

Tracy is tugging my arm, trying to get my opinion on some pleated shirt or pants or god knows, but I am gone. Buried alive someplace in that guy's mouth, unable to turn away, until, what the hell?!

"Ow!"

Tracy flicks me in the nose. "Snap out of it."

"That hurt. Dang. Where did you pick that up? Touchstone torture camp?"

Tracy isn't listening, she's too busy eyeing the smiling guy, her face a scrunch of disapproval.

"Let's go," she says, pulling my sleeve again, practically dragging me out the door and back toward the Quonset hut of doom.

"What gives?" I yank my arm free. "I was just looking around."

Tracy inhales sharply, sucking her breath as if through a straw. "It is too soon for you to be initiating romantic relationships."

"Wait a minute. Hold the phone. I wasn't initiating any—"

"There are procedures and policies, and I know you haven't bothered to memorize them, but they nonetheless still exist," she scolds. "Also, commandments 1, 2, and 6 ring any bells?"

"What are you yammering on about? This is stupid. I was looking at the counter. No biggie. The dude had a lot of bags. Is there a policy against looking at bags?"

"This isn't a joke, Drew. Your time for intimate relationships has yet to arrive. We can't have chaos. And chaos is what will result from wantonly ignoring the rules. We—you—are better than that."

"So you think I was *into* that dude? Because that is totally off-base. *Gross*. I mean, really?" I scoff.

"Just keep it together until the Changers Mixer. I'm not kidding. You do not approach, initiate, engage, or, most vitally, touch any other person until after said mixer. Are we clear?"

I narrow my eyes. "This is bullsh—"

"Are we clear?" she repeats.

"Yes, commander. We're clear. No letting my eyes wander in public spaces."

"Drew. Sometimes you are . . ."

She doesn't finish. She doesn't have to. I understand that for her, my doing *whatever* I was doing, reflects on her Touchstone performance, and G forbid she get a single demerit. I can deal with all that. I can even deal with the fact that I'm going to be inhabiting a girl's body for a year. It bites. But I can deal.

What I can't deal with, if I'm honest, is the fact that for what seemed like a century today I was transfixed by a guy smiling in a shop. Who am I? One of the Brontë sisters? I mean, what went down there? It felt cosmic. Big and otherworldly. You could have told me anything in that moment and I would have believed it. He's from the future. Of course. He's immortal. He's a god from *The Odyssey*. It was the first time since this whole thing began that I was completely outside of myself. Buoyant. In flight. Nothing heavy. Nothing wrong. Looking at him, I ceased to be.

It was the best feeling I have ever had in my life.

Tracy was right.

I gotta stay the hizell away from that.

CHANGE 1–DAY 15

Okay, I'll say it. The bar is lower for boys. I know for girl-born-girls this isn't news. But for us newbies, it is a real awakening to have your hand up in pre-algebra waiting so long to get called on that your blood starts to pool in your neck. Mrs. Walsh must have asked every single boy in the room for their answers before she even considered calling on me, or Michelle Hu, who probably learned algebra in her crib.

(And yes, I know Changers are supposed to be ridding the world of reckless stereotypes like "Asians are good in math," but for reals, Michelle Hu is like the Stephen Hawking of Central. Ask anybody.)

Let's see, what else? Ah yes. When a guy makes a joke in class, the girls always laugh. It could be the lamest punch line in the universe, and still, here come the ha-has. Which I guess explains Howie Mandel's career.

Also, girls aren't allowed to fart. Ever.

On the plus side, I made JV cheerleading. So did Audrey. And all of the Bees who tried out. And Chloe is captain, shocker, as well as the only freshman on the auxiliary varsity squad. So if, like, one girl on varsity gets swine flu, the Chlo-ster is moving on up. Which she mentioned no less than a dozen times when we were getting ready for our first official practice this afternoon. (If I'm on the varsity squad,

I'm not eating any Chloe-prepared gift-basket brownies, if you know what I'm saying. I bet she's Googling *untraceable poison* as we speak.)

After we get our uniforms and are assigned our (slightly bigger than standard PE) lockers, Chloe comes into the locker room with a clipboard and announces that we have to be on the field in sixty seconds. The fourteen of us kick it into high gear, yank on our matching skintight nylon shorts and baby tees, and head out, clapping in unison. We have to thread through the packs of athletic teams running and warming up around the track. About half of our squad gets through before the rest of us get stalled by the girls' soccer team.

I watch them scramble by, their cleats stirring up red dirt around their ankles, and I'm thinking, *I am an idiot*. The competitive part of me is glad I made the cheerleading team, but another part of me wonders why I even tried out in the first place. The girls on the soccer team look so much more like me, like Ethan, the kind of girl Ethan would like, the kind of girl *I* like. The kind of girl I guess I thought I was.

In all my experience of being one for two weeks.

The rest of our squad crosses after the soccer girls pass, but I'm not paying attention and am left alone on the outside of the dirt track, now waiting as some cross-country runners zip by. In the center of the loop, I see sets of red-and-white pom-poms resting in the grass in a neat row. I can hear most of the girls screaming and clapping with excitement as soon as they spot the poms, running up to their desired pairs and hovering over them, unsure as to whether they are allowed to touch.

"Go ahead, girls!" Coach Lois shouts.

They do, even Audrey, whom I'm watching in between flickers of individual runners: boys, girls, JV, varsity, tall, skinny, short, squat. They are all in the same sensible relaxed shorts and breezy T-shirts, some in tank tops with *Central* emblazoned across a stripe of red bisecting their bodies. I look down at my short-shorts, my too-tight T-shirt. I feel stupid.

"Drew," a couple of my squad mates holler, "come on!"

"Sorry," I call back, forcing my way through and tripping a girl who looks like a senior.

"Watch out!" she snaps, her long brown ponytail whipping behind her as she recovers and sprints on.

When I rejoin the squad, Coach Lois is asking everybody to gather in a circle. "Ladies, I am so proud of you," she begins. "Every year I think to myself, *This has got to be the most talented squad of all time,* but then the next class of girls comes in and blows me away all over again. The sheer skill level alone!"

Then, in a flash, her normally exuberant expression clicks off, and she asks us to join hands and bow our heads. I catch Audrey's eye across the circle and we both grimace. I put my palms out to my side, Brit takes one, and a girl I don't know very well, Josie, takes the other. I notice most of the girls are closing their eyes. I decide to focus on my shoes.

Coach Lois continues: "Being a Lady Falconette is not something to be taken lightly. I was a Falconette for two years, and then a proud Lady Falcon for another two years after that. This was, of course, many years ago." She peeks up at the other coaches, all younger, who smile extra sweet. One pops a bubble inside her mouth, and Coach Lois flinches like somebody just slapped a kitten.

Now her voice goes warbly and thick: "Those were the most formative years of my life. I know it's hard to understand, but I promise you right here, right now, that all the hard work you put into this squad, and the friendships you make while doing so, will be one of, if not *the* most influential part of your high school lives."

Doubtful, I think.

"Now let's go out there and make it the best Lady Falconette season ever! Can I get an amen up in here?"

Everybody shouts "Amen!" (except me) and claps. I lift my head, and there in the distance are the soccer girls, doing push-ups. Chloe catches me.

"See something you like, Bloody Mary?"

I ignore her. Which, unlike what it swears in every anti-bullying strategy pamphlet I ever got handed, does NOT make her give up and go away. Instead, she leans in tight to my ear, her breath damp, and hisses, "If it were up to me, you wouldn't even be here right now. But you are. And because you are, you are going to stay on the squad, and you are going to worship the squad, and you are not going to make me look like a fool by devoting anything less than your complete and full attention to the squad. Got it, bitch?"

And then she draws even closer, her voice an eel.

"Don't make me tell everyone in school who you really are," she warns, after which she pulls away grinning ear to ear like she's just shared some delicious secret.

I am trying not to freak out about Chloe, and have been studiously avoiding being alone with her for the last couple days. The *CB* has a whole section on being "outed" and various "stratagems for denial," but Tracy said not to worry until there was an actual reason to worry.

To which I said, "Have you met Chloe?"

Tracy assured me she'd keep an eye on the situation, told me to act normal, which, *okay, sure.* But it is still hard not to imagine all the fresh hells Chloe and her alpha twadgettes could unleash if they were to reveal to the whole world that I am a mutant.

Of course, who would believe her? Right?

Thankfully, I have other ridiculousness to keep me busy and not worrying, like more homework than I've ever had in my life, and interminable cheerleading practices where Coach Lois keeps us as long as it takes for every single girl on the squad to learn a new skill—plus, all this Chronicling, which you know what? I'm done with tonight, because I have a math test tomorrow that I haven't studied for yet, plus like a hundred pages to read in *The Odyssey* in order to get caught up for Mr. Crowell.

Speaking of whom—today in class we talked all about succumbing to temptation and how that leads to wasting your life, like when Odysseus spends another whole goddamn book boinking yet another goddess, this witchy lady named Circe, who had magically turned all of Odysseus's crew into pigs. Which isn't ideal, because pigs don't know the first thing about sailing ships across treacherous waters back home to Ithaca. So then another controlling god shows up and tells Odysseus he can eat some herb which will prevent him from being susceptible to getting turned into a pig when he confronts Circe to try and get her to turn his pig-men back into regular men. Which she does after Odysseus essentially gives her a beat-down, and then the next thing you know, they're all madly in love, and he and his men abandon their journey to Ithaca, living with Circe in the lap of luxury for a WHOLE YEAR.

I need to keep reading, because maybe there's a clue in the book about where to find said magical herb that makes you resistant to getting changed into a pig against your will.

I am screwing up in math. I used to be good at math. And now I am bad at math. I attribute this to Mrs. Walsh and her reflexive, subconscious sexism. And to my preoccupation with other things, like not getting killed by Chloe. I try to make this clear to my folks when I tell them about the D+ I got on my first pop quiz.

"This is an insane time for me. I started high school. I changed genders. Do the *math*, Dad!"

No laughs. Not even a titter. Instead a rant about how those are just "excuses" and this family does not "tolerate" excuses, to which I want to say, *So much for that fabled Changer empathy*, but I don't. I just sit there and count (ha!) the ways algebra will not matter in my life in any way, shape, or form.

What *does* matter? The social ladder. The girls I've met and grown friendly with, Shuba and Em and some others from the JV squad, Audrey of course. They are all smarter by a mile than any of the dudes I ever used to roll with. (Sorry, Andy.) And yet, all day every day it's: who likes who? Who hates who? Who is a slore, a geek, a dorkfiend, a Fatniss, a Lohan. Which girls' lady parts stink like expired yogurt. Whose haircut is so ugly it looks like it was chewed up and vomited out? On and on, this endless calculus of who is on top, all these idiotic turf battles that amount to who knows what—a date with some moronic football player, I guess. *Totally worth it.*

Worse than all of that? I am starting to act the same way. Not entirely, obviously. I'm not a total beyotch. But if this whole Changer mission is about improving the human race by making everyone kinder or more understanding or some crap, then they shouldn't have involved teenage girls. Maybe if the idea were to learn the fastest way to destroy a person's life, then yeah, stick me in one of the alphas' bodies, because those girls could take down the Red Army in two days.

Like, there was this afternoon when all of us cheerleaders were exiting the locker rooms en masse, and we passed Audrey's brother Jason and some other jock tormenting this sweet, kind of endearingly cheesy guy, Danny. They were standing really close, pressing him between their two chests, chanting, "Looks like we made ourselves a fairy sandwich."

"Any of you girls want to take a bite out of this?" Jason asked as we shuffled by. Some of the cheerleaders laughed. But I could tell from the dread in Danny's eyes, he didn't think it was so amusing.

"Maybe we should help him out?" I suggested. But the girls just kept on strolling.

"Mind your own business, Boner," Chloe spat as she brushed by.

So I did nothing.

I heard later that Jason stuffed Danny into the soiled-towel bin and sat on top of him so he couldn't get out for twenty minutes—threatening that if Danny fought back, he would shave Danny's head.

When I asked Tracy at our next meeting if I should have

done anything, she said elliptically, "What do you think?"

"What could I have done?" I whined.

"Well, now you'll never know," she answered, all matter-of-fact. Which made me feel like a monster. Worse, the person who stands by and allows the monster to terrorize its victims.

So yeah, I am having my moments. It's just so confusing. The rules. The shifting loyalties. The minute bursts of, I guess, power. For instance, the other day, when I was in my JV uniform for the pep rally before our first home game, I was cruising down the hall and I noticed that I felt . . . *special*. Which is irrational. But then I saw other kids eyeballing me like I *am* special. And it felt good.

Which felt bad.

Before that game I asked Audrey if she minded wearing the uniform, and she snorted at me and said, "Are you kidding? I tried out *for* the uniform."

In summation: the concept of cheerleading is terminally horrendous. But the trade-off is that you are queen of the world. (A really shitty, awful, confusing, heartbreaking world.)

Ready? O! K!

CHANGE 1-DAY 20

After cheering (Central won), Audrey and I went to the post-game keg party, something we never would have been invited to if we weren't on the squad. It was at a senior lineman's house in the hills. His parents were attending a Joel Osteen salvation Weekend of Hope retreat, so while the parental cats were away, basically, mayhem.

We arrive around nine p.m. and there is already puke in the pool. Cheesy rap music is blaring through the yard, and all the white dudes are bumping along, eyes narrowed into slits of self-regard. The black team members are in the living room, battling it out playing *Modern Warfare 3*, which looks off the chain, but I can't exactly pull up a chair. Some kids are dancing. Others are making out against doorframes and on lawn chairs, their elbows popping through the plastic lattice. Every surface is littered with cans and bottles and hastily ripped open bags of pork rinds and nacho cheese–flavored chips.

"I haven't touched anything that isn't sticky," Audrey says, wincing and holding her hands curled up in front of her like a velociraptor.

"Maybe there's some Purell in the bathroom?" We loop our way over and around the bacchanalia. By the line for the bathroom, we spot Jason, using his phone to take pictures of a pretty girl who had passed out on the floor.

"Lift up her skirt," he commands one of his bro-friends, who quickly kneels down and hikes the girl's denim mini to her hips, revealing Hello Kitty underwear.

"Meow," Jason purrs, clicking shot after shot.

I turn to Audrey. Her face is stark white. She marches over, slaps the phone from her brother's hand. It skitters across the floor, landing at my feet.

"The eff, Audrey? I was Tweeting that!"

"You're a pig, Jason."

His buddies laugh. Jason does not.

"Pick that up, Drew Bone-me," he snorts, jerking his head toward the phone.

I look at Audrey, her eyes pleading with me not to. I glance at Jason's gang of friends, drunk meatheads who won't even remember most of this conversation, let alone the night. Then I turn to the girl, bend over, and gently tug her skirt back down, crossing her legs as I do.

"Let's go, Audrey," I say, *accidentally* kicking the phone into the next room when we walk by.

"Good luck getting a ride home!" Jason shouts.

"Good luck explaining to Mom what you were just doing!" Audrey screams back, but her voice is shaky. She seems spooked.

"Are you really going to tell your parents?" I ask when we're a safe distance away.

"I don't know." Audrey drops her head. "Sometimes it's so hard to know the right thing to do."

I nod.

"Please don't hate me because of that," she adds.

"Because of what? Confusion? Because I can top you—" I start.

She gestures to Jason, now down the hall, tubing a beer through his nose. "No. *Him*."

"Oh geeze, Audrey, I never would. Not for that or any reason." I resist the urge to wrap my arms around her and make her feel safe.

"He's my brother, you know?" She's crying now, feverishly wiping the tears as soon as they fall, so no one will see. At a loss, I hand her the edge of my shirt. It's at this precise moment that Chloe sidles up, grinning like a baboon.

"What's wrong, little lamb chop? Catch a glimpse of yourself in the mirror?" She is slurring her words, listing a bit to the left.

"Not now," I snap.

Audrey sniffs hard, trying to pull herself together.

"Why are y'all even here anyway? This is supposed to be a party for cool people."

"Did you really just say that out loud?" I say.

"You know what, Drew? You may be cute on the outside. But on the inside? So. Much. Boring." Her eyes droop for a second, and she stumbles. I grab her by the shoulders, keeping her from planting chin-first into the coffee table.

"Here, sit down," I coax, and she does, one eye open now, glowering at me. "You have a friend with you?" I ask. "Someone who can—"

"Shut the freak up, freak," she spits, struggling to hold herself upright. "Of course I have a friend. I have hundreds of friends. I have more friends than you will ever—" And then, with no warning, she projectile pukes into my face.

Audrey and I are gob-smacked. (Well, me more like

puke-smacked.) Chloe, humiliated, bolts from the sofa, her hands over her mouth.

"That was the most amazing thing I have ever seen!" Audrey squeals, tears coming down again, this time from joy. And even though I stink of bile and synthetic peach, and will likely never get the vomit smell out of my hair, I am filled with happiness. Because my best friend is laughing. And I have never seen her look more beautiful.

I've been thinking a lot about love. Which is odd because Ethan never gave love much consideration. Sex, sure. That was a preoccupation. Having it, eventually. Sooner better than later. Not being horrible at it. That thought certainly crossed. But love? Yeah, no. There were no fantasies about falling in love, being in love, swirling in circles through yellowing woods while a symphony soared in the background providing a soundtrack to the love. Ethan loved the Yankees. And his dog.

Okay, it's possible Ethan would have started thinking about love. Guys do fall in love. I've listened to Maroon 5 lyrics. So maybe Ethan would have met Audrey and then gone home and put on "She Will Be Loved" and thrown himself on the bed in a heap of unmanageable longing. Not that that is what I'm doing as Drew.

What am I doing? That's a good question. Another one: what does what I'm doing even mean? In History we read about Viktor Frankl, this Jewish psychiatrist guy who survived the concentration camps. He wrote, "If there is meaning in life at all, then there is meaning in suffering." Which means no life escapes suffering, that suffering might even be a prerequisite for meaning, if I'm doing the math right. And also that Viktor Frankl is a hero we can all get behind. Because he saw light and purpose in the middle of the darkest world. He took hate and fear and sculpted it into a reason to go on. And here I am all, *Oh, being a Changer is sooo hard.*

I'm a jerk. I may even be a bad person. Sometimes it feels that way. When I careen out of control. When my mind cracks open and all these horrible thoughts come tumbling out. When I realize I will never be able to fulfill whatever mission I'm meant to be on. When I wish it weren't me who was chosen. Why does it seem like all the choice always belongs to somebody else?

Free will versus destiny. What a joke.

I don't want to feel the need to be around Audrey. I don't want to feel my stomach do a somersault when I catch a glimpse of some random dude smiling in a used clothing store. I don't want to feel anything at all that I can't control.

If that's what love is, you can keep it.

CHANGE 1-DAY 27

"I'm supposed to go out and make friends and be a normal teenager, and you're not letting me!" I hear myself shouting at Mom and Dad. My voice tilting high the way it does when I'm arguing for something I want but know I'm not going to get.

"Of course we want you to make friends," Mom says, laboring to keep her own voice calm. "That's the whole point of the mixer."

"I thought the point of the mixer was indoctrination."

Mom shoots me a check-the-attitude look.

Whatever.

"Listen, honey," Dad breaks in. (I still can't get used to him calling me pet names like that. He never used to call me anything but *Eath*, or maybe *buddy*, and now it's *baby* or *darlin'* or *thanks sweetie*, like I'm a waitress passing him a Denver omelet.) He goes on—oblivious to my rage. "I understand you're upset, but you're not going gallivanting with your girlfriend. You've got far more important things to do today."

"I am so *over* having *important* things to do!" I holler, impotent. "And she's not my *girlfriend!*" I storm off into my bedroom and slam the door, something I'd done maybe once in my life before changing, and now seem to do anytime the wind blows a funny way.

Which is where I am now, Chronicling this bullshit because, I don't know. I don't like admitting it, but I guess it does make me feel a little better. Score another one for Tracy.

This afternoon is the first Changers Mixer, and I thought I wanted to go until Audrey invited me to hang with her, and I immediately realized that no mixer is going to be as much fun as that, definitely no mixer that includes my parents, who are supposed to attend "transition support workshops," while we kids go with our Touchstones to "self-discovery seminars," which sound so freaking lame I can barely stomach thinking about them. The whole thing supposedly ends with a giant party, but again, a party with our parents and Touchstones . . . so, like, an Amish party.

I suppose I'm mildly curious. Maybe stuff/my life will make more sense after the mixer like Tracy and the *CB* says, but I'd really rather go into town with Audrey and her friend Jed—a dude who doesn't go to our school, who I assume is just a buddy of Audrey's—I mean, what else could he be?

Scary Jason was going to drop the three of us off— the plan: to chill on our own in East Nash. Eat noodles from the Thai lunch truck, check out some of the vintage record shops—I don't know, just be away from school and everything for a few hours. And now it will be Audrey and Jed alone, without me.

I just texted Audrey to let her know I couldn't go.

Bummer. Why? she texted back, right away.

Because I'm a freakazoid alien who only recently turned into a chick called Drew but still pretty much feels like a dude named Ethan, a basically decent guy who'd be totally crushing on you had he not turned into a GD girl, and in a couple hours I have to go to this convention where I'm supposed to hang out with other freakshows like me and talk about how awesome it is to be us. Thanks for the invite tho!

Kidding.

What I really texted Audrey: *Parents :(*

Her: *Sorry :(Will miss u.*

Me: *Have fun, get me a skinny tie if you see a good one at the thrift store. See you Monday. How do you know Jed?*

CHANGE 1–DAY 28

I was so exhausted when we got back from the mixer last night that I fell into bed without changing into my pajamas or brushing my teeth. I just now woke up—ten past noon. Completely disoriented. Okay, maybe not as disoriented as a particular morning four weeks ago, but still, I'm pretty out of it.

Where to start?

Maybe the car ride? I'm so tired, I can barely think . . .

Okay, before we even get into the car, it takes me about a million years to get dressed. I have no idea what I'm supposed to wear to a mixer. Is it formal? Am I supposed to be trying to impress somebody, like am I going to meet the Wizard? I opt for some jeans without holes, a knit top, and my black Converse high-tops.

Then Mom pops her head into my room. "Is that what you're wearing?"

Dang.

"Yes," I say, feigning confidence.

"Do you want me to help you put on a little makeup?"

"No, I do not," I say, beyond sure.

"No pressure, you're lovely au naturel. I was just checking."

Dad drives. It's more than an hour away, in the sticks. When we pull off the highway, there are fewer and fewer buildings, then just fields. After a series of hairpin turns off rutted dirt roads, we come upon a row of tightly planted trees. A virtual wall of greenery. We loop around one edge and I spot a massive compound that resembles a huge warehouse facility. Bigger than Cost Plus. There's a border-style barbed-wire fence around the whole place, and a line of cars waiting to get through a security checkpoint, where some dude in a uniform is ticking names off a clipboard. He has a walkie-talkie. And what looks like a gun, but more sci-fi. *Sweet.*

"I haven't been down here since we moved," Dad says, leaning forward and checking out the length of the facility through the blue strip at the top of the windshield. He whistles. "It's big. Serves the whole middle-southeast region."

"I'm glad we picked the South," Mom says, rolling down the window and cutting the A/C. "I like it hot."

Dad pinches her on the thigh and she jumps, starts giggling in a Mom way. As we creep closer to the entrance, I roll down my rear window and clock license plates from Georgia, Kentucky, Alabama, North Carolina. "How many Changers are here?" I ask.

"You know, I don't know," Dad says. "But I bet that's something we can ask today."

"It's okay."

"Are you nervous?" Mom asks.

"I guess. Not really."

"Well, lucky you. I am!"

"Why?" I ask.

"I'm nervous for you—"

"What, you don't think I can handle it?"

"That's not it at all," she says.

"Look at these schmo-hawks," Dad interrupts. Just outside the facility gate, a group of about a dozen kids are walking in a circle behind a barricade. They're all wearing the same T-shirts, in bright colors and bearing the same emblem, a Roman numeral IV turned on its side, which actually looks like a greater-than-or-equal-to symbol, plus slogans like *No Shame in Change* and *I Changed: So Will You.* Some of them carry signs that say *Change Happens* and *I'm not a Changer, but my boyfriend is.*

"Who're they?" I ask.

"Idiots," Dad pronounces, but won't say more. He puts his arm through the open window and presses his thumb onto an electronic reader that the attendant presents, and we are waved in, just as I catch the eye of a pale redheaded kid in the line of picketers. I'm close enough to read *Silence = Death* on his snapback hat, and he lifts his hand to shoot me a peace sign as we drive by.

Once inside, the building is teeming with kids, parents, Touchstones, and various executive-looking people in fancy business clothes. I wonder if they are part of the Council. Everyone except for the Council-types seems anxious, like this is one giant blind date and nobody knows what to do or say. In no time, I spot Tracy power-walking down the hall, a cluster of files under one arm. She's wearing a black pantsuit and matching braided black headband and stacked heels that make a clacking noise on the floor as she races along. I have never been so happy to see her.

I cling to her when she greets us in the main entry hall. She pins on our name tags, and then she and Mom blab about I don't even know what, while Dad schmoozes with some other parents of new Changers. I look around the giant hall and wonder why there are ship models, diagrams, plans, and parts everywhere beneath Plexiglas.

Tracy notices and whispers, "It's not a ship-building company *officially*, but it sure looks like one from the outside."

Next thing I know, it's time to break off into adult and kid groups. Mom hugs me goodbye, Dad pats my arm, and the Touchstones lead us toward the north end of the building. As I funnel through, I realize everybody here, probably almost a hundred of us, is a new Changer. Every kid woke up as a new person a month before. I was still nervous, but it was the first time in what seemed like months that I didn't feel on guard, or like my biggest secret was suddenly going to blurt out of my lips, leaving me to blame for the ruin of all Changerkind.

We all file into an auditorium and take seats next to our Touchstones, one of whom, a guy dressed in a too-tight suit, hotfoots it down to the front and flips on a giant LED screen where the da Vinci Changers emblem pops up.

Damn, that thing could use a makeover, I'm thinking while staring at the dated glowing logo, when I hear a guy in the row behind me whisper, "Cheese-tastic." I laugh, then turn around to read his name card: *Chase*. I look up into his green eyes, and he smiles.

Oh Christ. It's *him*. The guy from ReRunz. The smile guy. The smile guy who is now smiling right at me. With his smile.

"Well, hello there," he says, his eyes panning to my name tag, "Drew."

(OMFG!)

"What's happening?" he asks.

"Nothing. Just mixing, mixer-ing, mixy-ing it up," I spaz.

He smiles again, and it seems at once like I've both known him forever, and that I will know him forever. My mouth turns to cotton and I pivot back around and pretend to watch the presentation.

"You okay?" Tracy mutters. She has yet to let her eyes leave the presenter. She's also taking notes. Without looking down at the paper.

"What? I'm fine."

"*Conducere.* In Latin, it means *to bring together,*" too-tight suit guy begins, and some incredibly stylized, ultra-modern graphics replace the emblem and cycle on the screen above him. "You are Changers because that is what you did. You changed a month ago. Boy—or girl!—did you." Random nervous tittering from the audience.

"But that doesn't quite explain why you are on this planet. As Changers, you are conduits; you bring people together, various disparate people whom you never dreamed could exist in one household, much less one body. You are living proof that humans can indeed understand one another, can in essence *be* one another, can ultimately share this planet, not in spite of their differences, but *because* of those differences. Which, as you are coming to grasp, only exist in our fearful imaginations. You have certainly changed, and you will no doubt change again, and in doing so, you slowly, steadily, *undeniably* change others. As it says in Book One of our *CB, In the many, we are one.*"

As he speaks the last bit, all the Touchstones quietly chant with him. Behind me, smiling guy leans forward, sticks his hand out. "I'm Chase."

"Drew," I say back, twisting uncomfortably to touch his hand.

"I know," he says, smiling *again*. Sucking me in like one of those spinny hypnotism circles. Tracy elbows me and nods toward the front. I whip back around to attention, a sharp cramp stabbing into my neck. I start massaging it with the same hand that shook Chase's.

"Now, today isn't going to be all about how important you are. Or how important your mission is. Today is focused on today." Suit guy deepens his voice. He sounds like Zeus. "The possibility of creating yourself is the possibility of being. We are the stream that erodes the rocks, the wind that carves the channel. We are invisible to most. But over time we prevail. Because once we've done our work, there is no denying where we have been."

He coughs a bit, switches gears.

"Oh, there is one small issue that we feel we do need to address, namely because it was confronting you as you arrived today." He's trying to sound casual, but his jaw flinches, like he's clamping his back teeth together. "The young men and women you saw outside the facility, flashing their signs and actively undermining our—not to mention their own—purpose."

He coughs again, louder this time.

"They are disappointments to Changers everywhere, and we don't want you to worry, as they are not a large coalition. But they are a rowdy one, and you should be informed about the misguided tenets of the Radical Changers movement, so you can avoid the pitfalls that many of them, tragically, could not. I'm sure most of you are familiar with our rivals, the

Abiders, from that section of your *Changers Bible*. Because of the Abiders' rabid hatred and intolerance of our race, it is extremely important that we do not give power to the RaChas faction, whose activities are regretfully exposing the Changers race before we can completely fulfill our mission on this planet." He pauses a moment before resuming. "In a perfect world—the world we someday hope will exist—there will be no need for secrecy for any type of individual. But the more visible we Changers are in these times, the more of us meet potential harm at the hands of the Abiders, who do not value difference, and who will fight to the death to keep their blood unmingled with ours."

The room falls silent, but for a few stray stirrings, a squeaky chair, some feet kicking seat backs when crossing or uncrossing legs. My neck feels even stiffer than before.

"Which brings me to the first commandment in your *CB*, which I know you've heard your Touchstones and parents repeat over and over: *Thou shalt not reveal yourself a Changer to those who are not Changers.*" Again, the Touchstones recite it along with him. "Lives depend on it. And on top of that, today we're going to emphasize the second commandment. And this isn't always the most popular one, but it is a foundational tenet that preserves and broadens the Changers race. *Thou shalt not lie down with other Changers.*" Another chorus of Touchstones parroting back, Tracy rotating and arching her eyebrows at me like, *Get it, you whore?* (I'm translating, roughly.)

Suit dude offers a weak smile, glances around the room for a few seconds, then continues: "We wait until the first mixer to go over the second commandment in detail.

You've just spent a month feeling like the only person like you on the planet, and then all of a sudden, *poof*, here you are surrounded by scores of others like you, and it's easy to mistake a feeling of recognition with romantic attraction—or even love. But believe me, nothing good can ever come of a Changer-Changer union. Period."

He's silent for a few more seconds before taking his seat. After another appropriate pause, Tracy hops up and prances down to the front along the left-side steps. I sink in my chair, bracing for G only knows what's going to come out of the girl's mouth to embarrass me.

"Okay, ready?" she begins, like she's coaxing us off a diving board. I cut a look back at Chase, who smirks wryly, seeming to know exactly what I'm thinking. "Time to break out into orientation groups . . ."

My first seminar is "Feints and Friends, What to Do?" where we're told how the Changers Council explains our disappearance each year, when our current V goes away and a new one is enrolled in school. The Council provides the specific "feints" (a.k.a. lies), which are the stories our family will tell to our friends and any other curious parties. These range from exotic (sent to European boarding school) to tragic (drug overdose). I wonder if rebellious Changers are given terrible feints. Like, if you never read the *CB*, do they tell everyone you were in a drunk-driving accident? Food for thought.

We are advised to conduct the usual and customary friendships with whomever we wish, but we should always keep our parents and residences as separate as possible from our school friends, to reduce the likelihood of inadvertent discovery. (So, no slumber parties at the old homestead for Drew, unless they are with other Changers.) Also, it seems the whole foreign exchange student program thing was invented by the Council as a simple way to shuttle children in and out of families without arousing suspicion. Which is kind of genius.

Our seminar leader explains there are never more than two or three Changers assigned to each high school, so there should be few, if any, suspicions raised when a kid doesn't come back the next year (it happens all the time). Which of course sets my mind into overdrive. Two other potential Changers at Central High? Who are they? Can I meet them? Would Tracy tell me if she knew? Is there a Changer signal? Like, could I put that stupid multiple-arm-and-leg emblem dude on a spotlight and shine it into the sky like they do at movie premieres, and then all the local Changer spawn will come running?

The class ends with a nod to potential conflicts with particularly integrated Statics—a.k.a. close friends. Audrey pops into my head. I've been so wrapped up in my own torment that I haven't considered the fact that when I change again, I will be leaving her behind. She'll be without Drew. I mean, not technically. I'll still be around, unless my parents split town again. Just in another body. But Drew will exist no longer. And it is Audrey who will shoulder the loss alone.

The more I mull it over, the lousier it feels. Here we are being told we're spreading love and empathy with an eye toward some as yet unknown larger mission, when what it seems like we're really doing is jacking people around and breaking hearts. Including our own.

Up front, the class leader is explaining something about the procedure for submitting special requests for feints to the Council, which understands that these are human lives, and thus not everything can be neatly and tidily sewed up into a simple fiction every time.

I'm dubious. But it's time to move on to . . .

"Emergency! Just in Case!" (Who names these things? Coach Lois?)

Here we learn what to do if for some reason we end up in a medical emergency—say we are hit by a car or get a concussion playing football—and our clothes are removed and our emblem possibly revealed. Every hospital in the area apparently has at least one Changer doctor and nurse on staff, sometimes more. If needed, our implanted Chronicling chips will send an urgent alert through the medical equipment that a Changer has entered a hospital's care, and a Changers rep will be on our case immediately.

We aren't told much more than that, only not to sweat it too intensely, because along with all the body-shifting and whatnot, Changers are exceedingly robust. We don't get debilitated by colds or flus. We almost never break bones. Our cuts and scrapes heal in a matter of hours, not days.

"This is NOT an invitation to test your corporeal limits," the seminar leader admonishes. "You are not Superman and you can sustain mortal injury. Got it? You can still feel pain."

And everybody else's, I want to interject, but I don't.

Next up is "Monos and V's: Don't Worry, Be Happy," which

117

is maybe the dumbest advice anyone has ever been given in the history of the universe.

And yet—we are told not to fixate on our Monos. To be patient, to live these four lives to the fullest and trust that at the end of our Cycle, when we look back over our Chronicles, it will be clear what permanent choice should be made. Also to remember that whoever we choose to be "on the outside," we will still be the same person on the inside. (*Puke.*) And NO, there is NO way to know in advance what V you will be given on the first morning of each school year. So don't bother asking. (*Annoying.*)

There are a bunch of other mini-lectures. One called "Parental Guidance Required" is about how valuable our parents can be, how they're there for us and us alone (that's why Changer parents are given just one child), and how we shouldn't be afraid to ask our Changer parent about his or her old V's. Another is entitled "Chronicling: Your Story Is Our Story," where we hear how Chronicling is not only valuable to us personally, but it is also our unique contribution to Changers history and culture. (Fact: our pitiful little records will be encrypted and stored in some Armageddon-proof type chamber, like where Walt Disney's head is kept cryogenically frozen, and only we will be able to access them; they will not enter the Changers public domain until seventy-five years after our deaths.) Mainly it is impressed upon us how vital our Chronicles will be when it comes time to choose our Monos. We should feel free to include anything we want, to be unself-conscious in our recollections and analysis. To trust *ourselves*. Which is rich, especially after taking stock of the room. We look like a pack of terrified lemurs.

Then the talks turn serious. In "Abiders: An Ounce of Prevention," we are shown photographs of Changers who have been lost to Abiders' deprogramming camps. If we come in contact with an Abider, we are told to report to the Changers Council immediately, and further action will be determined at that time. We are shown images of a modified Roman numeral I, which is an unofficial Abiders emblem that some adherents might have tattooed on their bodies. (It symbolizes homogeneity, and the single identity and body they want each human to inhabit.)

"Make no mistake, the objective of every sworn Abider is the eradication of the Changer race," we are told.

Mmm-kay. I'm thinking the seminar planners maybe should've led with this one. I mean, what good is any of the other crap if we could be snuffed out by a pack of organized bigots at any moment?

"We do not tell you this to frighten you."

Too late.

"Only to make you aware, so that you can avoid putting you and your family in harm's way."

They conclude with some lame reassurances about how the Council is always watching, tracking Abider pods and developments. So really, don't lose sleep unless you encounter one, and then run like freaking hell.

Just when I think I can't swallow any more revelations, we are led into the last lecture, "Keep It Under Wraps," where a handful of Touchstones demonstrate various techniques for concealing our Changers emblems in circumstances when we need to disrobe in the proximity of Statics—the locker room, swim practice, a sleepover, etc. Two guy and two girl Touchstones get up and perform jerky dances and maneuvers with towels and clothes that actually do seem to cleverly keep their emblems out of sight during different scenarios. It is emphasized that "practice makes perfect," and one of the presenters promises that we'll likely have it mastered before we wake up on the first day of junior year, Change 3–Day 1. In a pinch, there are also "Bare Necessities," essentially large bandages you can use to cover your scar—"the very same ones that actors use to obscure their tattoos while filming!"

The seminar ends with a frank discussion about being "intimate" with Statics we might find ourselves attracted to. I can barely listen and feel my lungs tightening when they say something about how sexuality is natural, but it is not to be taken lightly, especially given the added risks for Changers, and how we should proceed with caution before jumping into anything flesh-related, yadda yadda *gross*.

The breakout seminars culminate with all of us reunited into the larger group for a final presentation. This time a handful of adults are in front of the auditorium waiting for us. They look authoritative. When Tracy and I enter, I scan the audience for Chase, but he and his Touchstone aren't there yet. Tracy directs me to the front row, naturally.

"We'll wait a couple more minutes for everybody to get back," a thirty-something man wearing a distressed T-shirt and blazer says into the mic, checking his chunky silver wristwatch. He looks like one of those mega-rich dudes who invented Google. I feel a breeze on my bare arm, and I turn just as Chase takes the seat next to me, his Touchstone on the other side of him.

"I think the best part was learning that they can keep tabs on us Big Brother–style with those little chips," Chase whispers, jabbing his thumb toward the back of his neck.

"I liked the whole swiveling out of bed and bunching a sheet up while pulling on your underwear like they do in the movies thing," I whisper back.

"Shhh," Tracy shoots in our direction, holding a finger to her lips.

The room goes dark and silent, but for spotlighting up front. The head of the Regional Council is introduced—it's the lady standing next to the Google guy, a husky woman with tidy brown hair and perfectly straight bangs that hit her eyebrows.

"My name is Lisa Vandenburg, and I would like to personally welcome you to the family," she starts. Everybody claps. Tracy is on the edge of her seat like David Copperfield is going to appear spontaneously in a puff of smoke and then vanish a '57 Chevy or something. "We couldn't be more proud of you and all that you've accomplished already." More clapping. I notice Chase's forearm mere millimeters from mine on the armrest.

"I know it's been a long afternoon with a lot of information thrown at you, but we have one more piece we need to talk about. Now, I want you to feel like you can be honest with us, honest with yourself, and if any questions arise, this is the time to ask them. That's what we're here for. I'm going to let Charlie take it from here . . . Charlie?"

Charlie, a.k.a. Mr. Google, steps in front of the lectern. He's obviously the "cool" one on the Council who can "keep it real" with the youths.

"Welcome, Changers . . . In the many, we are *one!*" he calls. Raucous applause. Charlie nods his head vigorously. I find myself nodding with him. "Now. You didn't think we'd turn your lives upside down and ask so much of you without giving you a little something in return, did you?"

Everybody's eyes are ping-ponging around the room, at each other, at our Touchstones, at Charlie. Beside me Tracy has a smug-as-hell, something-up-her-sleeve smirk spreading across her face.

"This is always my favorite part of the inaugural mixer," he continues, grinning in that slightly creepy way powerful people do. "I'll start by posing a question. Have any of you, and I'm talking in the four weeks since your Change, have any of you maybe, perhaps, found yourself in the position of *kissing* somebody?"

Discomfort all around.

"Really? Not a single one of you?" he prods. Waits a little longer. A couple hands reluctantly go up. "Great! So, just you two, did you notice anything a little *unusual* when kissing these other people?"

Everybody is staring at the guy and girl who raised their hands. The girl lowers hers slowly.

"No?" Charlie prompts.

"Uh, I guess it was more like a peck on the cheek," she says, eyes darting back and forth. Which sets everybody to laughter.

"Okay. So. And you?" Charlie asks the other kid, whose hand is still up.

"Well, yeah, now that you mention it," he offers, genuinely confounded.

"Tell us what happened."

"Me and this girl made out after we went to a movie, and I suddenly had this really weird dream, even though I was awake. It was like another movie was still going in my head. But then it was gone."

"And what was the vision? What did you see?" Charlie asks.

"A pretty girl diving into a crystal-clear blue pool, by a big glass house. The sun was bright so I couldn't really see, but she lifted herself out of the pool and this tanned, buff guy was there and took her hand."

"He dreamed a cologne commercial?" Chase whispers in my ear. Tracy shoots him a look.

"That's it?" Charlie asks.

"Pretty much."

The room was silent, everybody rapt.

"Do you know what you saw?" Charlie asks then, and the kid shakes his head. After a good twenty seconds of looking around the room, he answers his own question: "That was a flash of that girl's future."

"Ohhhhh!" all around. Anxious chatter. "We're mind readers, man!" I hear one dude in the back say. "What happens if I kiss my dog?" a girl with glasses considers aloud. A chorus of questions and excitement. It is mind-blowing. We have a superpower. Sort of.

Charlie steps aside, his face shining with triumph, as Ms. Vandenburg returns to the lectern and speaks into the mic, her voice sounding like that of every school principal I've ever known.

"*With great power must come great responsibility.* Does anybody know who said that?"

A skinny girl in the third row raises her hand. "Spider-Man's uncle. Well, technically, Stan Lee, since he wrote *Spider-Man.*"

"That's true," Ms. Vandenburg says solemnly. "Also Voltaire, and the thirty-second American president, Franklin Delano Roosevelt. A version of it appears in the *CB.* No matter who said it first, it is the truth. And I want you to think about that responsibility while this news settles over you." She twitches slightly, her bangs vibrating like blinds. "So now. Any questions, concerns? About anything?"

A hand goes up in the back, a Latina girl. "What if you kiss another Changer?"

Good freaking question.

"Second commandment. You don't get intimate with other Changers. It is not part of your mandate. And it is potentially dangerous," she recites sternly. "A Changer-Changer offspring kills the lineage for both families. All parties revert to Static status. We are in the business of producing more Changers, not fewer. There is also the risk of poisoning. Changers have been known to infect other Changers. It is rare, but not impossible. If in the unlikely event you kiss someone for the first time and you see nothing—assume you've intersected with one of your own kind. And end the relationship. Immediately."

"With great power comes really controlling rules," Chase mutters beside me.

"Listen, there are billions of Statics out there in the world," Vandenburg emphasizes, lightening it up now. "And it is a Static with whom you will eventually partner and hopefully have a Changer offspring."

Another hand. "Does a vision happen every time you kiss?"

"Yes, to varying degrees, with any new person. It does not happen every time with the same person."

"What if you kiss, like, your mom?" The room explodes, cutting the tension.

"If you kiss your Static parent, you could experience a vision, but we don't really recommend it. The visions are not always positive. Anyone else?"

"Is there going to be a time when we kiss a Static and we see ourselves in the flash of their future?"

"The million-dollar question. I'm going to pass on that one, though, because it touches upon the single most magical aspect of human life—one that cannot be explained or taught or prepared for. I'm going to let that be a mystery for you to uncover on your own. Now, any more questions?"

Everybody's frozen. Mr. Google struts over, commandeers the microphone. "All right then!" he shouts. "Let's party!"

Most of us Changer kids don't budge after being excused. To be honest, it feels like a rhino is sitting on my lap. Some Touchstones, including you-know-who, go up to network with the Council members. They all seem so abnormally upbeat; my initial instinct about this being a cult starts creeping in again.

"Wanna bust a move?" Chase asks me.

"Where?"

"I dunno, just out of here," he says, surveying the auditorium.

I follow him up the stairs and out an emergency exit, which empties into a stairwell, where we immediately smell smoke. We look down through the handrails and see a couple kids sitting on the gun metal–gray steps and passing a cigarette back and forth.

"Yo!" Chase calls down. It echoes.

"Yo," comes back up the stairwell.

Two flights down, we meet Gwen and Pickle, a sophomore and junior from Atlanta.

"Fresh meat, huh?" Pickle says after we all share our names, offering Chase the cigarette. He waves it off, but gestures toward me.

"No thanks."

"They just lay your special kissing power on you?" Gwen asks.

We nod as Pickle laughs, takes a long drag.

"It's actually pretty major," she finally says, smoke billowing around her face. "I kissed a teacher once, saw he was quitting his job in a month. No more sucking up to him. Big time saver."

"It's banana boats," adds Gwen.

I look to Chase, who seems as skeptical as I am. Also, who kisses a teacher?

"Well, see you up there," Chase volunteers after a beat. "Which way's the party?"

Gwen points, then fishes around for another cigarette.

We push through the exit door and enter an internal grass courtyard with stone paths. There are picnic tables with umbrellas, some bicycles, a volleyball court, and a community garden plot. As the door slams shut behind us,

Chase says sardonically, "I think they maybe aren't totally grasping the Changer mandate."

"I think maybe they aren't totally grasping where they *are*," I joke back.

Through the glass panels above, we see a bunch of our fellow Y-1s leaving the auditorium and heading toward the reception area in the center of the facility. We stroll in their general direction, but outside. When I look up again, I notice Tracy frantically waving at me and pointing me in the direction I'm already going.

"What's her deal?" Chase asks.

"Tragic type-A."

He snorts, almost surprised. "You're funny. Who were you?"

"What, like, *before*?"

"Yeah."

"A guy. Ethan."

"No way, I was a girl! Brooke," he says. "What were you like?" he asks after a few seconds.

"I don't know. I guess the same. Maybe a little more outgoing. Fewer boobs. What about you?"

"I was—I guess," he hesitates. "I mean, I think I was a little bit like you."

I don't know what to say. I glance toward the glass windows, and there's Tracy, shadowing us.

"I'm kind of jealous of these other clowns who get the same genders for their first V, you know?" he says.

"Me too." Although, underneath, looking at Chase, I am considering for the first time since becoming one that maybe it isn't so terrible to be a girl after all.

* * *

The party itself was a blur. There was a deejay; almost all the Touchstones and some of the older Changers danced. I remember walking up to my parents and my mom kissing me on the forehead and me sort of collapsing a little into her. I talked to some Indian kid who's a junior at a school across town from Central and works at ReRunz. I drank two glasses of purple punch and ate crackers and miniature corn, which looked good but was disgusting. I did a spit take when I noticed Tracy was even wearing out Dad with her ceaseless up-with-Changers routine. (Now who has the empathy?)

And then there was Chase. Smiling guy. Who used to be Brooke. Who was apparently like me. Me *now*.

The two of us acted right. No funny business. Not that he'd have wanted to anyhow. I'm sure he wasn't that into me. Or me into him. Besides. The second commandment and all. Hate to burn in eternal Changer hellfire because some guy smiled at me.

It's all just so confounding. I don't know what anything I'm feeling means or where it's coming from. But I do know that I feel less alone. Not because of the mixer so much. But because of Chase. Knowing he's out there. A guy who gets me. Maybe that's enough. I guess it has to be. Anyhow, this is what I was thinking as I drifted off to sleep in the backseat of the car on the way home from the mixer.

If I had a dream, I don't remember it.

"**Y**ou guys, seriously, we have a freaking show in two weeks. Can you stop making googly eyes over there and start from the bridge?" Gen is bossing around Chase and me for about the twentieth time in two hours. He starts fingering the bassline and bobbing his head in that annoying way, more forward and backward than up and down. Chase signals me, and we come in right where we're supposed to, and we are all in tune and totally clicking. Gen's original masterpiece, "Siri (You Only Want Me When I Don't Want You)" flows out of us perfectly this time.

Which is good, because I'm tired of being his little drummer girl when I don't even know whether I've made the band yet, and plus, my mom just walked in at the end of the song and is perched on a sawhorse listening to us, and bobbing her head along with Gen, which is so thoroughly embarrassing, I don't quite know what to do. We finish the song, and she starts clapping, the only noise in the garage except for a little whine of feedback from Chase's guitar.

"I gotta go," I say, as Mom's claps wind down.

Chase peers eagerly at Gen. "Good, right?"

Gen nods. "She's got a lot of power. I like that."

"So?" Chase prompts.

Everybody's staring at Gen during a good dramatic pause. He looks like he's really thinking hard about something. Probably the speech he's going to deliver when he collects his first Grammy in a few years. "Yeah. You're in. Can you make it to practice on Sunday? We have to learn 'Baby' for the gig, plus a lot of other stuff. It's a sweet sixteen party, special request," he adds, not at all shamefully.

I look over at Mom, who's hopping off the sawhorse and coming over to where we're set up on a dirty old Oriental rug in Gen's parents' garage. "Can I?"

"I think we should be back from Nana's by then. What time?" she asks.

"We can make it later if that helps," Gen offers, giving his best sincerity impression. "Four?"

"She'll be here," Mom says, tapping her fingers on my cymbal. "Do we need to pack up?"

"Naw, she can leave the set here," Gen says.

"I'm Drew's mom," Mom inserts.

I hop up and come around my kit. "Uh, sorry. This is my mom."

Mom reaches her hand out. "Connie," she says to Gen.

"This is Gen," I say, way too late.

"That's Gen with a G." He shakes Mom's hand.

"And this is, I think you met him before, Chase?" I say. Chase swings his guitar around his back and shakes Mom's hand, super polite like.

Mom holds onto Chase's hand a little longer than a usual handshake. Studies his eyes. I can tell she's thinking something, which I'm no doubt going to hear about in the car.

"And over there is Raymond," I add, then whisper, "He doesn't seem to share much." Ray-Ray is bent over unplugging his keyboard, pretending we aren't talking about him. Which I know also isn't going to go over very well, and I'll likely be hearing about that later too.

Gen is appraising me, approvingly. "How do you two know each other again?" he asks Chase.

"I told you, just around town and stuff," Chase replies quickly.

"Well, I gotta go," I say. "Are you sure it's cool if I leave everything? I can't practice until I get back into town anyway."

"Totally *cool*, Drew," Gen says, possibly like he's making fun of me, or maybe I'm just in on the joke but don't know it yet. "Welcome to the Bickersons."

"Yeah, thanks." I'm trying not to smile too big.

My first band! I hadn't even unpacked my drum set and hauled it into my room until a few weeks ago, and now I'm "in a band." Like, I'm going to have to paint *The Bickersons* onto my kick drum and everything.

I look at Chase. "Thanks," I say to him quietly, and my armpits feel instantly sweaty.

"See you Sunday" is all he says back. But I can tell he'd like to say more.

In the car on the way home from Gen's house, Mom is silent for the first five minutes while navigating the unfamiliar neighborhood: big old wood houses in rows, with little squares of green in front and stone steps down to the sidewalks. It's recycling day. Kids are playing outside, clearly psyched about Thanksgiving break. While we're at a stop sign, I watch a boy about my age land a varial in front of a big green house—he's decent. I'm wondering what Mom's thinking. No, I know what she's thinking. I'm just waiting for confirmation.

"So," she starts, just as we pull onto the Interstate.

I focus on downtown shimmering in the near distance.

"Ahem. Chase . . . ? I didn't know you two were in contact."

"Oh, I thought you knew. We've just e-mailed a few times since the mixer, you know . . ." I trail off, nonchalantly.

"I thought this band was with kids at Central High."

"Not this one, no."

"I see. Well, Dad didn't tell me it was a Changer band either."

"It's not. I mean, Chase is, but the other two aren't. I don't *think*."

She's quiet.

"And Chase wasn't there yet when Dad dropped me off," I add. "We just unloaded my equipment and Gen helped me bring it in."

She's quiet for a couple minutes.

"What?" I finally ask when I can't take it anymore.

"Nothing, honey."

"It's not like I lied or anything." I'm defensive, even though I shouldn't be. I mean, not if I'm not doing anything wrong. Which I'm not.

"I know," she says. "I just want you to feel like you can come to me with things, like you're not going to get in trouble when you do."

"I *do* feel like I can come to you."

"It's natural if you don't. I'm just saying I want to do

whatever I can to create the space where you feel you *can*," she says in her shrink voice. "I mean, this is a whole friendship you've been conducting over the last month or so, and your father and I don't even know about it."

"It's not a big deal. Honestly, we've just e-mailed a few times, like, *Blah blah blah, isn't it weird when this happens, or when people say that?* or, *Doesn't Chronicling bite?* or, *Hey, maybe we should exchange our old wardrobes, ha ha,* whatever, just stupid stuff," I say, spilling too much.

"Okay, okay," she concedes. "I just want you to think of me as a resource in your life if possible. Not as someone who's going to judge you."

"I *do*," I insist. But I don't really. I'm not even sure why.

I change the station on the radio. Everything's damn country around here.

After a few more minutes of silence, Mom asks, "Well, I think it's awesome you're going to be playing in a band. What kind of music is it? It sounded a little reggae-ish there at the end."

"Gen calls it Neo-Emo-Ska," I say with a chuckle.

"Is that supposed to mean something to me?"

"Not really." I start laughing. And then she does too. And then we're both laughing together at the expense of Gen (with a G).

At home, I go to my room and immediately open my laptop. Chase's signal is green on Skype. I go to the door and listen for Mom. Dad's not home yet. I push the door shut, sit on the bed, and initiate a video call with Chase.

He pops onto the screen, and immediately I realize how

much of a buzzkill it is to see him back in two dimensions and pixilated, when forty-five minutes ago I was standing next to him in 3-D and in the flesh, for the first time since the mixer.

"Hey!" he says.

My breathing quickens involuntarily. "Hi," I say back. I am suddenly completely shy and don't know what to do.

"You did really good," he says enthusiastically.

My bedroom door swings open then and I jump, totally startled, like I've been caught and Mom is going to kill me because I'm hiding something I told her I wasn't actually hiding. And it's not even something that needs to be hidden in the first place, so why the hell am I hiding it? I hop to my feet in a mini-panic, preparing what I'm going to say in my head, but then I realize it was just Snoopy who'd pushed the door open.

I pat a spot on the bed and Snoopy jumps up.

"Sorry, it's my dog," I say, now back in front of the screen.

"Let me see him," Chase says.

Snoopy is circling for his spot. "Snoop! Snoopers, Snoop-Dogg!" I try to get his attention, but he won't look at the computer. He doesn't care about such things.

"Hey, buddy, what's up?" Chase is cooing on screen. He looks so goofy. Snoopy doesn't even twitch an ear. "Hey, Snoopster!" I'm holding the laptop so he can watch as Snoopy finally finds his place, plops down hard on the comforter. Sighs.

"I want to meet him sometime. Damn, I want a dog so bad, but my dad's allergic."

"You can get a hypoallergenic one," I say. "Like a

snickerdoodle or whatever." But this is not what I want to be talking about.

We're silent for a few seconds. Which always makes us both laugh. It's so awkward to be talking and seeing each other, but then not really being together at all.

"Anyway," he says.

"Anyway," I echo.

A few more seconds of giggling.

"Seriously, I'm so psyched you're in the Bickersons. Our last drummer was such an ass-wipe. Plus, not hot at all."

"Ha," I say, because I am totally taken aback and nothing else will come out.

"After you left, Gen was all, *It'll be so sweet to have a hot babe playing drums. It's totally going to make us stick out, and everybody's going to wonder which one of us is going out with her. It'll be like our thing.*"

"He didn't say that!"

"He actually did," Chase laughs. "He's so insane."

Yeah, he's totally crazy, I'm thinking.

"What was up with your *mom*?" Chase asks out of nowhere.

"Yeah, uh, she . . ."

"Was she pissed?"

"Kind of. Not really. I guess she was just a little surprised you're in the band. That we're friends."

"We're allowed to be friends. I mean, what the hell? No Changer commandment against that," he says, then intones in a deep baritone, "*Thou shalt not Skype with another Changer.*"

"I know. I just didn't tell them. It felt weird for some reason."

"Why?" he pushes.

Isn't it obvious, dumb-ass?

"I don't know," I say defensively. "I don't tell them everything."

"Okay."

"Anyway . . ." I hear my mom coming down the hall. "I should probably go. Soon as my dad gets home, we're going to my nana's for Thanksgiving."

"Where is she?"

"On the beach in North Florida. It's really fun there . . ." I trail off. "I mean, I guess I used to have fun there when I was little."

"Have you seen her since—"

"No."

"Dude, I saw my uncle for the first time a couple weeks ago. He was all punching me on the shoulder and saying, *Hey, fella!* and, *What's up, my man?* Stuff like that. Bizarro."

"I'm kind of expecting the same. Well, with more cheek pinching, but, you know, the same," I say. But again, I don't really want to talk about it, and I think Chase can sense it.

Also, did he just *Dude* me?

"Call me when you get back," he says then. "Or, how cool is it I get to say this? I'll see you at practice on Sunday."

I smile, but I feel down. I was all high at Gen's, and after. Feeling good about myself, psyched about how the chips are falling, and all excited to Skype with Chase. But now I just feel . . . *bleh*. Like the cloud rolled back in. The dark gray one fixing to throw up on me. I'm getting used to those—you know, every so often one moves in and sits right over my head and follows me around for a day or two, like Charlie

Brown. But this particular one caught me unawares.

I thought seeing Chase would be amazing. And it was. *Was* being the operative verb tense. Everything just feels so—I don't know, I thought I really *knew* him after e-mailing and Skyping and stuff, but sitting here powwowing through a thirteen-inch screen, I'm realizing that between meeting him at the mixer and playing music for a few hours today, I've spent maybe fifteen minutes total alone with him in person—and between those two times there's been essentially electronic emptiness filling up said space. And talking to him now is only making me lonelier. Emotional piñata, party of one.

I guess the sad fact is that nobody really knows me—because Audrey can't ever, not *really*, and plus the thought of having to give her up at the end of the year is looming large, and now I'm realizing Chase doesn't really know me either, what with this technological gulf between us. And to top it all off, he's calling me *Dude*. All of this makes me feel like crying, which would be the absolute worst thing I could do in front of him, so I start rubbing my eyes really hard like they itch, then spit out, "Have a good break," and act like I need to go.

"Okay. Bye," he says.

"Bye," I say back, embarking upon our customary goodbye battle of wills: who will be the last to disconnect.

"Bye now," he says, as though it is the final word.

"B'bye," I reply.

"Goodbye . . . Bye now . . . Bye!" He sounds like he's sending somebody off on a cruise.

"Toodles," I say halfheartedly.

"Ciao, adios."

"Bye-*bye*," I say finally, and click the red *Hang Up* button. I lose.

I look at the screen. There's his silly face, frozen on a crooked smile with a flamboyant pageant wave, and I decide I don't care if Mom walks in; I am leaving the screenshot up of the last confirmed instant I knew for sure Chase was thinking about me. He might as well be a zillion miles away, but at least for now I can fool myself into thinking he's sitting on the bed right here in between me and Snoop.

CHANGE 1–DAY 90

We just got back from Florida. I know Nana's a Changer like Dad and all, so it's not supposed to be a big surprise to her that I used to be her grandson and now I showed up as her granddaughter. But. It was kind of a surprise to her.

Maybe it's because she's old and she forgets more, but she kept calling me Ethan by accident, and there were all these weird moments at the big Thanksgiving dinner when her buddies from the Pickwick Place retirement community were totally confused by their friend calling her granddaughter by a boy's name.

It was kind of confusing for me too. I mean, not that I don't miss the guy and wasn't quite fond of him, but the fact is, Ethan's not really an option in my life anymore, so I'm trying my hardest to forget he existed. Like I've pretty much ditched Andy, who has sent three e-mails so far that I haven't responded to. In his last one he was getting ticked at me for not writing, but I haven't known what to say. The *CB* says that it's best if these friendships naturally atrophy, that most Static teenagers go their separate ways in high school anyway. But Andy's not entirely cooperating with that whole setup.

He wrote something like, *Dude, WTF? Alien abduction much? Smell you later.* Which I know doesn't sound like he's *devastated* or anything, but I can tell he has hurt feelings, even though he'd never admit it. It just seems like I've aged about twenty years, and he's still spending his lunch breaks trying to get a peek up unsuspecting girls' skirts.

Anyway, so, Florida.

I had to wear a bathing suit. I thought my cheerleading uniform was a perv magnet. Training wheels! A bathing suit is a complete creep beacon. It's the bat signal of creepers. All these old dudes, as in older-than-my-dad old, staring at me, like I don't have eyes and I can't see them gawking. Like I'm a doll or something. I ended up keeping my T-shirt on, even though Nana kept telling me I should "show off that fabulous figure" in one breath, while referring to me as "Ethan" in the next. (As the *CB* says, *In the many, we are . . . confused.*)

Everywhere other girls my age were slathering themselves with baby oil and "laying out." All that skin cancer–awareness public service stuff? Not really registering with the teen girl demo. Babes want to be *bronze*. And they want to do little more than sit on their oversized towels and text. Maybe take a picture of their group, fake surprise– smiling and sucking in their already perfectly normal stomachs. I brought a Frisbee and a football to the beach like I always used to, but the only people doing any activity at all were older guys or toddlers in soggy diapers. I didn't want to fry like an egg in the sun. And I didn't want to hang with the dudes tackling each other as close as possible to the girls' towels. Basically, I belonged nowhere. Big shocker.

Another (not) surprise? Walking by yourself up and down the shore with no one to talk to, or point out sharks' teeth to, or kick cold water on . . . pretty much puts the cherry on top of the cake of suck. And the double-cherry on top of the cake of suck? Doing that with your dad because he feels sorry for you.

I did have one encouraging moment with Nana, though, when she told me she barely recalled her V's, and that once you choose your Mono, all this painful awfulness fades like old newspaper. "Time heals all wounds," she croaked out in her husky smoker's voice. "And for everything else, there's alcohol."

She was kidding. I think.

"Dudes—sorry. Um, dudes and *dudette*," Gen starts saying as we're setting up for practice. "I got word from the venue, and we're only allowed to perform two of my songs at the gig."

"It's the Veterans of Foreign Wars community room," Chase says, "not a venue." He makes air quotes when he says "venue."

"Whatever. A sweet sixteen at the VFW today . . . headlining the House of Blues tomorrow. Anyhow, they've asked that we limit original material to two numbers. One's going to be 'Siri,' of course, and the other, well, I'm trying to decide between 'My Personal Petting Zoo' and 'Soft Serv.' Drew, this is going to be a lot for you to learn, but the rest of the lineup is pretty simple four-four pop stuff, so you'll be fine."

"Such as?" Chase asks, smiling wide, like he knows this is going to be good. Ray-Ray's expression is inscrutable; he's just sitting there behind sunglasses with his arms crossed, waiting for something to happen.

"Well, 'Baby,' of course," Gen says, then starts digging around in his pockets. He fishes out a crushed-up piece of notebook paper, reads from it quickly and quietly like ticking off items on a to-do list. "'Miss Independent' by Ne-Yo. 'Sweet Sixteen,' Hilary Duff. Britney's 'I'm Not a Girl, Not Yet a Woman' . . ."

Chase shoots a look at me, and we burst out laughing.

"What?" Gen asks, thinking we're mocking him.

"Nothing!" Chase and I sing—literally in chorus.

Gen shrugs, continues, "Kanye's 'Good Life,' 50 Cent's 'In da Club.' Uh, 'We Are Never Ever Ever Getting Back Together'—"

"I think it's just one *Ever*," Chase interrupts.

"Okaaay," Gen says, taking a pen from behind his ear and crossing out one of the *Evers*. He's taking his job totally seriously. "Anyway, I ripped CDs for y'all to take home, but I figure we can knock out a few of these today."

"How much are we getting paid for this again?" Chase asks. Which garners a mild snort from Ray-Ray, who punctuates the sentiment with an electric pop while plugging in his amp.

"Five hundred bucks, smart-ass. Plus gas. That's one twenty-five apiece."

"I guess this recession's way worse than I thought," Chase says to me.

"Yeah," I chime in, "this poor girl's dad obviously doesn't love her enough to pay for the real Kelly Clarkson to perform."

"You two should really think about giving up music and taking this little comedy routine on the road," Gen says, sliding a CD into a busted-up boom box.

He presses play, and suddenly the garage is filled with the mad beats and dulcet tones of Fiddy murmuring, *"Go shawty, it's your birthday, we gonna party like it's your birthday, we gon' sip Bacardi like it's your birthday . . ."* and I start banging along, and Chase comes in too, just riffing over the track, and we are really feeling it and suddenly all about those one (and a quarter) Benjamins.

Practice went late, this time with my dad coming in at the end and catching the last song, eyeing Chase pretty much exclusively. Poor guy, I could tell he felt the extra weight on him, because he flubbed a couple licks. Dad was stressing me out too, but I didn't really mind, because time disappeared and I never wanted practice to end—it was so fun to play with Chase and the other two Bickersons. Okay, mostly Chase, who kept looking over and, like, mind-melding with me and my drumming the whole night. A couple times it felt like everything else around us actually dropped off, and it was just the two of us jamming together in some dark, out-of-the-way blues bar in New Orleans or something ridiculous like that. Only less Louis Armstrong and more Britney, bitches.

And now I'm sitting here in bed, cannot fall asleep no matter how hard I try, because—and I know this is crazy and I never thought I'd hear myself actually saying it, but I miss school, and I pretty much couldn't wait to get back the whole time I was away. A few days of Florida sunshine definitely lightened me up, gave me a different perspective on Audrey and Chase, and even Chloe and Tracy—and it made me feel, if not *warm* exactly, then somehow *connected* to something. Like I had a reason to come home.

At least people seem to think they know who I am here. Maybe I'm starting to, as well.

When Mr. Crowell stopped me after school and asked whether I had a couple minutes, I was certain I was in trouble for something. I don't know why that's my first thought, but it almost always is.

"Is this okay?" he asks, pointing to a corner bench in the quad. "Or, too cold for you?"

I say "No worries," sit on the icy concrete bench. He does the same.

"I mean, not that anyone around here knows what *actual* cold feels like. Speaking of, it seems like you're settling into Genesis and Central High rather well," he says, apropos of nothing. *Is this what he wanted to talk about?*

"Sure," I reply. "Tennessee's okay."

"You know, I don't know if it's ever come up in class, but I'm from New York too—well, upstate. Buffalo," he says, then adds weakly, "Go Bills."

I make a face. "No way. Giants or death." I realize this is the first time somebody has talked to me about sports since I turned into Drew. "Hate to be the bearer of bad news, but you know the Bills suck, right?"

At that he starts untying his left brown-and-tan saddle shoe, grinning while I watch, wondering what the hell he's doing. There's a hole in the heel of his red sock, which he also peels off, revealing . . . the blue-painted nail of his big toe. He wiggles all of his toes.

"You see this?" he asks, brown floppy curls falling over his forehead in an absentminded professorial way.

I stifle a laugh. *What the hell?*

"When I was in high school, we lost four Super Bowls in a row," he starts. "And after that fourth and final heartbreak, I vowed to my friends that I'd paint my big toenails blue until the Bills pulled off a championship."

"Is the other one painted too?"

He nods.

"It's sad that you're going to be lying on your deathbed with blue toenails."

He fakes a wounded look, but then concedes, "You're probably right," and starts pulling his sock back on. A couple students walk by us carrying their loaded-down backpacks, headed for home.

"So . . ." I say.

"Oh, right." He finishes retying his shoe and turns to me. "You're probably wondering why I asked you here."

"Kind of."

"I know you already saw your A in class today, but I wanted to take some extra time to tell you how great your *Of Mice and Men* essay was. I've been teaching that book to freshmen for years, and I have to say, I've never seen an essay with so much insight into, well, humans."

"Thanks?" I respond, like it's a question. Not that I've been a dolt all my life, but Ethan was never the type of scholar who collected A's with heaping side servings of extracurricular praise.

"I don't believe in A-pluses," Mr. Crowell continues. "But that paragraph about power and vulnerability almost changed my mind."

"Wow. Thanks," I say again, this time managing to punctuate with a period.

"Good to know you connected with the book so profoundly . . ."

A weak agreement sound falls out of my mouth.

"Our whole country is full of mutts," he adds, referring to the line from the book that I talked about in my essay's conclusion. "And your paragraph about isolation was uniquely poignant."

I'm wondering where he's going with this. Wait, does he think I think I'm like *Lennie*?

"It, uh," he struggles on, "it, uh, makes me want to tell you, or offer myself—no, that's not the right word, but okay, *offer* myself as a refuge for you, you know, whenever, if ever, you need help with anything that might come up."

"I'm in a band!" I suddenly share, more enthusiastically than I'd intended. *See? I'm cool! I have friends!* I'm not as sad as Crooks and Candy and Lennie—or, god forbid, Curley's sad sack of a desperate wife. I can just sort of sympathize with them, is all.

He looks surprised, but takes the hint. "Oh? What do you play?"

"Drums. I've been playing since I was six," I report, happy to change the subject. "I actually dropped it for a while, but I just started playing again, and a friend of mine from . . . another school is in a band that lost its drummer, so I auditioned a few weeks ago, and I made it."

"What's your name?"

"The Bickersons."

"I like it," he says. "What kind of music?"

"It's not really an official genre."

"I know my way around a record store. Wait, you know what records are, right? They're like these flat, round black plastic things that have music on them—"

"Funny," I say. "Well, Gen calls it—he's the lead singer, I guess it's his band. Anyway, he calls it Neo-Emo-Ska."

"Ah, so sort of Fishbone meets Dashboard Confessional meets, what—*American Idol?*"

"Exactly."

"I have no musical talent," Mr. Crowell offers. "But if I had a band, it'd be called Boba Fetish. Get it?"

I shake my head.

"No? *Star Wars?*"

"Oh yeah! The helmet-head guy who brings back Han Solo when he's on serious punishment."

"The one and only," he laughs.

"Well, I should probably get home," I say then. I guess kind of abruptly. But this is veering into things you don't expect to talk about with your English teacher territory, and I don't really know what else to add.

"Of course," he replies, standing. "Well, thanks for the little chat. Again, really good job. Keep it up."

I showed Mom my essay when I got home. She was busy with some patient charts, but when I set my paper with the *A* scribbled on it on top, she took off her reading glasses, sat back, and beamed.

"I am so proud of you," she said, flipping through the essay. "I loved Steinbeck. Can I hold onto this? I know Dad will want to read it too."

"Sure."

It feels good to be decent at something. I know it shouldn't be the motivation behind doing stuff, but I can't lie and say I'm not enjoying this tangible shred of proof that I'm getting at least one thing right.

You know who always gets the booty end of the stick? Kids with December birthdays. Well, ones after about the tenth—because everything always gets collapsed into the holidays, and you end up getting a combined gift for the whole month. I'm lucky my birthday isn't in December. In fact, wait a minute. When is my actual birthday now? Is it going to be the first day of school every year? And then after I pick my V, I can go back to having my normal birthday in June? I don't remember *The Changers Bible* saying anything about any of this.

Anyway, tonight's our first gig, and I don't know what to wear. It's stressing me out, and I'm staring back and forth between two very divergent outfits splayed out on my bed. Shredded punkish rocker girl who could not care less about her looks—*It's all about the music, man* . . . Or dark, unripped stretch jeans and a cute silky blouse, like, *I sort of do care, but not in any tragic, self-conscious way.*

I know it's just some stupid thing at the VFW, but Audrey is coming to watch my first show, and (annoyingly) Tracy said she's going to show up too. And I don't want to eff it up, because Chase really stuck his neck out to get me an audition with the band, and no matter how good practices have been going, you never really know until performing live in front of an actual audience.

So I'm Chronicling now to get it out of the way because I know it's going to be a late night. What else can I say? Um, I'm currently in the red tent, as Audrey sometimes calls it. So this is my, what, third, fourth period? Not getting easier.

What else? I ate a slice of pizza earlier. Plain cheese, if you must know. Replaced my Velcro duct-tape wallet with a sort of non-gendered but definitely not masculine wallet that I bought at ReRunz from Chase's Touchstone, who manages the place on weekends. Walked Snoopy to a dog run, where some lady was squatting down and petting him and swooning about how cute and sweet he is, but then when she asked me what kind of dog he was and I said pit bull, she completely jumped out of her shoes and was all wigged out thinking he was going to suddenly SNAP and lock onto her face with his jaws. Forget the fact that her purebred Pomeranian was essentially drawing blood from any creature—canine or human—who came within two feet of it.

Is that enough Chronicling? How long has it been? Gen's going to be here any minute to load my kit into his van, and then we have to drive all the way across town and set up before the party starts at seven. So, this is just going to have to be it for today, Chronicling Authority. I'll report back tomorrow about our first show. Wish me luck. Wait, I'm essentially wishing myself luck.

Well, Future Me: just know Drew was nervous as hellfire about playing live music in front of more than five people. And that she is going to go with the "I do care" outfit, plus the skinny vintage tie Audrey bought her a couple months ago, for luck.

I feel like I need it.

CHANGE 1-DAY 105

Turns out it was a Winter Wonderland–themed sweet sixteen party. And let me tell you, those kids were not expecting to hear Taylor Swift and Justin Bieber—at least not as interpreted live by a Neo-Emo-Ska band with Gen's reedy ironic vocals, as opposed to a simple iPod playlist and a set of speakers. That dad could've saved himself the five hundred bucks (plus the fifty extra he tipped us because he felt bad that his daughter's escort threw a Mr. Pibb at Ray-Ray when he started playing the keyboard intro to "Soft Serv" as an encore), had his daughter spent a little time compiling a playlist on her computer before the party.

As we were finishing sound check before the show, we started seeing all these kids filing in to the community room through an ice-arch hastily constructed out of blocks of ice from the Stop & Shop. Looking around at my bandmates, it's immediately obvious I'm not the only nervous Bickerson in the joint. Chase's hands are shaking slightly, even though he's trying to play it cool. And Ray-Ray has said more words in thirty minutes than I've heard him speak in six or seven practices. Gen just keeps bouncing around pounding Red Bull after Red Bull, standing too close to everybody and whispering, "Do I need more eyeliner?"

Just before we're about to start, some kid in an ill-fitting golf shirt and khaki slacks comes up to me, goading, "You're in the band?" and I answer, "Yeah. So?" And he just starts cackling hysterically and runs over toward his buddies repeatedly screaming, "There's a chick in the band! There's a chick in the band!" and jumping around like he just dunked on somebody for the first time.

Chase sees all of this going down, and I can tell his first thought is, *Let it go.* But then he studies me for a minute while I try to ignore the guy by keeping busy behind my drums, and suddenly Chase hops off the stage, heading right toward the golf shirt douche bag with an exaggerated manly strut, and confronts him all aggro: "Is there a problem here?"

The kid—*okay*, I'll just say it: he's obviously kind of the ookey-repulsive kid in school who probably only has friends because they're scared of what he'll do to them if they reject him. Anyway, golf shirt turns around and snipes, "You talking to me?" all puffing up close to Chase's chest, and I'm adjusting my kicker, thinking, *Wow, Brooke-slash-Chase certainly got with the dudes-roostering-around program really quick, didn't s/he?*

"Why don't you shut up and listen before you start acting like such a loser?" Chase says.

"*I'm* the loser?" The kid turns to his friends, who in all honesty don't look like they'd be willing to back him up if push came to punch. "That's funny, because you're the one in a band with a *girl.*"

"And you're the one who's so threatened by anything new that you have to make a big show of it, and insult my friend and make her feel like crap when she's never done anything to you," Chase growls.

Damn, I guess he's really cottoned to the Changers mission too.

"What are you even saying?" golf shirt ridicules, then begins walking away.

"Apologize to her," Chase calls after him.

The kid keeps moving.

"I said, *apologize*," he repeats, louder. A few people look over.

I have no idea which way this is going to go, but mercifully, Gen has just gotten the thumbs-up from the birthday girl's dad that she is about to make her entrance to "In da Club."

"We're gonna get this party started!" Gen hollers into the mic. There is terrible feedback, then the room falls completely quiet. No "yeahs" or hoots or whistles. Not a single clap . . .

Chase is still standing there, rigid, boring down the back of golf shirt's thick buzz-cut head as he slips into the crowd. And then the lights go down, a disco ball starts spinning, and Chase finally turns around, hops back up onto the stage, and swings his guitar strap over his head. He doesn't even turn back to look at me. It's the first time I've seen him angry. That kid isn't even worth it. But I've got other problems now, because Gen is cuing me to start, and I think my heart is maybe going to explode, it is beating so rapidly.

I click my sticks together so Ray-Ray knows when to come in, and we're off. *"Go shorty!"* Gen starts hollering into the mic. A few kids recognize the song and start half-clapping along, but most seem stupefied, confused as to what's happening and where they should be looking.

The spotlight is broken, so a few country-looking guys crowd around and flip on these powerful camping flashlights and aim them through the ice-arch, where I can see the front quarters of a horse standing there, pawing the ground with his left hoof. Somebody's holding the reins beside the horse—I think it's the birthday girl's older brother (he's in a camouflage baseball hat)—and he starts leading the animal out into the light, and soon the flashlight beams reveal the birthday girl mounted atop it bareback, with both legs dangling over one side. She's wearing a long white veil thing (like when you're getting married), which flows over the horse's rump and trails behind, plus a sparkly, too-tight stretchy-white dress, which she has to keep pulling down her thighs.

I'm trying to concentrate on playing the song, but it's clear that the ice-arch wasn't built high enough for her and the horse to clear, so the girl's mom and dad and other next-of-kin are scrambling over, trying to get her to duck without falling off, and the horse is getting spooked by the crooked, steaming ice blocks, plus the veil thingy trailing behind him, and he's prancing around trying to do the right thing the way horses do even though they could trounce the whole crowd at any moment, and I know he's supposed to be white, like snowy-white, but he's more a yellow flax color, and *phew*, the birthday girl has finally cleared the ice sculpture, regained her balance atop the swayback horse, yanked down her dress again, and now they are standing in the middle of the dance floor while all of her friends make a circle and clap along to my beat.

Some kids join in singing, *"We gonna party like it's your birthday, we gon' sip Bacardi like it's your birthday, and you know we don't give a fuck it's not your birthday!"* and I can

157

tell the parents don't love the swearing, but now this girl is sliding off the horse into her escort's arms, and we are just about done with the song. Time to transition into "I'm Not a Girl, Not Yet a Woman," which is when Chase finally seems like he's having a little fun, tossing a smile over his shoulder at me as he plays the intro.

It's at this point I notice Audrey, dressed real cute, headed toward the stage followed by her friend Jed, who I'm realizing from this vantage point isn't hideous, sadly. He's sporting that longish-but-not-too-long, dirty-blond, "I rock-climb and clear trails in my spare time" type of haircut. Audrey starts jumping up and down fist-pumping, so excited about the music. She's right in front of Chase and me now, close as she can be, and as I'm playing, I'm sitting there thinking, *Goddamnit.*

I had been all worried: Is Audrey going out with Jed? Is she just friends with Jed? Does she want to go out with Jed? What's the deal with Jed? And now Gen is moaning his emo Britney impression into the mic: *"All I need is time, a moment that is mine while I'm in between . . ."* and it just hits me, I completely forgot to worry about another horrible possibility: that Audrey is going to be all about Chase when she sees him in action, and he's of course going to be all about her as soon as they meet—and where's that going to leave me?

I mess up. Gen looks back at me, sweat covering his forehead despite the long kerchief he has tied around his head.

Sorry, I mouth, then catch back up.

The birthday girl has just been passed from her dad

to her escort to continue the slow dance in the flashlight spotlights, and I make a mental note never to do an icky slow-jam anything with my father—ever.

We finish the song and everybody's applauding, parents, relatives, friends. The petrified horse is led away. We move into a more upbeat Kanye track, and Audrey and Jed start dancing like mad on my and Chase's side of the stage. They're freaking right up against each other, being totally crazy and what my mother would call *inappropriate*—to the point where these other yahoo kids and some stray adults are staring at them and wondering who the hell they are— and more so, who invited them. Audrey catches my eye and squeals, "I love you!" with this crazy jokey face, then points at my tie and forms a heart shape with her hands. Seconds after, she swivels and wraps her arms around Jed's neck, dipping back dramatically. He's not expecting it, so he practically drops her, but he recovers, bracing her with his thigh. Not that Audrey notices. She's on another planet, having the best time in the world.

We get through about eight of the requested songs to a mostly empty dance floor, and then it's time to bring out the cake, which is one of those large sheet cakes from the supermarket bakery, this one with a big action-figure Pegasus pressed into the top, which I think is supposed to be a unicorn, and also sugar-cube igloos, and a couple of the flashlight guys are wheeling the thing out on a cart. Lights come up, and we're signaled to start playing "Happy Birthday," which Gen starts belting out a little like Marilyn Monroe did for President Kennedy, until a bunch of people start looking over with contorted faces; then the mom lights the candles, and everybody's singing to the birthday girl, which thankfully drowns Gen out.

We get a break while they're serving the cake. I hop down to talk to Audrey and Jed, who I've heard so much about, but have never met (except chatting on the phone a couple times when I've been with Audrey; I had no idea what she was doing, but she just handed me the phone and said, "Talk," and I was like, "Hey," and he was like, "Hey," and that was pretty much it).

"Howdy," Jed says, nodding at me, and I don't know if we're supposed to shake hands.

"Ohmigod, you guys are *awesome*!" Audrey screams, and wraps herself around me.

"Yeah, really tight," Jed agrees.

"You didn't tell me how *good* you are," Audrey says, so sincerely it almost hurts.

I don't know what to say, so I just sort of turn around and, thank jaysus, Chase is coming over with two dripping cold bottles of water, handing me one.

"Thank you," I say, for the water and the interruption. "Chase, this is Audrey—and Jed."

Everybody shakes and meets. And then we stand around. I gulp down half the bottle. Worlds colliding.

"I like your band," Audrey mumbles to Chase, and then gushes, "Drew is *so* talented."

Chase takes a long swig of water himself. "Yeah, she's great. We're lucky to have her."

"You *totes* are. She's the star!" Audrey shouts. If I didn't know otherwise, I'd think she'd been drinking spiked punch. Then she puts an arm around me and guides me toward the bathroom. I don't have to go, but I'm assuming I'm about to get an earload about Jed or Chase, since a lot of vital information in life seems to be delivered and received in girls' bathrooms.

Audrey goes into a stall, talking to me through the door. "Who's that Chase guy?"

Knew it.

"Just a friend. I told you about him." I stand there gawkily while a partygoer in a frilly pink dress dries her hands and stares at me dead-faced in the mirror over the sinks, chewing gum.

"No you didn't," Audrey shoots back. I can hear her tinkling and have to fight the urge to wait for her outside.

"He's just a guy in the band. I barely know him myself," I lie. Sort of.

Audrey flushes, and then comes out to wash her hands. She smiles real big at me, like she knows something I don't. "He likes you a lot," she says, nonchalantly leaning into the mirror and reapplying lip gloss. "Want some?"

I wave it off. "I have to get back on stage."

We re-enter the room just as the birthday girl is being presented with her big gift. She is really excited, fluttering her hands in front of her face like she's on *The Price Is Right*. The dad takes his time unzipping a long pink (I'm guessing fake) Louis Vuitton designer case, and pulls out a massive (also pink, not fake) shotgun with the birthday girl's name engraved on the barrel. *Oohs* and *Aahs* all around, as the dad places the weapon in his daughter's perfectly manicured hands.

"You have got to be joking," Audrey spits out, rolling her

eyes, as the girl swings around, sweeping the barrel full circle to show everyone.

"What? No matching pink grenades?" I snark as Gen catches my eye and waves me back to the drums. I turn to go, but Audrey grabs and hugs me real tight for a few beats before freeing me. I jog over and *(please don't face-plant in front of all these people)* take a leap onto the stage, and then I settle behind my kit and spot Audrey rejoining Jed, a big grin spreading on his face when he sees her.

And then: *gulp*, there's Tracy, leaning up against a wall with a cup of punch in her hand. She points a finger at me, like she's been watching the whole time. I sort of acknowledge her with one of my sticks, then Gen counts us off, and we crank out a kick-ass performance of "Siri" while nobody listens to us because they're all too excited about the birthday girl's new firearm.

After we thought we'd finished our entire set, the hosting dad climbed up on stage, commandeered the mic, and thanked everybody for coming out, thanked his wife, "the unicorn wrangler," the VFW, etc., and then went on to profess his love for his daughter in about a hundred ways. He started tearing up when he ended with, "I'll kill anybody who tries to hurt her." Which I believed. While he rambled, his daughter just stood there blushing innocently in the middle of the dance floor with all the flashlights aimed at her, where ten seconds before she'd been bending over in front of her escort and letting him pelvic thrust against her from behind while they danced.

Before finishing his speech, the dad asked for another

round of applause for the Bickersons ("another" being quite the misnomer), though nobody really complied. And then he asked us to play one more song, even though it was obvious nobody wanted us to. But Gen of course didn't ascertain this, so eager to try out his newest song, "Soft Serv," which is how Ray-Ray ended up completely drenched by a full cup of Mr. Pibb while singing backup, *"Hold the phone, my sugar cone, the bottom is the tastiest bit."*

Chase and I were cracking up when the lights flipped on, and Ray-Ray didn't really seem that put-out by the incident because his keyboard was spared, but when I looked over at Gen, he was completely devastated.

"This just isn't our crowd, man," Chase tried, but Gen wasn't buying it. He jumped off the stage and flew out the rear exit, where I'm assuming he chain-smoked the kinks out of his ego before coming back in to break down the equipment.

I couldn't get out of there quick enough, immediately started packing up my drums and schlepping stuff to Gen's van, while Audrey was trailing me, gushing about how transcendent we were and how she couldn't wait to see us when we get to play our own selection of covers and original songs, blah blah. She snapped her fingers at Jed to get him to carry the heaviest stuff like amps and whatnot, and he obeyed right quick.

I bent down to pick up my snare, and the next thing I knew, both Chase and Audrey had put a hand on it, so I let go, and then they were holding it aloft, sort of tugging at it from two sides, like a couple dogs with a Frisbee, trying to get the other to give up.

"I've got it," Chase said casually.

"That's okay," Audrey said.

"It's all good," Chase insisted, louder.

"I totally have it," Audrey snapped, yanking again, which made Chase release, and Audrey stumbled back onto her butt, the snare rattling in her lap.

"Seriously?" I said, looking back at Chase like, *What the hell, dude?* I reached a hand out to Audrey. "Are you okay?"

She hopped up without taking it, red-faced, and raced the snare out to the van.

Chase shrugged. "Accident."

I didn't really know what to say, so I said nothing, and he picked up an amp and followed her out. Then Tracy suddenly appeared from nowhere like a secret agent (minus the fedora), and sidled up next to me.

"Double trouble?" she said, raising an eyebrow.

"Pardon?"

"Don't be naïve," she remarked solemnly. "The greatest enemy will hide in the last place you would ever look."

"Hey, thanks so much—I'm glad you liked the show," I said.

"I know it might seem like a good problem to have," Tracy continued, furtively glancing around to make sure she wasn't being overheard, "but you're playing with fire, Drew."

"I'm playing with a *band*, Tracy. That's all."

We could hear Audrey and Jed coming back in to haul the final load. Tracy's eyes darted back and forth. "More later," she mumbled, then bolted back through the VFW and out of sight.

"Who was that?" Audrey asked, hefting some cables.

"Who?"

"That lady in the headband," she said, pointing over my shoulder.

I turned to look, but Tracy was vapor. "Oh, that," I said. "Nobody."

I got my midterm report card, and you may as well know, the news wasn't good. My studies are suffering, apparently. Well, all but English—where I'm pulling an A-.

"Just because you're going through an emotional and physical upheaval does not give you permission to slack off on academics," Dad said tonight, after eyeballing my lackluster grades. "I was, *am*, a Changer, and I made the honor roll all four years."

"This just in, Dad: I'm not you," I sniped back.

"Maybe not, but you represent me, this family, and your greater Changer family. In the many, we are one. And I will not have you failing in school. Period."

I wanted to say, *What about failing in every other way?* But instead I stormed off into my room, jammed in my earbuds, and cranked up MC Fatback loud enough to give me a raging migraine.

It's not that I want to suck at school. But I'm preoccupied. By other attentions. Like they warn you shouldn't be on that ubiquitous airplane-safety announcement. It does feel like I am crashing. I guess I should have put on my oxygen mask first, before worrying about everybody else's.

One thing is certain: I could have used one last night.

Audrey and I have been studying together. Which is about as productive as it sounds. Yesterday, I went over after school. We holed up in her room, snacking on potato chips and cheese. She likes to construct these little towers with the chips and cheese chunks, see how many she can stack and bite into without the whole thing splintering into a million pieces. It sounds gross as I'm describing it, but in actuality, it's kind of adorable.

So, I'm sitting on the bed, trying to care about algebra and the Civil War, when Audrey plops down right next to me.

"Can you believe Chloe tripped Miranda today? All her animé sketches went flying across the floor."

"Chloe's ass-hattery knows no bounds," I reply, as Audrey scoots even closer.

"What's her damage anyway?" she asks, twirling her hair around a finger. "How much alpha is enough alpha?"

"I think she might be satisfied when she is given a literal crown to wear, and we all have to avoid making eye contact with her like she's royalty."

"And she parades around in clothes sewn exclusively from the pelts of nerdy freshmen and subsists only on the blood of dead virgins and frozen Pinkberry," Audrey adds.

Now we're giggling, and we both shake a bit from the effort, our elbows and shoulders and thighs bumping in a sort of dance. After a bit, the shaking ceases, but I notice neither one of us repositions our thighs or shoulders; they continue to touch slightly, heat passing between us.

"She goes to our church," Audrey says flatly.

"Chloe?"

"Yeah. You can imagine the outfits."

"I can't imagine her as a person of God," I say.

"I don't think she's in it for God so much as the superiority."

"Ah."

Downstairs we hear Jason come home, announcing his presence by dropping his school stuff in a clatter and yelling for his mother to make him a snack. A chill seems to come over Audrey, but we both ignore it, look down to the open books in our laps.

"So, the Gettysburg Address," I try. But Audrey is even less interested in studying now.

There's a knock at the door. Her mom cracks it open. "Does your little friend want to stay for supper?" she asks.

Audrey looks to me, pleading.

"Um, sure, I guess," I say weakly. "I'll need to ask my folks first."

"Maybe Drew can sleep over?" Audrey presses. "It's silly to have y'all drive her home so late. She can borrow my clothes. And she has her schoolwork!"

"I'll need to confirm with her mother to make sure that's okay. Drew, do you have a number I can ring?"

I'm not sure what I'm supposed to do. Are Static parents allowed to have Changers' parents' phone numbers? It feels like I should say no, but I look at Audrey's beseeching face and cave. "Sure. Sounds great."

Audrey squeals and does a little jig. "Sleepover!" And I am immediately seized with regret.

Two mint face masks and several trays of Tater Tots later, Audrey and I are back in her room.

"Truth or dare?" she asks me.

"Truth," I say, reluctantly.

"Have you ever tongue-kissed a guy?"

My stomach flips. "Ah. No."

Audrey looks pleased. "Truth or dare?" she goes on.

"Hey, wait, isn't it my turn?"

"Ack. Yeah. Go ahead. Nothing horrible? 'Kay?"

"Truth or dare?"

"Truuuuuth," Audrey drawls.

I ponder, wondering what, if anything, I really want to know. What answer I could stand to hear. I want to ask about her brother. Why she seems afraid of him. I want to ask if she believes love really is blind. I want to ask if she believes in magic, in powers greater than every human, if she could ever see herself with someone like me.

But I decide to go with: "Do you think mint face masks really minimize pore size?"

"*Drew*. Don't be lame. Ask something real!"

My brain buzzes. Maybe I *could* ask something real. Maybe. No. Forget it. *I know.* "Do you have a crush on someone right now?" I ask.

Audrey grabs her pillow and smooshes it into her face. She starts making this goat noise, writhing around on her bed, like she's been possessed.

"Well?"

"Okay. Okay. Okay. Truth." She sighs super slowly, like a leaking semi tire. "Yes! *Ack!*" She wriggles and convulses again, throws out more barnyard sound effects. "But you can't ask me who. Okay? That's not the game. It's my secret."

"Okay . . ." I concede.

"No, seriously, Drew. I can't tell you. Totes private. Okay?"

"Aud, I'm not asking."

She falls quiet, an uncomfortable silence blooms. I scratch my head. She goes over to the window and looks out into her backyard, even though it's too dark to see anything.

"You want to keep playing?"

She shakes her head. "I'm cool."

"You want to minimize more pores or something? Exfoliate? Pluck?" Now I'm totally lost.

Nothing.

"Please don't make me read about the Battle of Fort Henry," I say.

"What I want, Drew, is to practice kissing." She says this slowly, with stolid conviction, turning from the window as she speaks, looking me dead in the eye.

I feel a sudden urge to flee.

"I want to know I'm doing it right," she continues, strolling toward me now, her back weirdly straight, almost like Frankenstein. "Don't you?"

"Define *right*," I say.

"You're my best friend. I trust you to tell me the truth. Like, if I'm excruciatingly gross. You'd tell me. Right?"

I feel my body pushing back into the pillow behind me.

"I can't be one of those girls who does it *wrong*," Audrey implores. "Come on. It's a win-win for both of us."

Yeah, but only one of us will possibly have her head overtaken by a vision of the other one's future.

"Why not?" I say, shrugging my shoulders.

I totally can't believe I just said that.

"What's the worst that can happen?"

Or that! Who am I? Whoever I am, zip your pie hole.

"Awesome," Audrey purrs, a crooked smile breaking across her face, as she plants her palms on the bed, clears her throat a little, leans into me, toward my mouth, closes her eyes, and—

"SHUT THE FRONT DOOR!"

And like my worst nightmare, it's Jason, barging into the room, wearing only flannel pajama bottoms and preppy man slippers, his emergent chest hair on full display. "Are y'all lezzing out, or what?"

Audrey and I fly apart instantly, me absently raising a hand to my lips, Audrey stomping toward her interloping brother.

"Get out!" she shouts. "Get out, *now*!"

"No way. I am *not* missing the rest of this show," he says, pulling over Audrey's desk chair.

Audrey sighs, clearly rattled, but keeping it together. "There is no show, deviant. She had something in her eye."

"Yeah. Your saliva," he shoots.

"You wish," Audrey says.

"*You* wish. Maybe I should tell Jed? Let him know you're switching teams now?"

At that, something shifts inside me, and I can't help myself. "What exactly are the *teams*, Jason?" I ask. I should know better than to push, but I don't care. Jason rises from the chair and positions his furry chest inches from my face. He smells like menthol.

"Well, Drew, there is *this* team," he says, pointing a thumb at his slightly twitching pectoral muscles. "The good-with-God team. And then there is *that*." He jabs a finger in the direction of Audrey's crotch. "The against-nature team."

I'm considering rattling the hornet nest even further, when I hear Audrey say, "Jason, just leave us alone." Her tone is completely different now. Tired, resigned.

He ignores her. Busy hammering holes of hate into my eye sockets.

"What's your problem anyway?" I ask, acting calmer than I feel.

"It's *you* who's going to have a problem, little girl." And with that, he swivels on his slippers and oozes out the door, smacking a hand on one of his butt cheeks.

I turn to Audrey, who looks relieved.

"I see your brother got a tattoo," I say after the door slams shut behind him.

CHANGE 1–DAY 108

Day after the sleepover. All through school Audrey avoided me like hepatitis. Let's examine. Is it:

1) Because she has a secret crush I now know about?

2) Because we almost kissed?

3) Because her psychotic brother almost saw us kiss and then threatened us with permanent brain damage?

Or is it:

4) Because after Jason left and I mentioned his tattoo, Audrey started sobbing, saying that she just found out her family is forcing her to go to some strident church camp this summer in a backwoods town, that she couldn't say more about it, only that she didn't want to go. I asked if Chloe was going. Was that why she hated it so much? And she sighed, "If only." But she wouldn't say anything else. About the camp, the church, her brother, his new ink.

I guess she really didn't have to. I saw it for myself. It was the Roman numeral I.

It's Christmas! I added the exclamation point ironically. Which is a Rudolf the Red-Nosed bummer, because when I was Ethan I *loved* Christmas. *Un*ironically. The way kids are supposed to.

It's not like we were an overly consumerist family in the past. There were never mountains of perfectly bedazzled gifts under the tree like you see on holiday jewelry commercials. We lit candles for Hanukkah, learned about Diwali and Kwanzaa. And Mom and Dad were consistently righteous about getting me the one or two things I really, really wanted. My drum kit one year. My skateboard another. My watch when I was ten. We'd bundle up and go sledding or snowshoeing together, then open our presents later in the day—no BS getting up at the crack of dawn—and then we'd all go to a Chinese restaurant and order way too much food and talk about how nice it was not to be sitting around a table with family members we didn't like. Sometimes we'd see a movie too. Basically, a perfect, perfect day.

But, like every other freaking thing in my endless crap-stream of a life, Christmas has changed because I'm a Changer.

Allow me to present: *A Very Changer Christmas.*

It involves schlepping out to the non-ship-building "ship-building" facility in the woods for a looong, bizarro ceremony that blathers on about spirituality and the meaning of giving and the importance of acknowledging there is not a single God, just as there is not a single identity, that all is everything and infinite, and additional *Xanadu* nonsense, and how on this day more than any other day, we must come together as a people and stand firm in the Changer cause of peace through plurality. Basically, it's the *In the many, we are one* extended dance remix.

Then we form a circle ("the strongest of all shapes"), and pass the Changer "possibility of being" amulet from hand to hand to hand. This takes longer than evolution. I swear I grew an inch by the time that amulet made its way around. (I did a quick scan for Chase but he wasn't in the circle of hell, probably at home watching the Cowboys, lucky bastard.)

Anyhow, while we were passing that thing? A song. That's right. We have to sing. And not a catchy Christmas carol either. Not even the dreaded "Silent Night." No, this song is the official Changer holiday anthem, and it sounds like a cross between something you'd hear during a spa massage and the theme song to every Celtic country known to man. It is the elevator music of the damned. And everybody knows it! They sing and chant along like it's "Happy Birthday," smiling and nodding and just so filled with Changer joy, you want to flipping puke. At least I did.

By the time we got out of there, it was too late for Chinese food.

"Maybe tomorrow?" Mom offered, making her sorry-but-not-that-much face.

Oh yeah. I almost forgot. My present. They gave it to me

when we got home, in an envelope that wasn't even sealed. I opened it and read the card:

> *A donation has been made in the name of <u>Drew Bohner</u> to the Changer Continued Enlightenment and Education Fund (CCEEF) which helps improve the lives of millions of souls every year. Your gift will provide critical resources for both the outreach program and relocation efforts, without which our vital work could not continue. May the gods bless you and all the yous you've yet to become.*

Yeah. So that happened.

I think I may have made a terrible mistake.

I mentioned to Tracy something about Jason's possibly Abider-related tattoo during our last check-in at the Q-hut, and she tripped right into Council-automaton mode.

"You need to file a formal report."

"A wha'?"

"You need to report Jason—actually, the whole family— to the Council so they can take it from there. I can give you the forms if you need them, but there should be copies in your welcome kit. Do you still have your welcome kit?"

My mind is jumping. Report Jason, no problem. Where do I sign? But Audrey? Her parents? *Audrey?*

"I don't understand. What happens after I file the report?" I ask.

"It'll be in the Council's hands."

"Could you be more vague?" I'm getting a little pissed.

"Yes." Tracy not budging.

"Why can't I just turn in Jason?"

"It is highly unlikely that Jason became an Abider all by himself. You have to be taught to hate."

"Knock it off, Tracy. You know Audrey isn't an Abider. She's my best friend."

"Is she?"

I resist the urge to rip off Tracy's headband and stomp

it into the dirt. "Audrey doesn't discriminate against anyone or anything. She is the most charitable, open person I know. Present company included." I wait for that to sink in. "What if I refuse?"

"Refuse what? To see the truth? To obey the sixth commandment? *Thou shalt put the welfare of the Changer race before that of thyself.*"

I've never hated anyone as much as I hate her in this moment. "Screw you, Tracy. And screw your commandments."

Tracy just stands there, inscrutable. She doesn't even seem upset. It's almost like she saw this coming. For a couple minutes, neither of us speaks. Mentally, I rifle through my options. I could go to Mom and Dad, lay out my case. They know about Audrey. They'll see how ridiculous this is. Or I could do nothing, play a game of chicken with Tracy and the Council.

Wait, of course, I should have thought of it first! I could go to Audrey. I could tell her everything, come clean—it would feel so good, and then she could hug me and reassure me she isn't my mortal enemy, that she loves me no matter what I am, and we could go on being best friends and neither one of us would end up locked in some Council brig.

God. I can't let anything happen to Audrey. Not because of me.

"Can't we just wait?" I plead, my desperation on full display. "Surely we can wait. Gather more evidence? Maybe I saw the tattoo wrong. Please, Tracy. I think—I think I love her."

At this, something resembling compassion moves across

her face. She chews on her lip, says nothing for what seems like a decade. Finally, she tilts her head to the right, looks up, and sighs.

"You have two weeks. Two weeks to do whatever it is you feel you need to do, after which I will personally go to the Council and—"

And there I am, my arms wrapped around Tracy, weeping and snotting all over her blouse. "Thank you, thank you, thank you," I blubber. "You won't be sorry. I promise. I swear."

And to her credit, she does not flinch, or try to wipe away the stains. She just strokes the side of my head and whispers to herself, "I hope not. For all of our sakes."

Something awful happened tonight. I can't begin to comprehend it. Much less describe it. I'm actually scared to think about it.

I don't *want* to think about it.

I don't want Chase to get in trouble for doing the right thing.

I can barely get this out because I'm crying so hard into my pillow. I can't stop. I'm not even sure this is recording anymore—

CHANGE 1–DAY 139

(SECOND ATTEMPT)

Where to start?

I freaking hate myself, how about we start there? I shouldn't have had that drink. It was just one fruity cup that killed the paralyzing dread about playing for the first time in front of people from my school. My first mistake. The Jenga block that triggered the collapse of the whole night. Of my whole world—

I'm back. I just checked to make sure my parents weren't awake. I didn't see the light under their bedroom door. Maybe they're finally asleep after all that arguing. I've never seen Dad so angry. He wouldn't let me say a single word in the car on the way home. Mom just sat in the front seat and cried. Other than that it was silence.

Okay. From the beginning.

It was Baron (yes, *Baron*), the kid from the football team who threw the party; he was the one paying us. I think his parents must regret having him or something—they're always leaving him alone, and he has these massive school-wide parties that pretty much destroy his house every time, but then he hires industrial cleaning crews to come in the next day, and his parents never seem to find out. Or they do, and they don't care.

Anyway, I'm really glad we got the gig and all, and it's probably only because Audrey is so obsessed with the Bickersons that it went viral through the football team that we can turn a party out.

So I'm drumming, and everything's going fine. It seems like people are digging Gen's songs, and we're playing really well together, plus we're getting paid a ton (maybe enough for me to buy myself a phone, I was thinking). Then around midnight, the party starts to get out of hand, like an R-rated version of those John Hughes movies Audrey is always trying to get me to watch: *Pretty in Pink*, *Some Kind of Wonderful*. She's memorized practically every line. *She's an incredible individual . . . I don't want you to worry, because my only plans are to make sure that she's taken care of.* Poor Duckie. Sad tragic bastard. So out of his depth. Like me.

Half of the McMansion is within range of the Bickersons, and in the other half a deejay is playing electro-house and dubstep. Basically there are some serious decibels going on, the beats colliding in the vaulted living room in the center of the house. Kids from all grades, plus some older ones who've already graduated, are devolving into crazed baboons, making every other party I've ever been to look like a church picnic. There are broken lamps, paintings being ripped from the walls, crushed plastic cups and food strewn everywhere. Stains on rugs and furniture, heaps of clothing pooled in the corners, sweat, partial nudity. *Caligula 2.0*.

In the middle of our set I'm thirsty and out of breath, and somehow Audrey senses this and in a minute she's around behind my drums handing me a pulpy-orange drink—and I just gulp it down. It's the kind of party I'd be stressed to be at even if we weren't playing a gig, but being in front of all these people acting so unpredictably feral, I'm starting to wig out.

In the back of my mind I know my parents would be none too pleased about me being here. And, full disclosure: I'm sure a part of me knew the drink Audrey handed me contained vodka before I downed it, but I didn't really care at the time, not enough anyway. Besides, what was one drink going to do? I wasn't going to be driving home—when he picked me up at home and loaded my equipment, Gen promised my dad he'd get me back safe, and he's been sober since before he got his driver's license. Also, that time Andy and I snuck rum and Coke from his folks' liquor cabinet one night when they left us home alone, I had two of them and barely felt anything. We just fell asleep on the couch with the PlayStation's home screen glowing on the other side of our closed eyelids.

It's twelve forty-five a.m. I'm playing hard, banging through the set list, and *bam*, my head grows light. I strain to focus, and there's Audrey directly in front of me, pogoing and thrashing like she's the only person in the room.

I glance into the backyard and notice that Jason and a few of his teammates are trying to throw that kid Danny into the pool, but somehow he manages to shake them off and beat it out of the yard through the heavy iron gates. Jason and the guys drain another keg of beer and kick it over, fixing to toss it into the pool like a buoy. One of them mounts the keg into the water, trying to ride it, but he slides off, and the barrel shoots up out of the water and lands on his head with an enormous splash. I'm thinking dude's got to have brain damage, but Jason and his buddies don't seem too concerned, and seconds later they blow into the room where we're playing and start slam-dancing and knocking random people over on the dance floor. I spot Chloe and Brit exiting the scene, not down with the whole getting-toppled-to-the-ground vibe.

Jason dance-steps over to Audrey and hip-checks her a couple times along with the beat, which totally changes her mood, and I want to go to her, but I'm a little busy. I can tell Chase is keeping a close eye on Jason too; even from behind, I know when he's distracted by something other than the music.

As we wrap up the first set, I scan the sea of partiers and realize Audrey has disappeared, nowhere to be seen. Gen hollers into the mic, "We're the Bickersons, and we'll be back in fifteen!" A lot of kids cheer, but I'm not really thinking about that.

"Chase!" I holler. He can't hear me. It seems like the deejay turned up whatever he was spinning in the other room as soon as we stopped playing. "Yo, Chase!" I scream.

He turns around, irritated. "*What?*"

"I'm going to find Audrey," I say, thumbing in the direction of a separate wing of the house. My head is pounding from the bass. And the drink.

Chase points to his ears indicating he can't hear, so I just wave him off and go. Maybe it's the woozy feeling from the alcohol, or the debauchery in every room, but I'm weirdly concerned about Audrey. I grip my drumsticks in my fist and head down a hallway with a rug so long it wouldn't fit in the Taj Mahal. There are countless professional family photos hanging on the walls. One on the ski slopes, another on a pristine sandy beach, the whole family dressed in khaki and white. Yet another on safari in Africa, a giraffe running in the background. I crack open every door, poking my head in, and call, "Aud?"

She's not in the first four rooms I try. No answer in the last room either. It's a library of some sort, but all the books look fake, like a library in Disney World. There are about a dozen taxidermy trophies on the wall, antelope, bears, boars—a freaking zebra! Can you even shoot those? I never understood why people want dead animals staring at them inside of their houses. Much less why they want to kill them in the first place. What feels good about that? I look up and see a row of weapons mounted on the opposite wall— long shotguns and swords with tassels, like a royal castle collection.

It's dark and quiet in here, and I take a couple steps into the room, and, "Oh, gah!" I screech, jumping back, terrified, as a full-grown polar bear appears behind the door, rearing up on two legs looking like it's about to pounce on me. I laugh at myself for being so scared of a hollow dead thing. I remember there's supposed to be something really special about polar bears' fur, but I can't recall what it is, so I reach forward, gently resting my hand on the pointy bristles of his forepaw.

"There you are."

I know that voice. It's Jason, and before I can turn to face him, he wraps his beefy arms around me from behind, squeezing me in a suffocating hug. He reeks of beer and chlorine and sweat. He's also obviously drunk, and we almost fall down as he waddles me over toward the couch.

185

"What are you doing?" I ask, testing to see if I can break free without seeming like I'm trying to. I can't.

"You know what I'm doing," he taunts, slobbering on my neck. I try to wiggle out of his grip in earnest, but his hands are linked together tight in front of my chest. I can barely move. I fumble my drumsticks, watching as they roll under the couch. My thoughts turn to Tracy.

She was right.

I squirm harder, working to get an elbow in as leverage. He clenches even more.

"You think you're so funny, don't you?" he jeers.

"Jason, seriously. You're hurting me," I say, my voice on the edge of panic.

At that, he releases his grip, spins me around, and pushes me down onto the couch, hard. I break my fall with my palms, but I hear something in my right wrist snap. "Ouch!"

"Don't act like you haven't been wanting this since the minute you laid eyes on me," he says, starting to unbuckle his belt.

"Wanting what?" I am genuinely bewildered, struggling to get up, but he pushes me down, and I fall back on the same wrist, which is throbbing now.

"Drop the innocent act," he spits, unzipping his jeans.

I push-kick him with both legs, intending to nail him in the nuts, but my heels miss and graze his right hip before falling uselessly to the ground. He stumbles, off-balance, but then he's right back on me, pressing my shoulders flat. I can't stand up, and my mind goes blank.

"Cut the crap, Drew," he hisses into my neck, trying to kiss me on the lips, but I keep turning my head side to side so he can't land his mouth anywhere near me. He reaches for my waist, starts fumbling with my jeans, and before I know it, he's yanking them down. My ass cheek is bare, and I know my emblem is exposed as Jason climbs on me, and I am so terrified, but I can't scream. I open my mouth and nothing comes out. My body has separated from my brain, I am a ghost watching myself from above, shrieking inside, where no one can hear.

Jason squeezes my chest with one hand, while the other holds me down. The disembodied me yells, *Do something!* but my actual body freezes, like a computer shutting itself down. *I'm not here. This isn't me. This isn't happening to me.*

Jason's pushing and grinding himself against me, but I feel nothing. I'm not there anymore. I'm gone. I don't know where. I can barely hear him when he barks into my face over and over, "Come on now, come on!" Like I'm a recalcitrant animal, not following the rules.

I close my eyes. There is nothing left to see.

And then, from what feels like miles away, I register a door flinging open, and a savage roar, and Jason's weight is suddenly lifted off me, and I jolt back to the present, every fiber of my being instantaneously flooding with shame.

This is my fault.

It is my first and only thought.

This is my fault.

"Pull up your pants," I hear Chase's voice as he clutches Jason by the back of his shirt and flings him around and into a set of iron fireplace tools. They clatter to the ground, Jason's head bumping against the brick.

"WHAT THE HELL DO YOU THINK YOU'RE

DOING?" Chase yells, standing over Jason, arms out to his side, pulsating with rage like the Incredible Hulk.

"Well, if it isn't the little band faggot," Jason heckles, and starts to laugh.

The next instant Chase is pounding his fists one after the other into Jason's face. It sounds like punching brick. Chase is half his size, but Jason is so wasted he can't defend himself. Two, three, four thwacks, and now there is blood, but Jason keeps laughing, isn't even trying to resist, in fact is almost enjoying it.

"Chase!" I scream, bounding off the couch.

But Chase doesn't stop, just keeps battering Jason's face over and over, more and more blood spewing out.

"How do you like it?" *Slam.* "Yeah, you like that, you piece of garbage?" *Slam.* "You like being the one with no power?" *Slam.*

I pull up my pants and race into the hall, yelling at the top of my lungs, "Help!"

Some kids hear me, then dash to get Gen and Baron and another football dude, and I just point into the room, where Chase is still rearranging Jason's face, nearly unrecognizable now.

It takes three guys to pull Chase off. They hold him back, his knuckles swollen and bloodied. "I am going to destroy you," Chase hisses, then spits on Jason, who just rolls back and forth on the ground, still conscious but out of it, his eyes puffed shut.

"Answers. Now!" Baron demands, looking to me. And then a few more people come into the room, and everybody is glaring my way.

"He was—"

I can't say anything. I can't think. It was my fault. I *knew*.

"Get him out of here," Baron orders, and a couple guys drag Chase away, and Gen comes over, puts his arm around me. More and more people file into the room, Jason's friends ushering him into the bathroom, trying to clean his face.

Gen and I follow Chase out.

"Did he hurt you?" Gen asks.

I still can't answer. How do you answer?

The music has been turned off. Chase is in the living room sitting back on a couch, two guys lording over him like prison guards. Nobody saying anything. He's just panting, cradling his right hand in his left.

"Did he—?" Chase asks when he sees me, then suddenly breaks off, because now two police officers have arrived, wading through the mess of the house.

"He attacked my friend," Baron says, fingering Chase. Jason emerges from the hallway behind him, looking like a zombie, holding a blood-soaked towel to his face. He can barely walk, Chloe and a teammate supporting him on either side.

"We need a bus," one of the cops says into his radio as soon as he spies Jason's condition.

"I'm fine," Jason croaks. "I don't need to go to the hospital."

"Is this the gentleman who assaulted you?" the other cop asks.

"Yes," Jason replies, glancing between me and Chase. "It was him. He just jumped me out of nowhere when my girlfriend and I were in the study. I think he's jealous or something." He smiles, the whites of his teeth flashing in his bloody mouth.

What then?

The cops put Chase in handcuffs and took him away in the police car with red strobes going, lighting up the cul-de-sac. And when the EMTs wheeled Jason away and put him into the ambulance, Audrey reluctantly at his side, he told the police he wanted to press charges against Chase. And when Gen told the policeman I had something to say, I explained that Jason wasn't my boyfriend and that he was trying to hurt me—that Chase was only protecting me.

The policeman asked, "Well, *did* he hurt you?"

I didn't know how to answer the question.

He was about to, I was thinking.

And: *Yes, he did.*

But I didn't say either.

Not until just now.

My iPod was vibrating on the table beside my bed and jolted me awake.

Clock reads *12:38*. Wow, I really slept. My head is pounding, eyes stinging. I look over at the screen.

Are u ok?

It's Audrey texting. In fact, there are three texts spaced about an hour apart, all asking a version of the same thing.

I sit up in bed, squint at the window, where some sun is twinkling through the crack between the curtains. I don't feel like dealing with Audrey now. Or anybody. The iPod buzzes again, I look over: *J isn't pressing charges. I told parents what he did.*

Last night comes rushing back in.

What he did.

I turn the iPod facedown. Flip open my laptop. I look over. It's Chase on Skype. I thought he'd still be in jail or something.

I pad across the room, make sure my door is shut, put on my headphones, and answer. His face pops up on the screen. He looks half-alive. Or maybe half-dead.

"Hi," he says, his voice lower than usual. "Are you okay?"

"Where are you?" I whisper back.

"My parents bailed me out this morning. I don't know why, but the cops didn't want to hold me."

"I'm really sorry, I . . ." I trail off.

"What are *you* sorry for?" he asks, then falls into a coughing fit like he has TB or something.

"For everything, all of it," I offer as soon as the coughing stops.

"This is *not* your fault," he says deliberately, gravely. "You hear me?"

"I shouldn't have gone into that room and—"

"Do you hear me? You. Did. Nothing. Wrong. That son of a bitch . . ."

Then he looks like he's about to cry. We sit there in silence, just staring at each other on the screen. I feel like reaching out and touching his pixilated face.

"I wish I could hug you right now," he says, then after a few seconds: "That shouldn't have happened. You don't deserve to be treated like that. Nobody deserves to be treated like that."

And then Chase is full-on crying. I'm at a loss. I feel like I should maybe look away, give him privacy or something. But he just takes a giant breath, then lets go. "I was molested when I was in sixth grade. When I was Brooke."

It hits me like a punch to the gut. And now I'm crying too. I try to stop.

"It was a soccer coach," he adds, like he's in a trance.

"Chase, I'm so sorry."

"It's okay, it was a long time ago," he says quickly, rubbing the rims of his eyes with the back of a hand. "It felt good to beat the shit out of Jason."

I nod.

"I could've killed him. I mean, if you didn't get people in

there when you did, I think I would've killed him."

Chase starts sobbing again. I sit with it for a while. He recomposes himself, looks up. "I'm sorry. I-I don't mean to lay all this baggage on you."

"Are you kidding? I'm glad you feel like you can—"

"Drew." Chase sniffs hard. I can see him swallow. "Do you ever wish we'd met before?"

My heart jumps.

"Because if we had, I'm pretty sure I would have wanted to be with you."

"I feel the same way," I hear myself confess, a fresh dizziness coming over me.

"I'm not sure I don't want to be with you now," he adds, leaning closer to the screen. "I know it's forbidden. But I think about you all the time. It hurts when we aren't together."

"Oh, Chase." I'm reeling. So much is happening.

"I don't think it makes us bad people, do you?" he asks. "To be in—"

My bedroom door flies open. It's Dad. He spies my laptop screen. "What are you doing?"

"Dad, I—"

He looks closer at the screen, where Chase is just beginning to realize what's happening. "I told you not to be in contact with that kid!" Dad yells. "And what do you go and do first thing?"

"Sir, I—" Chase starts explaining through the tinny speakers.

My dad reaches for the mousepad, clicks *Hang Up*.

"Wait!" I yell, but it's too late. Chase is frozen trying to explain himself.

"Are you *kidding* me?" Dad asks. Then Mom pops her head into the room. "She's Skyping with him," he reports to her.

They both look like I've just told them I'm running off with a meth-dealing carnie.

"We've got a call into the Council, Tracy has been notified," Dad starts. "And in the meantime, I mean it more than I've ever meant anything in your life: don't talk to that boy until you hear differently."

"You don't even know everything that happened!" I shout. Mom looks like she's about to cry again.

"I know enough," Dad counters. "The rules are for your protection. The commandments aren't a joke, Drew."

I lower my head, too tired to deal with any of this.

"You are not to be in contact with him until further notice. Do you understand?"

"So you're saying I can't be in the band anymore?" I screech.

"Maybe not until we get this all sorted out, honey," Mom breaks in.

For a second I waver, and I want to tell Mom everything—that I had a drink, that there were no parents at the party, what Jason did—and, most importantly, how if it weren't for Chase, things would've gone way worse. But all I am is mad, so mad I can't string together a sentence. Mom pulls me into a hug, and though I am shaking with anger and don't want anybody touching me, I have no fight left, so I let her hold me.

Dad is still irate, hands on hips. "You're grounded. Indefinitely." He sighs. "I don't even know who you are anymore."

"Neither do I!" I wail.

Mom pats me on the back and watches as Dad, acting like he's the really wounded one here, storms out.

"Can I be alone for a little bit?" I ask Mom, and she lets go of me.

"I'm here, you know," she says tentatively.

"I know."

"You can tell me anything." She won't leave.

"I'm fine," I insist, the words feeling weird in my mouth.

She seems skeptical, but finally nods, "Okay," then just before closing the door behind her adds, "I love you, baby. I will always love you. No matter what."

And now I'm alone, T minus twenty hours until I have to go back to school and face everybody. All of whom will have heard some twisted version of what happened last night. None of whom will ever know the truth. Because I can't tell them. And Jason will lie. And he will be believed.

I'm searching hard. But I can't seem to find the lesson in this. At least one that doesn't involve my walking into the ocean and never coming out.

I've never seen Tracy so crushed. She is slouched into a folding chair, eyes trained on her shoes. We're at Changer HQ, for what is essentially my intervention. All of us— Chase, his Touchstone Tom, Tracy, my parents, Chase's parents, Council suit Lisa Vandenburg, the Council Lives Coach (or LC) Turner—are arranged in a circle (again, the "strongest shape") to "download and process" recent events.

We will not, however, be "downloading" Jason's attempted assault on me, because I have decided not to "process" that particular nightmare with anyone outside of Chase and Audrey. Thanks to Chase, Jason was stopped. So what else is there to say? Not a freakin' lot. To this crowd anyway. Besides, Jason has already done his PR blitz, spreading a load of horse manure about how Chase is bipolar and that's why he didn't defend himself. "I would *never* hit a retard," I heard him telling some chick in the hall who was asking about the maze of stitches on his face.

Also, I'm a "slut." Apparently. And a "tease." How I can be both, I'm not certain. But the practical impossibility of embodying both female stereotypes in one person doesn't seem to be a hard pill to swallow for the student body of Central High. Chloe was especially eager to embrace the new smears. And to pass them around like a plate of cocktail weenies. (I even made the bathroom stall: *Drew Bonerface,* underneath a horrible sketch of me with a penis for a nose. It looked like Chloe's handwriting, but I'm not totally certain.)

Across the circle, I try to catch Tracy's eye, but she isn't having it. As bad as I might be feeling, she looks even worse. She broke the rules for me. And she got busted. Her perfect record is ruined. She may get demoted as well. I feel terrible. She looks like a scolded puppy. If she peed on the floor I wouldn't be surprised.

"So, to recap, as I understand it," Turner is directing his gushing hose of empathy toward Tracy, "you chose to ignore statute 10-X9 and permit your Y-1 charge to explore and assess the level of threat on her own?" His voice is soft and relaxed. He sounds like he's asking about gardening tips, not how Tracy allowed a potential Abider assassin to walk free amongst us. Tracy just nods, her eyes still glued to the ground.

"It was my fault," I interject. "I made her wait to tell you."

"Drew, we are not here to assign fault," Turner says in the same tranquil tone. "Fault and blame are time wasters and energy drainers, and we are in the business of *creating* energy, not depleting it. Also, no one can make anyone else do anything. We are all the governors of our own free will."

I think about the party. I think about telling Turner he is full of crap.

"Tracy," he redirects, tilting his head slightly like a deer hearing a snapping branch, "are you open to the consequences of your decision?"

"Yes sir," she answers sharply.

Lisa Vandenburg stands up and Tracy follows her from the room, her posture now military-straight.

"Where are they going? What's happening?" I ask, worried.

"Your fear has no place here," Turner responds, smiling with his lips closed. "Or anywhere. Tracy has accepted her consequences. She is a highly evolved being. Now," he gestures a limp hand to Chase, "I'd like to hear from the two of you."

"What about?" Chase says angrily. His parents shoot him harsh looks.

"Are we in trouble?" I ask, just wanting the information already.

At this Turner laughs, again with the lips closed, his eyes squinting. He looks like Buddha. This may be deliberate.

"We are the water that shapes the stones," he begins, eyes at half-mast. "We are the wind that carves the canyons. We are as essential to growth as light and air. Ours is a noble and right mission. The extent of which you have yet to grasp. This is as it should be. You are an infant. And as an infant, we expect you to make messes. This is a mess. But it is one we are well-equipped to clean up."

"Are you on the nest?" Chase's mother asks anxiously. She is pretty, but looks ragged. We all do, I guess.

"Yes. We have been on the nest since the incident," Turner assures her.

Chase and I cut eyes at each other. I can tell we are both thinking the same thing: *Audrey*.

"Um, how big is said nest?" I ask, in my best fake-casual voice.

"The greatest enemy will hide in the last place you would ever look," Turner says in a near whisper. (Now I know where Tracy gets her catch phrases. The Touchstone doesn't fall far from the tree.)

"Yeah, I know, but listen, Audrey is not an Abider."

"Drew, that's enough," my father pipes in, still simmering, his glare never leaving Chase's face.

"No. It is *not* enough," I shoot back. "I couldn't live if anything were to happen to her."

"You could live, and you *will* live. So many more lifetimes than you comprehend." Turner takes a full, cleansing breath, presses his palms together at chest level, and leaves them there, hanging midair.

"What now?" My mother chimes in again, her irritation with this affair seeping through. "Do we initiate seclusion procedures?"

Turner's eyes open fully. He lowers his hands to his lap. "Indeed. The principals will divide, to reduce the risk of muddled intentions."

"Absolutely!" my father loudly seconds.

"And until the nest is contained, the principals will abandon all questionable Static connections for their own safety and for the safety of our people. In the many, we are one."

"In the many, we are one," everyone parrots back except Chase and me.

The circle breaks, folks start gathering their stuff, saying their goodbyes, my dad drawing Turner aside for some private G knows what. I feel a yank on my elbow. Chase is tugging me toward the empty hallway. I do a quick scan: no one is paying attention, so I pad silently to his side.

"What the hell did all that even mean?" I ask, so happy

just to be standing close to him again. I can't contain a smile, even though I know I should.

"It means we can never see each other again," Chase says, looking nauseous.

I shake my head. "I don't think that's what they meant." He brushes a hair from my cheek.

"We're the principals, Drew. They don't trust us together." He sighs. "Maybe they are right not to."

Reality hits. I start to cry. "I won't do it," I wail. "I can't."

From the other room we hear Chase's father frantically barking his name.

"I have to go," he says, reaching for my face again, but stopping himself. He begins to walk away.

"I CAN'T!" I am screaming now, I don't care who hears. I feel a ripping in my chest. A boiling over. A rush of longing that swells and begins to drown me from the inside. Chase keeps on walking, escorted by his parents. He glances back just once, and I can see his eyes are wet, and then he rounds the corner and is gone.

I do not stop crying on the drive home. I do not stop crying when we get to our building. Or when we ride the elevator. I do not duck my head in contrition or hide my tear-streaked face or pretend I am anything less than lost at sea.

In a matter of hours I have lost the only two people I have ever truly loved.

One I can never see again.

The other, I will have to see, and pretend that I don't.

Just *blah*.

Blah blah blah blah blah blah blah blah blah blah blah blah blah blah blah blah blah blah blah blah blah.

Two weeks since I've had a normal conversation with Audrey, besides just the minimum classroom chitchat. I'm supposed to avoid her, which is impossible given that our social and educational worlds intertwine like kudzu vines.

Dad says when I can't *avoid*, I am to *withdraw*, for what he insists is my own good. So now I'm treating my best friend the way Chloe treats the ninety-eight percent of the student body she can't be bothered to acknowledge. I hate being cold to Audrey. And I know she thinks it's because of Jason. Even though I promised her he could never come between us. So in addition to being a frosty beyotch, I'm a liar.

I've been dutifully laying low while the Council does its investigation, or "contains the nest." Whatever. It has taken everything in me not to flat-out ask Audrey about the camp she has to go to this summer, whether she knows what her brother's tattoo means—to confess to her that I'm a Changer and beg her to move in with me so she can rid herself of whatever jacked-up influence is obviously making her feel so sad in her home.

Yesterday I spotted this bright green sign on a telephone

pole that said, *TREE PRESERVATION AREA*. Behind it, for as far as the eye could see, was a stark, leveled lot. Just red dirt and flat land. Not a single tree. Not even a shrub. It was the kind of completely random absurdity Audrey loves, and I started to text her a photo of the sign and the barren landscape behind it before remembering I wasn't permitted to correspond with her in any extracurricular way. Because somehow my sharing a ridiculous photo of an ill-placed park sign could bring down the whole of humanity as we know it. I deleted the picture.

Just like I deleted my friends.

It's been two weeks since I saw Chase or heard from him either. His old e-mail address bounced back the couple messages I tried sending. The Skype account was deleted. His cell phone kicks straight to automated voicemail. I don't know why I even bothered. I mean, all my contact information had to be changed too. The Council is a lot of things, but it isn't stupid.

The one thing they couldn't alter, though, is where I live.

When my mom dropped my issue of *Vibe* magazine and a piece of junk mail on my desk, I hadn't bothered opening it for a couple days.

FIERCE MAGAZINE wants YOU! the junk envelope read in bright fuchsia, my name and address peeking through the clear window, though in a slightly different font from the rest of the envelope. I was about to recycle it, but then I flipped the thing over, and it looked like it had been resealed—there were tiny strips of tape holding down the flap. I opened it up, read:

Dear DREW: As I'm sure you know, some of the most beautiful girls in the country hail from the DEEP SOUTH, and as one of these lovely ladies, you have been preselected by our NEW YORK CITY expert scouts to take part in our National Teen-Model Search, coming to your region soon.

Then, in slightly different text:

That's right, DREW. Immediately after school on MONDAY, take the N14 bus to the Country Music Hall of Fame downtown, and meet in front of the Dolly Parton statue inside the lobby to the right. No, this is not your big modeling break; it's just your old buddy Chase, who misses you and would like to see you, despite the world telling him he's not allowed to. He (and Dolly) will be waiting, but don't take him for granted; he'll only wait, oh, all night for you to arrive. (It closes at 5, so get there quickly as you can.)

I read it over like fifty times, thinking it had to be a joke, even as I hoped with every chamber of my splintered heart that it wasn't. I decided to risk it, told my parents I'd be late coming home from school because I was thinking about trying out for a school play. Miraculously, they said okay.

When I get off the bus in downtown Nashville, I don't know which way to go, but there are a lot of tourists milling around Lower Broadway, and when I ask a bouncer outside one of the honky-tonks which way the Hall of Fame is, he gives me precise, detailed directions, more like a tour guide than the mean, tattooed tough it seemed like he'd be.

I step into the museum, peer left then right, and there's faux Dolly Parton, who's pretty much a saint around these parts. A really busty saint.

Leaning on her shoulder—Chase. He swoops me in his arms immediately. He feels good, strong.

"Here you come again," he starts singing, *"looking better than a body has right to."*

"I didn't know you were such a Dolly aficionado," I quip.

Chase lifts one brow, like, *Girl, please*, links his arm in mine, and then we exit the museum and walk for what seems like about half an hour, the neighborhood getting less and less touristy by the block. Chase is buoyant, still singing Dolly, now on "I Will Always Love You," when we start passing these old warehouses, big brick monstrosities three and four stories high, some of their doors flung open with industry going on inside, others abandoned and in disrepair.

"You know she wrote that song for Porter Wagoner," he says. "As a sweet way to break up with him, professionally speaking."

"No, I did not know that. Nor would any human born above the Mason-Dixon line," I tease.

"Do you even know who Porter Wagoner is?"

"No. Do you know who Jim Boeheim is?"

Chase grins. "Touché." Then, "Who is he?"

"The legendary yet divisive head coach of the Syracuse men's basketball team."

"Of course," he smirks, adding, "You're *such* a dude."

"And you're such a chick!" I reply, as we both start giggling. Chase embraces the moment, begins swaying his butt back and forth.

"Oh my god. Is that how you think girls walk?" I say, feigning repulsion.

"I think if anyone knows how girls walk it is probably the dude who was a girl for the first fourteen years of his life," Chase counters playfully.

"Well, someone needs a refresher course in sashay, shanté. Hey, maybe next year?" I joke, and Chase rolls his eyes.

We keep walking, but my comment hangs in the air. Neither of us seems to want to think about the year after this one, when we will both change again, into who knows what.

Chase stops in front of an abandoned depot with an iron façade. "Let's go inside," he says.

"Let's not and say we did."

"Come on. I have a surprise for you." And then he disappears, swallowed up by the darkness just inside the mammoth sliding iron door. Reluctantly, I drop in after him.

"This is the part in the horror movie where the young, too-curious-for-their-own-good couple gets stabbed in the neck by a hillbilly psycho," I murmur into the pitch black. No answer. I begin to waver. "Chase? This seriously stopped being fun five seconds ago."

"Hey there!"

I shriek.

Some redheaded guy has leapt out in front of me, Chase just behind him, doubled over in hysterics.

"Really funny, Chase," I scowl. "I hope you have a spare pair of pants to lend me for the ride home."

"I'm Benedict," the redhead says, extending his arms theatrically. It's then I recognize him from the protest outside the Council HQ the day of the mixer. "Welcome to the Thunderdome!"

As he bellows, more kids appear from various dingy corners, most dressed in some version of urban street punk, more than one sporting the anarchy emblem on their tees. Piercings and dreadlocks abound. Also, BO.

"Hey, uh, everybody," I say, spinning to take it all in.

"I'm Peaches," a girl in a long flowy dress and combat boots introduces herself. "For now."

I say hello to Peaches, and also to about a dozen other kids who approach me seeming alternately blissed out or seething with hostility. I catch Chase's eye, mouth, *RaChas?* and he nods excitedly.

"Can I get you some kombucha, or a spelt muffin?" Benedict is asking, but I am having trouble focusing, trying to connect the dots from when Chase left the Council intervention to when he dropped out of normal society and joined a band of rebel miscreants.

"No, no thanks. I'm good."

"That's good to hear," Benedict says. "We are all about good here, right, gang?" A few RaChas whoop and whistle. "We are all about the *greater* good, the good that comes from living a life of transparency and brotherhood, of living out and proud and, when situations call for it, *loud!*" He yowls the last word, and the RaChas join in, their eager bawls echoing through the warehouse like a tribe of howler monkeys.

The RaChas stomp their boots, jump up and down, banging on crates and random sheets of metal, and just as the noise reaches a fever pitch, Peaches skips to the center of the floor and throws herself around Benedict and begins vigorously kissing him on the mouth. I feel like I may faint.

Chase senses my impending psychological/physical meltdown and swoops in, leading me off the floor to a crusty futon set up beside a camp stove.

"Sit down." I'm already sitting. "Take a breath." I do as I'm told, inhaling and exhaling in a controlled yogic fashion, waiting for the supposed calm to wash over me. It does not.

"When?" I sputter. "How? Why?"

Chase bites his lower lip, considering. "Let's start with why. I guess, after the intervention, I really found myself questioning what the Council is all about. I mean, you have to admit, their message seems a little convoluted."

I nod, still breathing, in, out . . .

"Anyway, I'd met Benedict a couple times at my school. He went there, before he declared, so he had friends, and he could sniff out the Changers there without arousing suspicion."

"How could Peaches kiss him like that?" I shudder. "People could die now!"

"Well. Ain't nobody dead yet."

"You don't know that," I argue, furtively skimming the room. "The *CB* clearly says—"

"The *CB* is BS," Chase says flatly.

Oh boy.

"Says who?" I push. "Your new friends?" I drop my voice to a whisper. "Chase, you don't even know these people."

Which prompts a mini-rant about how "these people" have leveled with him far more than any Changers he's met (*ouch*), and that unlike the Council, their mission actually makes sense, that living in the shadows, afraid of discovery, is never the way to spark change. That change, real change, only ever comes from action, from *taking* power, not from waiting for power to be *given*. He says they are gearing up to launch wearechangers.org, a website that will outline their mandate without putting Changers in jeopardy. Eventually, "Benedict hopes to sit down with Matt Lauer." I make the *Seriously?* face.

"Don't you get it, Drew? The Council just wants to control us with fear. They lie to keep their authority. No different than it's always been throughout history."

"No. I don't get it. And I don't get you. I don't even recognize you right now. What these people—what *you*— are doing is going to put Changers in danger. You can't just out a whole race on the Internet!"

Chase exhales, regroups. "Don't you want to embrace who you are?"

I shrug.

"Don't you want some control over your own life?"

"Of course," I say peevishly. "Everyone does."

"Well, this is how you get it. You grab it."

In the center of the floor, Benedict has at last quieted the howlers. He points to Chase, who nods and gives him a thumbs-up. At this, Benedict commands everybody's attention and begins outlining the evening's raid on a suspected Abider nest.

"We have reason to believe two abducted Changers are

being held in the basement of the church, where the Abider zealot pinheads are attempting to interrogate and de-program them. We know one of the priests, we've clocked him before."

Benedict goes on, outlining specific details, then assignments to different RaChas. "Chase, you up for driving?" he asks.

I whip my head toward him, but Chase is already nodding. "I'm in."

"You don't have a license!" I reproach under my breath. "You could get arrested."

"I've already been arrested, remember?" he snaps.

I swallow my breath, notice my hands are shaking.

"I'm sorry. That was jerky," he says, softening. "It's just, you don't have to worry. I can handle myself. I think this may be where I belong. I feel alive again. Like I know my purpose." Chase sighs, seems disappointed in me for something he doesn't say. "There is no drifting back to sleep once you've woken from the dream."

Good for you, I'm thinking, but keep silent.

"Come on," he says. "Let's get you home."

Which is where I sit now, frightened for Chase. Feeling like something awful is going to go down. Like he'll be thrown in jail again. Or abducted. Or worse.

My computer IM is blinking. It's Audrey.

Do you still hate me?

I ignore it, like I'm supposed to. She persists.

I don't blame you.

. . .

And then: *I'd try calling you for the 500th time, but my rents are taking us to hear some special speaker at a church on the other side of Nash tonight. :/*

I lurch to the keyboard.

Me: *Don't go. No matter what, do NOT go to the church tonight. Promise me.*

Her: *Why? Who even cares? I want to talk to you about what happened, not my weird family.*

Me: *Promise me. I'm not joking.*

Her: *Okay, okay. If it means we can be friends again, I'll do anything. I'll say I have food poisoning. :P*

I breathe a sigh of relief.

Her: *See you for lunch tomorrow.* And then: *OK?*

OK, I send back. It might not be the truth, but it's what she wants to hear. And for now, there is nothing else I can tell her.

CHANGE 1—DAY 239

"**G**O DREEEEW!"

A chorus of encouragement erupts somewhere, maybe up in the stands, possibly from the perimeter of the track. But I have five more hurdles to go, *now four*, and my head is pounding, *now three*, my feet are pounding even faster than that, *now two*, and there is just one chick ahead of me, her braids whipping all over her head, and I suddenly want more than I've wanted anything in life to catch this bitch and WIN this race.

Before I realize it, the race is over, and I'm slowing my pace, heels practically kicking my butt as I wind down around the bend, and I catch a flicker in my peripheral vision of Audrey and a couple of the other JV cheerleaders jumping up and down beside the track. I think they might be cheering for me. One of their own—an *ex* one of their own, that is.

Kenya jogs up and swats me on the butt while I'm bent over, trying to catch my breath. "You ran like you were running from *something*," she jokes. "You're a beast—hey, you okay?"

I cannot breathe, cannot speak. I look up at her and nod while gasping for air.

"It's all right, you're all right," she says, rubbing my back gently.

I might vomit. I have never run faster or tried harder at anything than during the seventeen-point-something seconds of that race.

"Do you even know?" she asks when I stand upright.

I shake my head, still gasping.

"You won!" she shouts.

I bounce up and down a little, slowly realize what she's telling me, and we hug, jumping and sliding against each other's sweaty skin. I can't believe it. I look back at the board. Yep, my number's up there on top. I beat the girl with the braids by less than half a second.

"What the hell," I finally say, completely surprised at myself.

"Yes!" Kenya hisses, pumping a fist. "Falcons, killin' it!" She's real competitive, takes track and field more seriously than most kids take life. She wants an athletic scholarship to Vanderbilt or Florida. She talks about it ceaselessly, says she has pictures of the schools' mascots next to the Olympic rings on her dream realization board at home. My win put us over the edge, and we've spanked our crosstown rivals, the Wolverines—one tiny step closer to Kenya's goal. "I knew you could do it!"

Now the coach comes over, also pats me on the back, kind of hard. He is smiling, his mustache for the first time inching up and revealing his teeth—which, I honestly wasn't sure he even had until just now. He's always so serious when I see him in practice, though he doesn't spend as much time with JV as he does with the older girls. "Welcome to varsity," he announces.

"Really?" I ask, chugging the cup of Gatorade he'd brought over for me. Kenya is sliding side-to-side in a victory dance, chin up, her glistening skin reflecting the sunlight like a river.

"You keep posting times like that, and I don't see why not," Coach says, checking something on his clipboard, then adding, "You're a real natural. Good recruit, Kenya."

He starts reviewing business with the officials and some other teammates, a few of whom come up and congratulate me before grabbing their duffels and heading off the field. My body is vibrating all over, my muscles are sore, in a good way. Like I can do anything. Which I know will pass, but right now I'm convinced no one can touch me, or ever will. Screw cheerleading. Track is the bomb.

I head over to the benches, my legs rubber-banding beneath me. Something catches my eye up in the mostly empty stands; it's Tracy in a Central High T-shirt, giving me a cheesy thumbs-up. She's the most dressed-down I've seen her, obviously making the attempt to "blend in" with the natives. Even so, she's still wearing a pleated tartan skort with the tee, and navy knee socks straight outta 1972.

Tracy's been showing up for everything in my life since she's been on probation with the Council, putting the "touch" back in Touchstone. And while I can tell she's conscientiously keeping tabs on me, it's also clear from the expression on her face that she's proud too. Which makes me feel good in a way I didn't expect.

For a second I remember that Nicole's broken collarbone in practice Thursday is the only reason I'm here today, but then something from the *CB* pops into my head—about how each of us on the planet is responsible for running his or her own individual race, and I say a secret wish that Nicole gets better soon, and we'll just worry about who keeps this spot on the varsity team if and when she comes back at the end of this season. (And if she doesn't, well then, it's really not going to be an issue next year, is it? Considering I myself could come back as a 275-pound kid with two left legs and zero hand-eye coordination. Note to the Council: if you're out there reading this, which you're supposedly not doing, that wasn't a dare.)

Tracy tilts toward the parking lot, like she's fixing to leave, then taps her fist against her heart twice and points at me, like she's Drake onstage at Yankee Stadium or something. It makes me smile.

Kenya comes back, this time with her parents. She introduces me; they are maybe the tallest and best-looking family ever.

"Would you like to join us for dinner to celebrate?" Kenya's mom asks me. "We're going out for hamburgers and milkshakes."

"Sure," I say, looking to Kenya. I kind of can't believe she wants to hang out with me, a lowly freshman. "Let me call and ask my folks. Thank you so much for inviting me."

Kenya and I beeline toward the locker room, and I am so high on the afternoon that I momentarily forget how stressful the prospect of showering at school is. Since track started a few weeks ago, I usually just change back into my school clothes after practice, and then shower when I get home. But now I've got no choice.

"You go ahead and get started," I say, "I'm gonna call my parents."

"It's cool, I'll wait," Kenya offers.

"I've got to talk to them about some other stuff too," I say, the amazing post-race feeling coursing throughout my body starting to drain away with each new lie I tell.

"Does Tracy know this girl?" Dad asks when I phone and tell him what's up.

"Uh, I don't know. I mean, she probably saw her at the meet, she's the best runner on the team," I say.

"Okay . . ." He doesn't sound convinced. He is constantly suspicious, like I'm a bad kid all of a sudden. I wish I could introduce him to some of the choice delinquents at Central. Two hours with cut-a-bitch Rhonda might give him a wee bit o' perspective.

"She's just a girl from Central," I say. "A junior. Her mom and dad are taking us out, and then I'll have them drop me back at school, and I'll walk home."

Mom gets on the line. "Hey, honey. How'd you do?"

"I won the 100 hurdles," I say nonchalantly, though it doesn't sound as exciting as before.

"Oh my goodness, baby, I'm so proud of you!" Mom squeals in a high voice.

Dad is quiet.

"Thanks," I say.

"That's so wonderful," Mom goes on. "I'm sorry we couldn't be there, but you know the rules about being seen at school."

"I *know*."

"Was everybody impressed with your performance?" she asks.

"I guess maybe a little."

"Drew," Dad breaks in then. "Why didn't you tell me?"

"Because you didn't ask."

The line is silent for a few seconds, then he says, "Of course you can go out with your teammate. Have a wonderful time."

"Where's she going?" Mom asks.

"Out with a friend and her parents," I say.

"With a new girlfriend from the varsity team," Dad says—at the exact same time.

"What?" Mom asks. Nothing more exasperating than a three-way conversation on the phone with your parents.

"Dad, can you just fill her in?" I try not to sound as annoyed as I feel. "I have to go shower. I won't be home late."

"Okay, baby," Mom says. "Have a good time. Be careful."

"Call if you want me to pick you up later," Dad adds, and I hang up.

Then, just as I'm headed into the locker room, Audrey appears from behind the concession stand, catching me off guard. "You were sickening out there," she says kindly, then comes in for a hug.

It is heartwarming to be this close to her; it seems like it's been forever. She holds on tight, and so do I.

"Thanks," I say, as things begin to get awkward.

"I was cheering so loud, did you hear?" she asks excitedly. We pull apart, facing each other, close.

"I don't know, I was kind of in the zone."

"Oh."

"I mean, I definitely saw you guys at the finish line," I try to compensate. Now it's *really* awkward.

"Well, I guess I just wanted to tell you that," she says.

"I really appreciate it." And: *I really miss you.*

"Well . . ."

"Yeah," I say, because I can't think of anything else.

"I—" she begins, but then stops herself.

"What?" I ask, even though I know I shouldn't.

"I'm not, like, on my brother's *side*," she says suddenly.

That night rushes back. I try never to think about it, but here it is. And with it, a hollowness.

"I mean, I'm your friend," she explains. "Or I *was*, right? I know it's supposed to be 'family first' and all, so that sounds crazy and you probably don't believe me, but it's true. I hate what Jason did, it makes me hate *him*, and I'm really sad—every single day it makes me sad, Drew—what he tried to do to you, and that it came between us. But I'm not him." Her voice wavers at the end.

"Aud," I start. "It's, it's . . . not you. It's not that." But I am lying. I don't know how all this lying is supposed to make me a better person. Maybe Chase had a point dropping out of school and joining the RaChas. "I wish I could say more. I just don't think you'd understand."

"Why don't you try me?" She looks like she's about to cry. "I might understand way more than you think."

For a second I believe her, and want to reveal more, about the Council, about their fear that her family has Abider sympathies. But I can't open the door to more trouble right now. I just want to go out with Kenya and her family and have a ginormous vanilla milkshake and talk about measurable things like winning or losing, or clearing a hurdle instead of knocking it over, or having a time that qualifies or one that doesn't.

"I have to go," I say. "But I want to talk. Maybe we can figure out a way."

Audrey looks wounded. "Up to you, I guess. So. Good job. *Again.*"

"Thanks. *Again*," I say.

As she leaves, I notice her cheerleading bloomers are hitched up a little on her left butt cheek. I want to call after her and tell her, but I don't.

Seeing Audrey threw me a little, but all told, I guess I had a pretty good night. Kenya's parents were hospitable. Funny, despite a practically visible shroud of sorrow around them, due to the death of Kenya's older brother a couple years back. He was stabbed for a pair of shoes, the week after he signed to play football at Florida, full ride. A goddamn stupid free pair of orange shoes that some trainer gave him when he visited campus.

You could tell her parents aren't going to let Kenya out of their sight, which she doesn't seem to mind. She values one thing, and one thing only. Being the best at something. She's the only kid in school I can think of who's driven like that. I'm certainly not.

I hated having to be evasive with Kenya and her family about where I live, who I was before coming to Genesis, Tennessee. *Who I am now.* Especially when they were being so honest with me about their past and present, their hopes for the future. It seems like that's all they focus on, Kenya's prospects—I guess because the past is too painful.

I realized sitting there at the Freezo with them, I cannot project and dream that way. I can't consider anything but the now. (I guess all Changers are sorta Buddhist by default.) I know maybe one-fourth of my future. Or not even that. I know one-fourth of the choices I'm going to have *about* my future—whom I'm going to live it out as. It's straight-up weird is what it is, and it made me feel like a misfit sitting there with them, a perfectly normal loving family who know who they are and what they desire, having perfectly normal responses to life and what's happened to them, good and terrible.

But I can't really speak to my goals, my desires, the drive to get good at something like running fast and clearing hurdles—which they all seem to think I have some exceptional aptitude for. If it all becomes moot in four or five months, why bother?

Which is the attitude I came in with when I got home a little while ago. My dad was sporting a Central baseball cap (I've seen him in a hat like that maybe twice before), and he and Mom greeted me at the door with irritating noisemakers and my favorite dessert: homemade peanut butter pie.

"Congratulations!" they hollered in unison, surprising me soon as I came through the door. Even Snoopy was dancing around and barking, his nails clicking on the kitchen floor, though he had no idea what all the excitement was about.

Join the club, *dawg*.

When I got home from school after track practice today, I checked my e-mail:

Dearest Drew,
Voila, your weekly pleading missive. WHEN ARE
YOU GOING TO FULFILL YOUR DESTINY
AND REJOIN THE BICKERSONS? We can no
longer make music without your killer chops, and seeing
how we are on track to accept the Billboard Magazine
award for Top New Group in approximately 3.5 years,
there's still time for you to get in on the ground level
now, before we all become addicted to fame and pills and
hair extensions and yoga (respectively) and start living
up to our name, unable to be in the same room together,
much less share a stage.

Sincerely,
Gen (on behalf of Ray-Ray and C-Rok too)

Ah, C-Rok.

Mr. Radical Changer Freegan Anarchist Squatter Spelt-Muffin Eating, Home-Schooled, Freedom Fighter for Visibility and Equality Everywhere . . . I'm surprised that playing for an alternative Neo-Emo-Ska band hasn't become too "mainstream" for him yet. I'm sure that day is coming.

I clicked *Reply* and wrote:

Dearest Gen (and fellow Bickersons),
Thank you so much for continuing to hold my spot in your esteemed band, but at this juncture, I still think it advisable to fill the position with some other (likely) subpar beat maker. I am sorry to inform you that my parental units are still boycotting my triumphant return to the stage, and there's no telling if or when they might relent. Maybe this summer? Hard to tell. Feel free to check back periodically (as I'm sure you will), but if you need to find another drummer in the interim, please proceed. I will not be hurt, and understand well that the road to fame and fortune is paved with difficult decisions such as this one. Good luck!

Sincerely,
D-Rok

I pressed *Send*. Felt a twinge of an urge to play with them again, a flash of anger at my parents and the Council for not letting me, and a deep longing to see Chase's stupid face, but I stuffed it all. Chase is becoming someone else now. As am I. And anyway, he knows where to find me, if he wants to. A girl can't sit around and wait to be rescued or loved, or any of that rom-com crap. And besides, I'm running my own race now. Literally. I know what it feels like to win. And I'm not giving that up before I have to.

Today in class, Mr. Crowell informed us that we would all be performing different scenes from *Romeo and Juliet*. As in, memorizing scenes and acting them out with other students in front of the entire class. In costume. For a grade.

Mr. Crowell starts assigning scenes, groups of four, six, three, two. He claims he's grouping kids who he feels will make a "fruitful collaboration," those most likely to learn something from one another during the process. I notice Audrey and I are among the few left as he's going down the roster, and he seems to be holding the main scenes between Romeo and Juliet for last. Chloe gets to play Juliet in the balcony scene. ("Holla!" she sings out and raises the roof soon as she hears she's been assigned the role of Juliet in the money shot, but then her arms drop and her face completely sours when she hears her Romeo will be this burner dude named Dave.)

Mr. Crowell announces last that Audrey and I will also be performing as Romeo and Juliet (I'm Romeo), an excerpt from Act I, Scene V: the dance scene when Romeo sees Juliet for the first time.

"Now, some of you might notice that we are doing some serious gender-bending for the sake of these performances," Mr. Crowell says after all parts have been assigned.

"So I have to be, like, RuPaul or something when I

play the nurse?" Jerry the joker shouts out.

"Not exactly," Mr. Crowell replies. "But I certainly wouldn't frown upon a wig and a little makeup."

Everybody groans.

"Does anybody know who played the parts of women when Shakespeare's plays were originally staged?"

"Hot chicks?" Dave offers.

"He wouldn't be asking the question if that were the answer, idiot," Chloe snips. "It's men, obviously."

"Mostly boys, actually," Mr. Crowell says. "During Shakespeare's time, it was considered morally suspect for women to perform on stage."

"I am so glad I didn't live then," Chloe sighs.

"Don't worry, you're morally suspect off stage too," Jerry quips.

"And you're a dateless wonder," she snaps back.

Audrey once told me that when Chloe competes in her glitz pageants, she always performs Scarlett O'Hara monologues for the "talent" portion of the competitions. Which explains so, so much.

"Yeah, the sixteenth and seventeenth centuries were pretty rough all around, but especially for women," Mr. Crowell tells us. "In fact, I wrote my thesis about gender play on the Shakespearean stage, and much of my research focused on the audience's fear of women's sexuality, and the notion of experiencing it in such an up-close and personal way in the theater. Interesting, considering how much of Shakespeare's work deals with the ambiguity of romantic love and sexual attraction."

Chloe nods her head in an exaggerated way, like she

already knows everything Mr. Crowell is saying—and concurs completely. Meanwhile, my curiosity is piqued. It sounds like Mr. C has dipped both feet into the Changer pool.

"Anyway, prepubescent boys were used, because their voices hadn't yet cracked and they were of course beardless, so audiences found them more believable in women's roles. An additional scintillating fact: the bright white makeup used by these boys was made of lead, and a lot of them ended up with the skin on their faces destroyed, or very ill from what we know now was lead poisoning. Some of them even died from it."

Chloe fawns, "I would die for my art too."

"I know I feel like dying when I watch it," Jerry cracks.

"Eff you, loser," Chloe retorts. "You should be so lucky."

"Wait, do I have to white out my face?" Dave interjects, actually concerned.

"No students will be harmed in the making of this play," Mr. Crowell assures the class with a wink.

I'm not so certain. My "playing" a boy who falls madly in love with a girl "played" by Audrey seems like an express train to crazy town.

"In the spirit of authenticity, I'd like you to let go of gender stereotypes, if you can," Mr. Crowell says, and it feels like he might be speaking directly to me. Or *about* me. Nervous laughter spreads throughout the classroom. "I know you are teenagers, and as such, that is going to be near-impossible for you to do, but your entire quarter grade depends on it, so figure it out, people."

I glance over at Audrey, whose attention has been on Mr.

Crowell exclusively. I clear my throat, shift in my seat, but she still doesn't look over at me. I start scanning our scene. I can feel sweat pumping in my armpits. Dang. There's a lot to memorize.

Finally Audrey looks over, and she curls up her lips tentatively, like, *Is this okay?* I nod encouragingly, and she relaxes. Almost like old times. I flip through our scene, notice that after the portion we are to perform, Romeo asks the Nurse who that girl is he was just talking to, and she tells him that she is the daughter of the Capulets, his own father's sworn enemy. Then Juliet asks the Nurse who the guy she was just crushing on is—and finds out that he's the son of *her* father's mortal enemy. It's quite a cluster-frack.

Juliet cries, *"My only love sprung from my only hate!"*
Oh boy.

I am studying the scene at home when an e-mail pops into my in-box:

O Romeo, Romeo, wherefore art thou Romeo?
Hey, you. Now we HAVE to hang out and you'll have to stop ignoring me, or we'll fail English. When do you want to start practicing? I can do any day this week after cheerleading. Plus next weekend nights. It's a lot to learn, and I SUCK at memorizing lines. But I'm glad we're doing it together. ;)

Love,
Juliet

"*If I profane with my unworthiest hand this holy shrine, the gentle fine is this: my lips, two blushing pilgrims, ready stand to smooth that rough touch with a tender kiss.*"

My hair slicked back, I am channeling *boy*, maybe even Ethan, standing at the front of the classroom in my purple stockings and fluffy Elizabethan man-bloomers and doublet that Mom rented for me from a costume shop in Nashville. Everything is so itchy, especially the gold cape tied around my neck—and stanky, as in the funk of fifty thousand teenage fears.

"*Good pilgrim,*" Audrey picks up, "*you do wrong your hand too much, which mannerly devotion shows in this; for saints have hands that pilgrims' hands do touch, and palm to palm is holy palmers' kiss.*" She inches toward me, her hooped, floor-length blue gown swaying around her legs like a giant bell.

We hold our hands up, palms out. They touch, the shapes perfectly matched. I can see my fingers trembling against hers, and Audrey looks right into my eyes, steadying me as I go on, launching into Shakespeare's clever argument for why Juliet should let Romeo kiss her.

"*Have not saints lips, and holy palmers too?*" I ask, sucking in Audrey's warmth through my hands.

"*Ay, pilgrim, lips that they must use in prayer,*" Aud shoots back, slightly smart-ass—onto my, well, Romeo's scheming.

"*O, then, dear saint, let lips do what hands do; they pray, grant thou, lest faith turn to despair,*" I go on.

"*Saints do not move, though grant for prayers' sake,*" she counters.

Another student coughs in the audience, which takes me out of the scene and causes me to forget completely what I'm supposed to say next. I can feel moisture building at the hundreds of tiny points where our flesh meets. I am standing there petrified, Elizabethan English phrases ricocheting around my brain. I feel Aud push her hands against me, and I look up into her eyes. In the background I hear Chloe sigh dramatically.

"*Then move . . .*" Mr. Crowell prompts.

"*Then move not, while my prayer's effect I take!*" I say, too enthusiastically and momentarily out of character. *Whew.* Then, *damn*, I realize this is where Romeo is supposed to lean in and kiss Juliet, a little fact Aud and I only ascertained once we got together and started practicing our scene. We never actually kissed during rehearsals; both of us just kept saying we'd save it for the actual performance, "to make it more real."

I gulp down a breath, terrified of what's going to happen, if anything. I mean, this whole superpower-vision thing must not apply to mandatory in-character, in-class kisses for a grade, right? I start leaning in, closer and closer, and I flash on the first time I saw Audrey in class at the beginning of the school year, merely a couple hours after I became Drew. How she stuck up for me when Chloe and the Bees were going for the jugular of the new girl wearing stained mom-shorts. Aud's lips so shiny and soft-looking, and me just mesmerized by them and maybe wondering if I'd ever get to kiss them, even though it was ridiculous to think at the time.

I keep leaning in, even closer, Audrey stock-still like Juliet's supposed to be, after Romeo convinces her to sit back and let him kiss her. I pucker up, close my eyes, and I can feel a flutter of warmth on my cheeks, my nose, my lips, and . . . CONTACT.

Wait, what? At the last second, Audrey turned her head to the side, and my lips land squarely on her left cheek. She ducked me. I am floored. And more than a little humiliated. I try to stay in character.

"Thus from my lips, by yours, my sin is purged," I fumble.

Audrey is red as Christmas. She is supposed to act like she enjoyed the kiss so much that she now wants another one—to give back the sin that she supposedly just took from my lips. *"Then have my lips the sin that they have took."*

"Sin from thy lips?" I ask, like, *I have you now.* *"O trespass sweetly urged! Give me my sin again."* I lean in again, this time more aggressively, and Aud moves toward me too. This time we're really going to do it, I know we are, and we're looking into each other's eyes, like, *This is really happening*, but right before we make contact that sentiment switches over to *Is this really happening?* and at the last millisecond, Aud wrenches her head again, but less severely than the last time, and I graze the corner of her lips with mine.

We hold it for a few seconds. I mean, I might not have landed on the bull's eye, but this is supposed to be the real deal, a life-altering moment that seals Romeo and Juliet's fate. Not to mention we are gunning for that A.

We pull apart. Me dizzy. Aud more flushed than before,

prettier, if it's possible. I watch her, and now it is she who seems to have forgotten what's supposed to happen next.

"*You kiss by the book,*" Aud says, snapping to, and I can't really discern how much is acting, and how much could be reality, whatever that is.

The room is silent, and we are locked into one another's gaze for a few beats, and then: clapping, spurred by Mr. Crowell. The rest of the class enthusiastically joins in. There are a couple hoots, a whistle or two. We shake off the trance we'd obviously fallen into, then turn to the class, holding hands and taking a little bow.

Mr. Crowell is smiling. "Now *that* is how it's done," he pronounces. "Lovely, ladies. An incredible job. Who knew we had such talent in our midst? Questions, comments?"

Chloe's hand shoots up. Mr. Crowell nods to her. "Um, they didn't kiss on the lips," Chloe says, real pissy. "They didn't stay true to the script."

Audrey and I let go of each other's hand. I glare at Chloe, who smirks, unmoved.

"Well, it's not a script, but a scene, which is different. And even though it wasn't absolutely spot on," Mr. Crowell concedes, "I believe they really conveyed the emotion and power of what's going on in that first meeting, an expression of the perfect love—yet one that is bound inextricably to a tragic destiny."

Chloe, not satisfied, crosses her arms and leans back in her seat.

"Any other observations? Anything?" Mr. Crowell asks.

"Ye-ah," Jerry says, raking his fingers through his hair. "Drew, you got game, man."

"Shakespeare has game, more correctly," Mr. Crowell says. "All right, Drew, Audrey, good job. You're excused."

We practically floated down to the girls' bathroom then, where I couldn't wait to get out of those ridiculously uncomfortable clothes. Sure, I'd thought it might be fun to dress up as a "guy" again for the assignment, but once I realized that prospect involved thick tights and poufy short-shorts, that theory sort of flew out the window. Elizabethan menswear? About as masculine as Tracy's wardrobe.

Audrey started gratefully peeling off all her layers too, her massive gown falling to the floor in a circle around her.

"We kind of hit that out of the park," I say.

"I know," Audrey chirps. "We are so getting an A."

"Did you see grody Chloe's face?" I laugh. "There's room for only one diva Juliet in this town."

"She is welcome to that title!" Audrey says. "Hey, help me untie this kirtle? I think it's in a knot."

Aud stands in her bra by the sinks, presenting her pale back to me. I try not to look at her reflection in the mirror while I relax the knot. And for that matter, I also try not to look at my own. Because for a while there—and I know this probably sounds a little bananas—but it sort of felt like I *was* Romeo, or even good old Ethan (RIP). Just a boy who saw a girl at a party and went up to talk to her for a minute. Nothing more complicated than that. (Minus the Olde English.)

Of course, my life *is* more complicated than that. It's the whack-a-mole of complication. I hammer one down, and another pops up, bearing its grimy yellow teeth.

That's what I was thinking as I stood there. Refusing to look at myself. Afraid to see who I was. *What* I was. Realizing that any reflection I saw in the mirror would be a lie.

"It was fun pretending to be someone else for a while," I hear Audrey say.

I don't answer. I worry if I do I'll blurt something like, *Not as much fun as you might think. Or, About that . . . have I got a crazy story for you! Or, I was a boy. And now I'm a girl. And neither one feels like the whole truth. And neither one feels like pretending either.*

After a minute I catch her staring at me, her face soft, concerned. "You okay?" she whispers.

I smile, faking. "Totally," I say. "Why wouldn't I be?"

Audrey tilts her head, seemingly unconvinced. "Are *we* okay?" she murmurs, her voice so quiet I can barely hear the words.

I clear my throat, turn around, suddenly obsessed with folding my doofy costume.

"Because if we aren't okay," she goes on, her voice wavering, "I don't know if I can deal with that. You know me better than anyone. I don't . . . I don't want to be in a world where nobody gets me. You're the only person I can be myself with. Does that make sense? At all? God, I feel like a creep. Do you ever feel like a creep?"

I drop my costume and embrace Audrey, her body going limp as I do. "Only every day," I say into her hair, which smells of lavender and brown sugar. "And you couldn't be a creep if you tried." I hug tighter. "Your brother, on the other hand . . ."

Audrey begins to giggle, and I let her go. She looks so

relieved. Pretty. And I decide in that moment, *Eff you, Council.* Audrey is my friend. Audrey has been my friend since the moment we first met. And I plan on being hers. As much as possible in the time we (okay, I) have left. So if you think that's wrong, or it breaks the commandments, you just go ahead and try to stop me.

Nana wrote me today. An actual letter. Her handwriting all chicken-scratch from arthritis. For as long as I can remember, her fingers have looked like gnarled tree branches, her wedding ring lodged beneath a knuckle swollen big as a walnut. When I was Ethan, I took morbid fascination in Nana's hands, reveled in how deformed they were. I remember telling her how they were "cool," that they could be a special effect in a horror movie. She always just laughed and started chasing me, her hands raised in front of her face: "I'm gonna getcha!"

Now I think about her hands differently. (Like practically everything else I think about.) I wonder if they cause her much pain, how she buttons a blouse, what happens when she needs to pick up something tiny, like a toothpick. She still makes homemade pies, fluting the crust between her thumb and forefingers. It can't be easy. Nor can writing, but she is nothing if not stubborn. Dad calls her "the mule."

Anyway, the letter:

Dearest grandchild,

Sure has been hot down here. Too hot to do much of anything besides watch the shrimp boats and drink frozen piña coladas. It's been bringing back old, old memories of when I was a boy one summer in the early

1950s, working at the docks, hosing down boats and stocking ice for change and free lunch.

It was monkey work, but I loved it. You've never tasted anything like shrimp boiled and peppered straight out of the net. Peeling back their shells, dropping them into the water for the catfish to gobble up. The sound of the mast chains clanking, the smell of fuel and seawater and fish and wet newspaper. I was sunburned every day that summer. I think I wore shoes once.

It's odd what sticks in your head. You live all these years, days upon days of memories stacking up. And then you get old, God willing, and you are sitting on your patio, drinking a piña colada, and all you can recall is one summer when you were fifteen, and the feel of the weathered planks scraping against your feet as you ran down the dock.

Now that I think about it, that was the summer after my first Change. Same as this year is for you. Funny it didn't hit me until now. Memory can be sweet that way. You should keep that in mind. Like I told you at Christmas, everything you are going through, all the mess and fuss and heartache—there is a good chance none of that will stay with you for long. Time is like the tide, sweetpea. It washes everything away, leaving behind only the glittering shells.

Well, I best be off to my Tai Chi class. Know that I love you and am thinking about you every day.

Hugs and kisses,
Nana

In the letter, she included an old, wrinkled square photograph. It is a picture of a boy crouching down on a reedy shoreline, a fleet of boats behind him, farther out in the water. He's shirtless, dressed in overalls, the legs rolled up to his shins. He's trying not to smile, but he can't seem to help himself. He appears to be flexing his biceps.

I flip the picture over. There's an inscription in the lower right corner:

To Chase, the boy of my dreams. I will love you forever.
—D

CHANGE 1–DAY 274

The Changers Spring Fling theme was the predictably earnest "Spring into the Future!" Like the fall mixer, tonight's event was a mandatory get-together for all the regional Changers at the old Council HQ, a chance for the powers that be to lay eyes on us, make sure we aren't stepping out of line or having nervous breakdowns. There was also an egg toss.

When I looked around the courtyard, decorated in an old-time fairground style, with dunking booths and long picnic tables, and a roped-off area for the trust exercises, it sure seemed like most of the Changer kids were having a fine time, horsing around, springing into their futures and whatnot.

I tried to resist, but I couldn't help scanning the yard for Chase. Not that he'd ever come, of course. (The best part of going rogue like he did has to be skipping these corny meetings.)

"Why don't you find a friend and try the wheelbarrow race?" Mom suggests. "It looks hysterical."

"Why don't you?" I answer in what has become my trademark lazy sarcasm.

Mom overlooks the attitude, says, "I'm not sure my bladder is up to the task."

"Really, Mom?"

"It's your fault." She pinches me on the hip. "You were the one who decided to be a ten-pound fetus."

"Are you talking about this so I'll leave and go do some stupid race?"

"Talking about what?" It's Tracy. She is decked out head-to-toe in canary yellow, hair scrunchie to flats, all the same glaring shade.

"Oh Tracy, you look so pretty," Mom swoons.

"It just said *spring* to me," Tracy trills back, cutting a look my way. "You want to do an event, Drew?"

"I prefer watching."

Tracy sniffs. "I think you should do an event," she says, sterner this time. I catch her eye, and notice she is bulging them to the right, in the direction of the popcorn cart. I swivel to see what she is pointing out, and she kicks me in the shin with her canary flat.

"Ouch!"

"Let's you and me do the sack race," she barks, grabbing my hand, wrenching me away and toward the competition field.

"You girls have fun!" Mom yells, waving as we stumble away.

"What is your fresh damage?" I ask, as soon as we are out of earshot.

"Lighten up, Drew. It's a picnic," Tracy sighs, still nearly dislocating my arm as we power walk to the starting line. When we arrive she finally drops my hand, grabs a couple burlap sacks, steps into the first one, and gestures for me to do the same, which I do. The fabric itches as I bunch it around my waist.

"Ready?" shouts the ref, who turns out to be Council member Charlie, a.k.a. Mr. Google. "One, two, three, GO!"

And we are off, a whole row of Changers hopping along in a fevered spazmodic rush to the finish line. My competitive instinct suddenly kicks into high gear. I survey my opponents, many of whom have already toppled over like bowling pins and are scrambling inside their bags. Last in the row is some beefy dude with a ball cap who seems like the only real threat. He is hopping with admirable control, with purpose, like maybe he even trained for this thing, which is just *sad*.

Beside me, Tracy is holding her own. Even in the flats. I'm impressed, but I lean in and inch ahead of her, and soon enough it is just me versus ball-cap boy, everyone else a distant third place. I hop hard, my thighs burning like they do on the hurdles. My heart jolts with every landing. It is hard to breathe. I keep pushing, hear Tracy in the background screaming, "Go Drew!"

I hop like my life depends on it, and then, with the finish in sight, the burlap girdles my ankles and I trip, thwacking flat into the dirt, carnival road kill.

I lift my head just in time to see ball-cap boy somersault over the line, jumping from his bag with his hat somehow still on his head. A friend comes to chest bump him, and the two of them hoot and holler and writhe in the ecstasy of victory. I pull the burlap over my face, panting, lame.

"You totally would have had him," I hear through the muffle of fabric. Before I know it, the burlap is being pulled off my eyes and hovering above me is a face I wasn't sure I'd ever see again.

"Chase?"

"Yo."

"What are you doing here? Do they know you . . . ?"

"The Council knows I'm here, of course. It's a favor for my parents," he informs me, then lowers his voice to a whisper, "Plus, it's a chance to do some RaChas recon." He winks, helps me to my feet.

I want nothing more than to crawl into his arms and never leave, but this is not the time or the place, and besides, it's been so long, he may not even want that. If he ever really did. Man, ten seconds in, and the romantic discombobulation is already back in full force. I thought I was over this guy.

Chase juts his chin upward, and I see it is Tracy he's signaling. "Your Touchstone is pretty slick," he says, brushing straw off my jeans.

"More slick than I realized," I murmur, still absorbing that it was she, of all people, who helped finesse this mini-reunion. "So."

"So."

Silence.

"What have you been up to?" I ask, struggling to appear cool.

"I don't think you really want to know," he says kindly.

"Probably not." He looks thinner. Tanner.

"And you? What are you up to?"

"I-I run track now," I stammer. "Hundred-meter hurdles."

"I bet you're amazing," he says genuinely.

"I don't suck." I'm fighting the urge to cry, the loss of

Chase hitting me anew, like I was done with him and now I'm not, just because I saw him and his stupid gorgeous smile again. I try again with the cool.

"Did you know my nana was a Chase? What are the odds?" I ask, like it's not practically a sign from above that we are meant to be together.

"Yeah. Benedict says some name and identity recycling does go on." He's still working the smile. I'm still combusting inside.

"Wait, so, like, Nana was somebody like you that year? Because that is veering into a territory I don't want to explore." I shudder.

Chase shrugs. "Nobody knows for sure. Hey, you should ask Tracy. She seems like someone with all the answers—"

"WHAT in the GODS' name is the meaning of THIS?" Oh no. My father.

"Sir, wait . . ." Chase starts.

And here comes Tracy, in hot pursuit directly behind Dad, arms outstretched like a *Scooby-Doo* villan.

Chase straightens, extends a hand for my father to shake. "Nice to see you again . . ."

My father eyes Chase's palm like it's a viper.

"Let me explain . . ." Tracy arrives on the scene winded, inserting herself between Chase and Dad. "It's protocol. New information came to light. We had to redress the wrongs, take accountability. I can have Ms. Vandenburg come over to download if that helps."

"That won't be necessary," my dad seethes. "Now, elaborate."

"Okay, well . . ." Tracy is breathing too fast, gasping.

"First. We found no evidence of commandment transgression. Any perceived misconduct—"

"*Perceived?* The boy was courting my daughter! And he publicly beat the hell out of another student, endangering all of us!" Dad, not having the semantics.

"Yes, that's *technically* correct," Tracy tries, her breath finally regulating some. "But deeper analysis revealed mitigating circumstances that ..."

And it is here that both Chase and I begin to fear losing the contents of our collective bowels.

"Tracy, don't," I plead.

"Seriously, *don't*," Chase seconds simultaneously.

Tracy, eyes on Dad, oblivious, "... changed our interpretation of said events. The trigger being Chase's experience as Brooke pre-Change ..."

"Oh god," Chase withers, a balloon popped.

"... which understandably led to his outsized reaction when the same event threatened to repeat itself with Drew. Therefore—"

"Wait. I'm not sure I understand what you're saying," Dad stops her, but from the despair flooding into his face, I think he does understand.

"As you know, these types of experiences imprint in our subconscious and can exert control in ways too deep to contain, in ways we don't even realize, like how a gene for a disease in humans can lie dormant for years, but then ignite under the right conditions." Tracy on a roll now. "We are just lucky that Chase was able to stop the event when he did."

"The *event?*" My father swallows hard. He's got to be wondering what I didn't tell him. *Why* I didn't tell him everything. Wondering just how terrible that night was, what really happened to his child.

"Don't feel bad, Dad," I say, and go to his side, burying my head in his chest. "It's okay. I'm *fine*."

He gulps back tears. "I didn't know," he mumbles thickly. "I should have known."

I squeeze him tight. Chase starts to walk away, but Dad reaches out a hand and stops him.

"Thank you," he says. And then, "I'm sorry for my ignorance."

Chase nods, respectfully extracts himself from the scene. From the corner of my eye, I see him shuffle across the field, getting smaller and smaller—until he vanishes into essentially nothing.

Again.

Want to know something I've never in my life given even a passing thought to?

Prom.

Want to know something that occupies nearly every waking moment of my life in these last weeks of the school year?

Prom.

Okay. I never considered going to prom. Prom is for girly girls. And for the guys who want to take advantage of the aforementioned girls, once they've downed too many rounds of hard lemonade. I am neither. Nor was I particularly drawn to this year's prom theme when it was announced a couple weeks ago: *Masquerade!* (Come on!)

And yet, the minute Audrey broached the subject in a note she passed to me in Algebra, we have both been consumed with going to prom—and going together as "friends." It's all we talk about; we are obsessed. But there is a lot of maneuvering that will need to occur to get us there. A cornucopia of obstacles we must overcome—all for one single night at a silly dance that, if Nana's right, I won't remember the details of in half a decade anyway.

Obstacle 1: We aren't juniors or seniors, and thus aren't automatically allowed to buy tickets to prom, unless escorted by an actual junior or senior.

Solution 1: Audrey is friends with her homophobic brother's perennial abuse target, Danny (a junior), one of the only "out" (sort of) kids at school. They got close when she joined the gay-straight student alliance last term. Danny is down-low dating a senior, also at our school, who is not at all out, who is in fact the opposite of out, and plays on the varsity football team with Jason the horrible (and is a first team all-league safety at that). This kid would, it seems, *die* if anybody found out—and I mean that literally, as in, his father would punt him out of the house, and the lunkhead contingent of the football team (led by the dark overlord of them all) would beat him to a pulp, string him up on a fence, and leave him to rot.

I wasn't supposed to know who this kid is, but the minute Aud told me he played on the football team, I immediately guessed it was Aaron. Not that you can tell from the outside or anything, I don't mean that—just that I always noticed something ever so slightly different about the way he moved through the world. Chalk it up to Changer intuition.

Audrey and Danny's genius idea (obviously cribbed from a horribly overwrought yet still tear-jerking after-school TV special): I go with Danny, and Audrey goes with Aaron—the consummate double-date that won't raise eyebrows on any side of the various equations (Audrey's parents, my parents, Aaron's parents, the football team, and so on).

Obstacle 2: Girls don't usually go with girls to prom.

Solution 2: See Solution 1.

Obstacle 3: Tracy.

Solution 3: A miraculous change of heart at our last weekly meeting at the Q-hut, during which Tracy admitted that she likes Audrey and thinks she's a "quality Static," and that she, Tracy, has been doing some careful observation and study of Audrey's lifestyle, and she has determined that Audrey's sympathies, at least at this time, do not seem to skew Abider in any way, shape, or form—and that keeping Audrey and me apart simply because her brother is probably a budding fascist doesn't exactly sit squarely with the overall Changer philosophy of acceptance and compassion.

"In the many, we may be one," Tracy said by way of explanation that afternoon, "but also, in the one, we are many. I feel strongly that Y-1 Changers should be allowed to make mistakes and learn from them, to carry all of those parts over into whichever single life they choose to lead after completing their cycles."

Yeah, I had no idea what she was saying either, but if it meant she was agreeing to chaperone the night and not go ratting me out to my parents or the Council, then I was good to go.

Which brings me to:

Obstacle 4: My parents think that beyond the usual casual contact in school, I have not been socializing with Audrey since the Changers Council intervention, when Turner the culty Lives Coach informed them that the Council suspects Audrey's family of being Abider stock, and that my being

247

close to her could put me (and other Changers) in grave danger.

Mom and Dad don't even know I did the *Romeo and Juliet* scene with Audrey. I just told them I'd been randomly paired with a girl from class I didn't know very well.

Solution 4: I'm not sure there is a fix for this one. It feels wrong lying, but I'm realizing that this dreadful feeling is a little by-product of the life I have to lead: I'm getting more and more skilled at shading the truth, bending facts, fibbing. I do it so much I'm sometimes afraid the cup will run over and I'll simply drown in it. It's getting to the point where I don't even think about it—half-truths come tumbling out of my mouth to random people:

"You can't come over to my place to study because my kitchen's being renovated and my family is crammed into two adjoining rooms at the Holiday Inn for a month."

"My dad had to have lower back surgery (his discs), and my mom is pretty much waiting on him hand and foot, so neither of my folks can come to the parent-teacher conference this semester."

"Of *course* I've never tried peeing standing up."

And so on.

The lies pile up, and after eight months of it, I can't remember whom I've told what. Tracy said there's a part of the *CB* that addresses this very issue, and sure, I skimmed over it, but there wasn't much more than, *There is no absolute truth. Reality is a social construct. Deception for the greater good is not a sin but a strategy. Etc.* Cold comfort per usual.

Which is why, when I was dropping off a paper in the

English department office and saw Mr. Crowell hunched over the table grading papers earlier this afternoon, I decided to stop and chat. He probably didn't even remember telling me back in December that I should—it seems like a hundred years ago now. But instead of quietly sliding my paper into his box, I say, "Hello, Mr. Crowell."

He looks up, his pen clattering to the linoleum. "Drew! Hello. Nice to see you."

"I was just handing in the *Antigone* paper. I thought I'd say hi, maybe talk a little, you know how you said—"

"Yes, of course." He shuffles papers into a messy pile, pulls out the chair beside him. "Have a seat. How's it going?"

I drop my messenger bag on the floor and sit, immediately regretting the decision. "Pretty good."

"You excited for this school year to be over?" he asks. "Not that I'm a fly on the wall, but from what I can tell, you—"

I interrupt him: "I have a question about a decision I'm trying to make."

"I'm great with decisions," he says, brightening.

"Well, I'm thinking of doing this thing that would be fun and I really want to do," I start. It's already so convoluted in my head, I can only imagine how loopy it's going to sound to him. "But I have to lie to somebody in order to do it, and I guess that's not really sitting well with me."

"I see, I see." He's frowning, really trying to understand. "Or, maybe I don't. I'm sorry, can you tell me a little more?"

"Not really."

"Is this about prom?"

"Oh my gosh, how'd you know?"

He looks pleased, starts talking meanderingly like a television psychic. "I'm thinking maybe there's somebody you think you *should* go with, but you really want to go with somebody else," he tries, "and you really don't want to hurt the first person's feelings, so you want to know whether you should tell that person the whole truth, knowing the information will probably upset him or her—or fib and say you're not going at all, taking the chance that the person finds out the truth and is hurt even more than he or she would've been in the first place."

I start laughing.

"What?"

"That's not it at all," I say flatly, and he starts laughing too.

"I'm sorry, I've been watching too many *Beverly Hills, 90210* reruns. Why don't you give me just a teeny bit more information?"

I consider it. Especially in light of how careful he was not to use specific gender pronouns . . . *Okay, let's do this.* "I want to go with a friend. Well, you know her—Audrey?"

"Of course, Audrey, another one of my favorite students—you two had quite the synergy in *Romeo and Juliet*."

"It's not like *that*," I say, flustered. "Not that there's anything wrong with that, I just mean . . ."

"It was heartening to see that you two seemed to patch things up after the assignment," he says.

"What do you mean? You knew we were in a weird place?" I'm starting to wonder whether Tracy or somebody is feeding this guy information.

"Teachers notice things. I don't mean to overstep."

"You aren't. It's true," I concede.

"But after that scene, I noticed you two were getting along better—so as far as I'm concerned, mission accomplished."

"You put us together on purpose?"

He doesn't answer.

"Well, anyway," I say. I'm getting flustered. I think I'm being so careful about information all the time, but maybe I'm an open book and everybody knows it but me. I take a deep breath. "I guess I'm just wondering whether you think it's ever okay to do the wrong thing for the right reasons."

He thinks on it. "I believe there are some situations where that is okay, yes."

"I think so too."

"Am I going to get you in trouble? Because if so, then I want to change my answer."

"Nah, not too much," I say.

"Because life is short," he adds, then seems to be considering whether to continue. "And make no mistake: convention is there to be flaunted. But that's just my two cents. Which are probably worth less than half that in today's economy."

"Thanks, Mr. Crowell," I say, and I mean it. "See you in class tomorrow."

"See you later, Drew," he says, scratching behind his earlobe. "You're a good one. And don't let anybody ever make you feel differently."

Dad wanted me to wear a gown. He actually went so far as to circle some likely candidates in the Delilah prom catalog, underlining the color he thought I would "really shine" in.

"I'll look like an Easter egg," I winced. "An Easter egg at her bat mitzvah."

"I don't think that combination is possible," Dad said.

"Neither is me and any of those dresses," I cracked back.

Hence my rented tuxedo, a fitted black number with a retro ruffled shirt underneath. I'm pairing it with a sequined scarf and my black Chucks. I let Mom blow out my hair, and even glue on some fake eyelashes. I look like an '80s Brit-pop star. Cool, full of swag. David Bowie when David Bowie was pretty. Exactly what I envisioned. This night is going to rock.

"Tracy's here!" Mom announces, already snapping photos as I walk into the living room, shrugging on my jacket.

I pop a pose, giving disco realness, and Mom seems utterly delighted.

"You'll never forget your first prom," she says, eyes misty. "I'm so happy you decided to go after all."

Dad is hovering in the background with a plastic box, Tracy behind him waiting in the entry.

"What's the deal, Dad?" I ask.

He shuffles over, produces a wrist corsage made from a

black rose. It's bad-ass. For a flower bracelet. "You don't have to wear it," he says, holding it out.

"Are you kidding?" I remove the wrapping, snap the elastic around my wrist. "It's great. I love it."

Tracy taps her watch. "We should get a move on if we are going to be on time."

"I don't think there's an *on time* for prom, Trace," I say.

"Well, I have been to four proms in my lives, and I can safely say the cake table is a disaster after twenty minutes, so I suggest we skedaddle *tout de suite*."

Hugs from the 'rents, and then Tracy and I head to the limo she procured from a "friend" (translation: the underground Changer nexus), to pick up Danny and the others before hitting Central and the impossibly unrealistic expectations of a thousand amped-up teenagers in cheesy masquerade drag.

We roll up on Danny's ranch house. He sprints down the sidewalk and hops into the limo, slamming the heavy door shut behind him. He's in shiny, skinny pants and a bedazzled jacket with enough sparkle to eclipse the sun.

"Drive!" he commands Tracy, before turning to me. "Where's your mask?"

"You can't tell? I'm already wearing it," I (sorta) joke.

"Nice. Aren't we all?" he intones with mock gravity.

"You on the lam?" I ask. "What's with the ground-speed record setting?"

"My parents were all up in my business about my new 'girlfriend' and insisting upon meeting her," Danny says. "I was sparing you from certain protracted interrogation."

I nod. "I feel your pain."

"Who's driving, Miss Daisy?" Danny asks.

"My name is Tracy, an old friend of Drew's, and her chauffeur-slash-chaperone for the evening," Tracy replies officiously.

"She's not serious," Danny says, wrinkling his brow.

"She's always serious," I reply. "But she's dope. Ish." I can see Tracy smirking in the rearview. "Have you talked to Aaron today?"

"Have I breathed today?" Danny snorts. "We coordinated our outfits."

I have a moment of panic. Was I supposed to do that with Audrey? Danny reads my mind.

"Mary, you didn't compare color stories?"

"I don't even know what a color story is," I say. I hear Tracy gasp from the front seat. I raise my voice, enunciating dramatically. "And I am comfortable not ever knowing, so neither one of you needs to spend another second stressing about my lack of fashionista cred."

"Bitchin' corsage, by the way," Danny offers. "Very Elvira, Mistress of the Dark."

I thank him, then awkwardly begin to apologize for that day at the beginning of the year when I saw Jason terrorizing him by the lockers and just kept on walking. "I was a coward, I'm a different person now—"

He stops me short. "From what I understand, we've both had more than our share of Jason's sad attempts to convince himself he's a real man." He flashes a knowing look. "Trust me, that turd cutter will get what's coming to him eventually. Karma is a bitch. And so am I."

"I think I might kind of love you right now," I say, relieved.

"Join the club!" he lobs back, giving me a high five.

Minutes later we collect Aaron, who is indeed dressed to complement Danny, though more understatedly, then head a couple more miles over to Audrey's. The two boys hold hands in the car, Danny resting his head on Aaron's shoulder.

When we arrive at Audrey's, I brace myself, but Jason is nowhere in sight. Instead, her parents are in the yard taking photographs of Audrey posing in front of the azalea bushes. She's wearing a knee-length polka dot dress with layers of ruffles underneath, a giant pink bow tied around her waist, and a feather thing sprouting out of the side of her updo. She looks like a sexy cupcake.

As we ease to a stop, Aaron and Danny separate. Audrey gestures from the lawn for us to join her, and we file out of the limo and over to the impromptu photo set.

"Everybody say *prom!*" her father coaches, and we comply, feeling ridiculous. "Okay, now just Audrey and Aaron." Aaron wraps his arm around Audrey's shoulders, and they both grin like donkeys into the lens. "What a stunning couple," her mom coos.

"Of *what?*" Danny mutters under his breath.

"Now just me and Drew," Audrey suggests, and her father at first looks perturbed, but then shrugs his shoulders, directing us under a pergola with wild vines climbing all over it.

We stand close, but not too close. He snaps a few shots.

"That's a fun look," Audrey's mom says about my tuxedo. "How daring."

"I *love* it," Audrey says, sensing her mother's insincerity.

Aud's father waves Danny over. "Hold her hand," he prompts, indicating me.

Danny inches over to me and puts his arm around my shoulders like we're buddies.

"A little closer," Audrey's dad pushes. "Just a few more ..."

Twenty minutes and twelve hundred photographs later, all four of us are spilling out of the limo and strolling into the barely recognizable gymnasium, the joint decked out in faux-French decadence, with paper chandeliers, fake candles twinkling, mirrors propped in all the corners, silver urns overflowing with masks on wooden sticks and costume jewelry, a Versailles vibe that truly transports us.

"They vogued the crap out of this place," Aaron says approvingly as he and Danny walk ahead, quickly scouting the best table and claiming four seats. Audrey and I follow, craning our necks to digest the spectacle of both the transformative decor and the sight of Mr. Crowell shimmying on the side of the designated dance floor.

"Coordination. Not a strength," I observe.

Audrey laughs. "Check out the Chl-horror show." She thumbs toward the middle of the floor, where directly beneath the shimmering disco ball, Chloe is spinning in tight circles, flipping her blown-out hair like a manic pony, while her crew of wannabes makes a ring of adoration around her and clap like they'll be executed if they don't. "That. Is. Troubling."

"Come on, let's throw down," I say, linking arms and skipping onto the floor, just as a slow jam comes over the speakers. I look for Danny and Aaron, but they have already vanished. I pivot back to Audrey. "Well?"

"Why not?" she says, a devilish grin spreading across her face. "We won't be the first chicks to dance without their dates at the prom."

And so we face each other, Audrey draping her arms over my shoulders, me wrapping mine around her waist, careful not to crush the bow. We sway, right foot, left foot, right foot. Giggling a little as we do. I survey the room. Audrey was right: no one notices two girls when said girls don't want to be noticed.

After a while of rocking back and forth like this, the song transitions into a sappy ballad, and I slowly spin Aud around. Over her shoulder, I spot a masked Jason roaching up on Chloe in a dark corner, and a chill creeps down my spine, but Chloe is clearly enjoying the attention, so I block it out, keep my gaze moving while we dance.

And there's Kenya by the punch table, smacking her thigh at a friend's joke, and Mr. Crowell to her left, head cocked like a spaniel listening to a high-pitched whistle audible only to him. Scanning further I see the cake display, a collapsed, gilded monstrosity that has obviously been attacked by a kagillion students in search of a sugar rush. It looks like a rhino has trampled the king-sized cake, but that hasn't stopped Tracy, who is hovering behind it in her rhinestone mask, inhaling a giant slab balanced on a napkin. Above her a banner reads, *Central Masquerade Ball*, in gold and black.

"Earth to Drew," Audrey chides. She's close to my ear. "You aren't even looking at me! You are the worst fake prom date ever."

"My apologies, m'lady," I play along. "Maybe you should call in Romeo."

"Maybe I should." She pauses, then: "Only problem is . . ."

"Yes?"

"Romeo was a *horrible* kisser." She smirks, eyes alit with mischief.

"Well, maybe Juliet was a horrible kissee," I toss back. "There's only so much passion one can extract from a cheekbone."

Audrey chews her bottom lip, trains her eyes on mine. I can see her brain cranking. Above us the ballad is swelling, a saxophone solo whining out some poor sap's approximation of love.

"Drew?"

"Yes, Aud?"

And then, without warning, she does it. And by *it*, I mean pitches her face forward into mine, where our lips finally meet, full on together, in a deep, lingering, *holy freaking cow*, KISS.

I keep waiting for Audrey to yank herself back, to say she tripped or something, but she doesn't. In fact, she presses in harder, and as she does, the whole prom washes away into a sea that is flooding my ears, and I can hear and see and feel nothing but the ripe softness of her mouth on mine; it is as if the entire universe has telescoped to that intimate location, this improbable moment, and I care about nothing else, and am fairly certain I never will again.

Until something else happens.

A vision.

I want to stop it, but Audrey won't pull away, and anyway, it came into my brain full-blown, an opera in a snapshot. In my head, clear as day, I see Audrey sitting in a car screaming, enraged. She's fighting with a guy leaning through the window. I don't recognize him, handsome, big. She screams, *I hate you, Kyle!* and he grabs her arm, but she frees herself, punching the gas and speeding off. And then. And then . . . No, that can't be right.

A crash.

At a distance, her car T-boned by a barreling delivery truck.

Smoke. Fire. A horn jammed.

"No!" I scream. "No!"

My eyes snap open. The vision replaced by one of Audrey gaping at me, humiliated. She covers her face with her hands and runs as fast as she can out the gym doors.

"Wait!" I yell after her, but it's too late. She's already gone.

I am considering pursuing her when I see him, right where she raced past. *Chase.* All cleaned up in a suit and tie. A bouquet in his hand. From his traumatized expression I can tell he has witnessed the whole episode. He gives me a curt nod, then disappears through the same exit as Audrey.

I stand frozen on the dance floor. Consumed by only one thought.

Who is Kyle?

"I have to do something!"

"No. You actually do not."

"How can you say that?"

"Because I know more than you do."

"Then tell me what you know."

"It is too soon."

And so it has gone for the past half hour. Tracy and me in the Quonset hut.

Her: evasive, uncooperative, annoying.

Me: doing my blind-panic thing over the Audrey vision.

"What good is this power if you can't use it to affect the future?" I demand.

"It isn't a *power*, it is a *gift*."

"Stuff it, Yoda."

"Visions allow you to feel an even deeper connection with the people you love. And they remind you to live in the moment. To be your best self now, because tomorrow may never be. The future is yesterday," Tracy recites.

I sigh dramatically. "Tracy. Audrey is my best friend. And if I can stop a tragedy from entering her life, I will."

"You don't know there is a tragedy, Drew."

"A massive auto accident is kind of a tragedy!"

"What you saw is a few frames of an entire movie," she says. "Context is everything."

"I'm going to tell her the truth. About all of it."

"Okay."

"I'm not kidding."

"Okay."

I consider strangling her. She can decompose in this hut for all I care.

"Drew, I can't control anything you say or do. Your life is about choices. Everything is a choice. Including how you *feel*."

Now she's gone too far. I didn't choose to fall in love with Chase—or Audrey. Or to loathe Jason. Or to adore my dog. Or to hate the color purple.

"In fact," she continues, calm as clams, "deciding how you feel about what happens to you is really the only choice that matters."

"Want to know how I feel *now*?" I snap.

Tracy laughs, gives me a look like, *Poor lamb*. "You have Changer homework this week. As school ends, all Y-1s are required to Chronicle a list of what they think they've learned. It doesn't need to be in order of importance, although it can be if you want. I always submitted mine in descending order of significance, with subcategories, but then, I do like my data to be organized and easily downloaded."

I pretend to ignore her.

"I found it immensely helpful to the process of choosing my Mono," she adds.

I am studying the dirt, kick at it with my shoe.

"You've come such a long way, Drew," Tracy says, changing tack. "Don't lose sight of that. I have to admit I was a little concerned when I was first assigned to you, but . . . I couldn't be prouder. Really." And then she rummages around in a pile of rusty junk and pulls out a present that looks professionally wrapped. "Here, a memento."

I rip the package open. It's my skateboard. The one I'd been missing since my first day as Drew. My last link to Ethan.

At that Tracy gave me a stiff hug and left the hut. I was on my own. She didn't even look back, which was a good thing, because if she had, she would have seen me crying.

Chase suggested we meet at the Freezo. Which I know was a little private joke to himself, but I didn't let him know I knew, which was a private joke to *myself*. Changer head games. Like a hall of mirrors in hell.

"How was prom?" he opens when I slide into the booth where he's been waiting. There is a pronounced sneer in his voice. So much for endless love.

"You tell me, since you were there," I smack back.

He says he wasn't planning to show up, but then he changed his mind, he wanted to see me, talk about the future, *my* future. "You're on the wrong path," he tosses out at me.

"That's rich coming from the dude whose best friends have rap sheets longer than Rapunzel's weave."

"Beats being an automaton," he snipes, then sucks on his milkshake straw. The shake won't budge, so he pops the lid and tilts the rim to his mouth, whereupon the shake unexpectedly releases in its entirety all over his neck.

"Holy crap!" Chase jumps up, palming at his chin to wipe the ice cream off, but it just smears and drips, and the whole situation is so altogether farcical we both drop the attitude showdown and burst into stomach-cramping hysterics.

"Good look for you," I say, handing him a wad of paper napkins.

"You think? I couldn't decide between this and Boston cream pie."

As he scrapes away the shake residue, I'm startled by how much I've missed him. Even if he has become a moody anarchist.

"How are you, really?" I ask.

He considers. "I've been better. I still believe in what I'm doing. It has its share of suck, though."

"Everything does."

He nods. "So. Is Audrey your Static GF?"

"No. Just a friend."

"A friend you make out with in front of the whole student body?"

"She kissed *me*." It feels unfair, even if it is the truth. "I don't know why. Maybe the magic of prom night possessed her."

"Did it happen?"

I know what he means, but I ask anyway: "Did what happen?"

"So, it did."

We sit in silence.

"It wasn't good," I finally say. And I can tell Chase feels terrible, but there is nothing to be done but wait and let life play out.

"I'm here, you know." He hunches his shoulders a bit.

"I know."

"I mean, I'm really here. Okay?"

"Okay." I reach out, run one finger slowly over the back of his hand. He watches as I do. "I'll always be grateful for what you did for me," I say, my eyes focused solely on our hands touching. "Do you ever wonder if, maybe, we—"

"Drew, don't. I'm-I'm-I'm broken."

I pull my hand away. "Don't be stupid, Chase."

"I should go." He pushes away from the booth, his shirt still sticky from the spill.

"Fine. Whatever. It's a choice you make." God, I'm an a-hole.

"I meant what I said. I'm here," he repeats.

"Really? Because it looks like you're trying to be anywhere *but* here."

"It's complicated, Drew."

"Not exactly news, Chase. Why did you even want to see me? Just to check if I would come when you called?"

He never answered. Just tossed a ten-dollar bill and his soggy napkins on the table and bolted. Leaving me alone to wonder if and when I'd see him again. And for the first time, I doubted I even wanted to.

Changer homework, or "What I Learned on My First Change," by Drew Bohner, née Ethan Miller.

   1) . . .

   2) . . .

   —-. . .—

I don't feel like doing this.

I mean, I could give a bunch of oh-so-clever answers that I guess is what the Council replicants are after. To put up on the shelf for all of history. Evidence that I've evolved. That I'm ready for C2–D1. But maybe I'm not?

I know it's the thing to walk around spouting off what you know for sure. To be solid in your convictions. To know right from wrong. But from where I'm sitting, life is one giant shade of gray. Tracy was right: context is everything.

Like my last meeting with Chase. Him acting all temperamental. Well, I heard through the ReRunz grapevine that he'd gone and knocked up some girl. Another RaCha. I don't know if I believe that's true. But I can't contact Chase to ask. And I'm not sure I really could ask, not in person. It must be a rumor. It has to be. Probably started by some jealous RaCha hop head. I'm sure he'll reach out soon, maybe in the summer. And then, I don't know.

I guess you could say this year was like a Rubik's Cube I

never solved. I'd get one side all yellow or green, but then I'd turn it over, and every other side would be a hot mess.

What else? At the end of the day, being a girl isn't all bad. I can scarcely remember Ethan. I wonder if it's the same for my parents. It never hit me until, well, just *now* that they had to say goodbye to him too. That must have been really tough. Like a mini-death. Only he's still here. Just different.

I suppose that's the point, isn't it? We are all changing all the time. And once we have, there's no going back.

So there. That's what I learned.

That.

And also that a kiss can stop time.

And love at first sight exists.

And there are some things worth fighting for.

And that you are only truly alive when you let people see you.

(Even though it sometimes feels like you might die if you do.)

At least that's how it felt to me, Drew Bohner, at the conclusion of her freshman year of high school.

It was the last day of school today. It's past midnight, and I've got my headphones on, streaming music on my laptop. An e-mail from Andy just popped up:

> *Eth,*
>
> *I know you haven't written me back in three or four months. But freshman year's almost over and we haven't talked once. Wait, do you Skype? You've probably become a hideous zit-ridden ape, so you're embarrassed to see me. No prob, bro. You can be my ugly wingman the next time we hang out.*
>
> *Anyway, I could use a friend, and even though you've dropped me like a fat girl, I thought of you. My dad found a bag of weed in my jacket yesterday. I swear it's not mine, but he doesn't believe me. I didn't mention it before, but my moms got really sick a couple months ago, and when Dad found the bud he was all screaming like, "How could you do this to her?" He actually kicked me out for the night.*
>
> *So, life kind of bites. I just thought you might be around sometime. What are you doing this summer? Come to New York! We got tickets for five Yankees games, so come up, and I'll take you, not like a date . . . I'm no 'mo.*
>
> *Our school gets out next week, when does yours? I'm*

getting a summer J-O-B, probably at the bagel shop. YES,
I'm going to have to wear one of those dorky paper hats.

Later,
Andy

Andy's never really shared anything serious with me
before. Much less said anything serious. I don't know
what to say, and I have enough on my plate right now, so
I'm probably not going to write back. Not now anyhow.
He sounds lonely. I feel bad for him. For how fast he got
replaced in my life. Or more accurately: how soon I decided
he wasn't enough.

I wonder if he's lying about the drugs.

I start flipping through my yearbook and reread some
of the notes people scribbled on the blank pages in the back
earlier today:

Ayo D-Girl,

You continued to surprise me all spring-long. White
girls can jump! I'm only sorry I didn't meet you earlier
in the year. I don't know why you're not coming to
Georgetown with me to train this summer. I mean, I
already picked out our dorm room, and I was going to
personally guarantee you'd shave a second off your 100m
by the end of training camp! Oh well, your loss. (Wait,
and mine, since you're gonna help us win State next year,
remember?)

Well, peace and love, and see you in September. I'll
call you the minute I'm back in town, and we'll go for

a long run and you can fill me in on any juicy Genesis details I missed while kicking up dirt in our nation's capital.

Love,
Kenya

~ ~ ~

Sexy Drew,

OK, I barely know you, but I've been staring at the back of your head all year long in English, and I've been meaning to tell you that you're really hot. Of course you're hot from the front too, and I guess what I'm saying is, if I'm not too much of a dumb-ass for you, I hope we get to hang out more next year. Have a dope summer. Skate or die.
—Jerry

~ ~ ~

Dear Drew,

It was lovely having you in class this year. Your "Of Mice and Men" essay remains one of the best I've read. So much insight from such a young lady. Have an enriching summer, and I'll look forward to seeing you around the halls next year.

Fondly,
Mr. Crowell

~ ~ ~

Boner,

Lady Falconettes rule! You should've stuck with it.
LYLAS (not really),
Chloe

~~~

Drew,

    I had the time of my life. And I owe it all to you.
Love,
Danny

~~~

Romeo,

    What's in a name? That which we call a rose by any other name would smell as sweet . . .

    Heh. What do I even say to you here in the pages of this stupid thing? You were my favorite part of freshman year. See? LAME! Words fail me. Wonder if that ever happened to Shakespeare? Prolly not.

Love,
Juliet

Audrey. By far, the hardest part about today was saying goodbye to Audrey. Not that she comprehended it was GOODBYE goodbye. But I did. I've been dreading this day since we started spending time together again. Which is—no coincidence—when life stopped sucking so hard.

Audrey and Jason are shipping off first thing tomorrow to their sleepaway church camp in Alabama for the summer. She pleaded with her parents to let her stay home, even offered to get a full-time job and pay the utilities at their house. No go. The camp sounds super regimented, as in, wake up at five a.m., do manual labor, meet, pray, play outdoor survival skill–building games, pray, eat, sing, go to sleep at eight p.m., then wake up the next morning and rinse, repeat. So much for s'mores and campfire stories.

It's killing me that I'll be missing out on two and a half months with her. E-mailing isn't the same. Aud says she'll be lonesome. She isn't friends with anybody going to the camp. Jason has a few gonzo moron pals coming with, and a cousin of theirs is going too, but Audrey despises the lot of them, especially the cousin, who used to pin her by the throat and threaten to spit on her face when they were younger.

It's also killing me that, let's face it, odds are this is an Abider camp, or at least an Abider-in-training camp. And yeah, I should probably report all the information I've gleaned to the Council, or at least to Tracy, but I won't. I just can't risk anything happening to Audrey.

As school was emptying out, I sat by the flagpole and waited for her, the ropes clanging against the metal in the warm breeze above me. Aud had promised to meet me there, so we could say goodbye in person. Kids splintered off, crammed in jeeps, ragtops down, music blaring. Others on scooters, bikes, skateboards. Everyone manic, wild-eyed, infected by summer fever. The gates to the zoo flung wide open.

Minutes pass. I keep scanning for Audrey, but no sign of her. In the distance I spot Mr. Crowell carrying a box full of school supplies and books from the teacher's lunchroom to the parking lot. *Please don't look over here, please don't look over here . . .* I like the guy all right, but I feel like I've said goodbye to him and everybody else about a hundred times already. He gets to his car, sets the box on his hood, pats all his pockets. Seems to have lost his keys (for the fiftieth time I personally know of this year).

Then Tracy appears, and I'm thinking, *Come on, you don't have to supervise my last minute with Audrey!* but I notice she's not even headed in my direction. She's . . . *What the hell?* Talking to Mr. Crowell, who is grinning at something she's said.

Come again? Since when is Tracy funny? I keep spying, and now Tracy is chuckling too. Just as I start to get really disturbed, I hear, "I'm glad you waited." I turn around; it's Aud.

"Where else do I have to be?" I say, shifting focus.

She apologizes. She seems sad. "I had to clean out my gym locker."

"It's okay."

We're silent.

"I'm really going to miss you," she says.

"I'm going to miss you too. I wish you didn't have to go to this thing tomorrow."

"I'd donate a kidney if it would get me out of it. And I read those surgeries are much worse for the donors. They, like, saw you in half or something to get it out."

"Ta-da! And for my next trick . . ."

She smiles, her eyes holding mine. I am considering what Tracy said last time in the Quonset hut. That it's my choice whether to break protocol and tell her. *Speaking of Tracy* . . . I turn back to the parking lot, but she and Mr. Crowell are gone. *Weird*, but not really one of my biggest concerns. Those would be:

1) Who am I going to be next year?

2) Will Audrey like this person?

3) If I'm a guy, will Audrey *like-like* this person?

4) If I'm a girl, will this person be as tight with her as I am now?

5) What feint will I get to explain Drew's evaporation? Not that a million people are going to mourn me or anything, but I know a few will notice I'm not around. One of whom is standing in front of me, her eyes as warm and open as the first day we met.

"Aud," I begin, then burst out with it: "Who's Kyle?" She looks confused.

"Do you know somebody named Kyle?" I press, sort of accusingly, even though I don't mean it that way.

"No, why? Who is he?"

I study her face for any clue. She seems genuinely stumped.

"Nobody," I say.

"Okaay." She makes a screwed-up face of comic confusion.

I should be relieved, but instead I'm engulfed by grief. We are breaking up. And she doesn't even know it. After a minute, I say, "I'm going to miss you so much."

"It's just a few months, silly."

"About prom—"

"We never need to talk about prom, ever," she stops me.

"You've been shutting me down every time I try to talk about it."

"*IT*," Audrey says, "was a massive mistake, an emotional aneurism, and the less said about IT, the better."

"But there's something I think I need to tell you—"

"So, summer plans?" Audrey interrupts again.

I sigh, she wins. "Besides taking a Greyhound out to the sticks to rescue you?" I suggest, not really joking.

"Shut up. Summer will be over in a snap, and we'll be back in school wishing we weren't before you know it," Audrey says. "Hey, I'm considering cutting my hair short. New look for sophomore year. What do you think?"

"I'm all about new looks."

"Me too," she seconds, and I say a prayer that she truly means it. "How awesome is it we will never be freshmen again?"

"Pretty awesome," I lie.

"You should get a job," she says, picking up on my malaise. "You need to do something besides mark black X's over the days on the calendar."

"Yeah, maybe I'll work at ReRunz," I shrug.

"You should rejoin the Bickersons! You'll have time now."

"Not enough," I say.

I hear the familiar roar of an eight-cylinder engine, and behind Audrey I can see Jason pulling up in his monster convertible. He stops far ahead of us, death metal blasting, so I know he can't hear us. I imagine shooting a spear into the base of his greasy neck.

"Here, I got you something." Audrey shoves a cardboard jewelry box into my hand. I'm sincerely touched and feel like garbage at the same time.

"I didn't get you anything," I stammer, thinking I should have. *What's my problem?*

"Shut up and open it," she chides. "It's not a big deal."

I yank off the Snoopy wrapping paper and lift the lid to the box. Inside, resting on a rectangle of white cotton, is a silver bracelet with a single charm hanging off.

"It's a friendship bracelet!" Audrey says, rocking on her heels a little.

I lift it to get a better look at the charm: a tiny, perfect silver drum kit.

"Do you like it?" she asks, eyeing me. "We can add a new charm for every year we're friends!"

"It's amazing, Audrey. Really. I love it. I love . . ."

My voice is drowned out by angry honking from Jason's car. Audrey springs into motion, embracing me hard. I wrap my arms around her and cling like a koala. This time I pray I'll get to hold her again. If not as me, then as someone else.

"See you real soon," she whispers into my ear before breaking away.

I want to respond, but the tears have begun, clogging my throat.

"Oh, Drew." Audrey squeezes me again, even tighter. "I never would have survived this year without you."

"Same," I say, swallowing hard. "Sorry to be such a punk."

After a beat she lets go, begins walking quickly toward the car, then freezes and turns around.

"I love you just the way you are!" she shouts over the noise. "Don't ever change, Drew!"

She doesn't hear me, but I answer: "I couldn't if I tried."

And oddly enough, in that precise moment, nothing feels truer.

(NOT) THE END

ABIDER. A non-Changer (see *Static*, below) belonging to an underground syndicate of anti-Changers, whose ultimate goal is the extermination of the Changer race. The Abider philosophy is characterized by a steadfast desire for genetic purity, for human blood to remain unmingled with Changer blood. Abider leaders operate by instilling fear in humans, for when people fear one another, they are easier to control. Abiders sometimes have an identifying tattoo depicting an ancient symbol of a Roman numeral I (*Figure 1*), the emblem symbolizing homogeneity and the single identity Abiders desire each human to inhabit.

FIG. 1. ABIDERS EMBLEM

CHANGER. A member of an ancient race of humans imbued with the gift of changing into a different person four times between the ages of approximately fourteen and eighteen. (In more modern times, one change occurs at the commencement of each of the four years of high school; see *Cycle*, below.) Changers may not reveal themselves to non-Changers (see *Static*, below). After living as all four versions of themselves (see *V*, below), Changers must choose one version in which to live out the rest of their lives (see *Mono*, below). Changer doctrine holds that the Changer race is the last hope for the human race on the whole to reverse the moral devolution that has overcome it. Changers believe more Changers equals more empathy on planet Earth. And that only through empathy will the human race survive. After their Cycles (see *Cycle*, below), Changers eventually partner with Statics. When approved by the Council (see *Changers Council*, below), Changer-Static unions produce a single Changer offspring.

CHANGERS COUNCIL. The official Changer authority. The Changers Council is divided into regional units spread out across the globe. Each Council is responsible for all basic decisions regarding the population of Changers in its specific region.

CHANGERS EMBLEM. A variation on Leonardo da Vinci's *Vitruvian Man* drawing, dating to approximately 1490 CE (*Figure 2*). The Changers Emblem contains four bodies superimposed in motion, instead of two (as portrayed in da Vinci's composition), and appears to the eye as both four bodies and one body at the same time—though all sharing one head and heart. An emblem of the Changer mantra: *In the many we are one*.

FIG. 2. CHANGERS EMBLEM

CHANGERS MIXER. Required events for all Changers to attend, during each of the four years of high school (a minimum of two mixers are required for each year). Council rules and regulations are emphasized at mixers (see *Changers Council*, above). Mixers sometimes require classwork and formal discussions, but Mixers are primarily designed to offer more informal camaraderie and problem-solving techniques, both of which help Changers address some of the difficulties that frequently arise during their Cycles (see *Cycle*, below).

CYCLE. The four-year period of different iterations, or versions (see *V*, below) that a Changer goes through between the approximate ages of fourteen and eighteen. One V per each of the four years of high school.

FEINTS. The story a Changer family tells the non-Changers (see *Static*, below) in their lives, to explain each V's (see *V*, below) absence during the following year of school. The specific details for Feints are provided by the Council (see *Changers Council*, above), unless a Changer and her/his parents submit a formal request for an alternative Feint, which is necessary under certain circumstances (i.e., when Statics are especially integrated into a particular V's life, or when a particular Feint will better protect the identity of the Changer and her/his family).

FOREVER CEREMONY. Regional "graduation" events held on the day after high school graduation for every Changer within a designated region. A joyous though private (from Statics—except parental Statics; see *Static*, below) occasion, as each year of ceremonies initiates more and more Changers to filter out into the world and eventually find a Static mate, with whom they will start a family and raise Changer offspring of their own. At the Forever Ceremony, Changers are introduced one by one, and each speaks a little about each of her/his V's (see *V*, below) before declaring in front of both the Council (see *Changers Council*, above) and their community whom they will live as for the rest of their lives (see *Mono*, below).

MONO. A Changer's "forever identity," a.k.a. the V (see *V*, below) a Changer ultimately selects for her/himself after living as each of the four different assigned V's. A Mono cannot be the individual a Changer lived as during the approximately fourteen years before her/his Cycle (see *Cycle*, above) began.

RACHAS. Common term for "Radical Changers," a small but growing splinter group of Changers tired of living in secret, as the Council (see *Changers Council*, above) dictates. RaChas are freegans, anarchist free spirits, often living in the margins, surviving on what human society at large throws away. RaChas philosophy calls for living openly and demanding liberation and acceptance for all, Changers and Statics alike. RaChas have adopted the ancient Roman numeral IV, rotated on its side (*Figure 3*), as an emblem, symbolizing their desire to shake up traditional Changers philosophy and call attention to the limitations of the four-V Cycle (See *V*, below; see *Cycle*, above) each Changer must go through. RaChas have been known to recruit Changers with the intention of indoctrinating them into RaChas activities. RaChas have also been known to battle Abiders (see *Abider*, above) and even stage secret missions to rescue Changers who have been abducted by Abiders and held in Abider deprogramming camps. [*Nota bene:* While the Changers Council is at odds with the RaChas movement, it can also no longer deny its existence.]

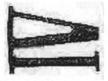

FIG. 3. RACHAS EMBLEM

STATIC. A non-Changer (i.e., the vast majority of the world's population). Particularly sympathetic Statics are ideal mates for Changers later in life. Once a Changer has completed his or her Cycle (see *Cycle*, above), s/he will be fully prepared to assess various Statics' openness and acceptance of difference. When a Changer feels certain that s/he has found an ideal potential Static mate, s/he may, with permission of the Council (see *Changers Council*, above), reveal her/himself to the Static. [*Nota bene:* This revelation can occur only after a Changer's full Cycle is complete, and s/he has declared his or her Mono (see *Mono*, above).]

TOUCHSTONE. A Changer's official mentor, assigned immediately upon a Changer's transformation into her/his first V (see *V*, below). The same Touchstone is assigned for a Changer's entire Cycle (see *Cycle*, above).

V. Any one of a Changer's four versions of her/himself into which s/he changes during each of the four years of high school. Changers walk in the shoes of one V for each year of school (between the approximate ages of fourteen and eighteen).

ACKNOWLEDGMENTS

Deserved thanks are due to a great many folks, all of whom helped Changers evolve from a lightning-bolt idea in the park to an actual book series we are proud to have our children (and others) read. The love and kindness of the following friends and family can be felt on every page:

Johnny Temple, Johanna Ingalls, Aaron Petrovich, Ibrahim Ahmad, and everybody at Akashic Books; Clay Aiken; Shannon Burke; Sarah Chalfant and Rebecca Nagel at the Wylie Agency; the families Cooper and Glock; Gabriel Crowell; Daniel Ehrenhaft; Elaine, Jane, Miss Kristy, and all at the Museum of Appalachia; Jeff Gordinier; John Green; Peggy Hambright and Magpies Cakes; Christina Jokanovich; Stephen Kay; Tom Léger; Téa Leoni and family; Langley Perer and Dawn Saltzman at Mosaic; Alex Petrowsky; Spencer Presler; Danny Rose; Adam Schroeder; Doug Stewart at Sterling Lord Literistic; and Scott Silver.

And, of course, our daughters Dixie and Matilda, whose empathy and wit continue to inspire and astound us every day.

T COOPER and **ALLISON GLOCK-COOPER** are best-selling and award-winning authors and journalists. Between them, they have published seven books, raised two children, and rescued six dogs. The **CHANGERS** series is their first collaboration in print. The two also write for television and film, and they can be reached at their websites: www.t-cooper.com and www.allisonglock.com.